BY SANDRA SCOPPETTONE

Some Unknown Person
Such Nice People
Innocent Bystanders
A Creative Kind of Killer
Razzamatazz
Donato and Daughter
Beautiful Rage
This Dame for Hire

THE LAUREN LAURANO NOVELS

Everything You Have Is Mine
I'll Be Leaving You Always
My Sweet Untraceable You
Let's Face the Music and Die
Gonna Take a Homicidal Journey

FOR YOUNG ADULTS

Trying Hard to Hear You
The Late Great Me
Happy Endings Are All Alike
Long Time Between Kisses
Playing Murder

THIS DAME *for* HIRE

Sandra
SCOPPETTONE

THIS DAME
for HIRE
a novel

BALLANTINE BOOKS · NEW YORK

Published in the United States by Ballantine Books, an imprint of The Random House Publishing Group, a division of Random House, Inc., New York.

BALLANTINE and colophon are registered trademarks of Random House, Inc.

Library of Congress Cataloging-in-Publication Data
Scoppettone, Sandra.
This dame for hire : a novel of suspense / Sandra Scoppettone.
p. cm.
ISBN 0-345-47810-X
1. Women private investigators—New York (State)—New York—Fiction.
2. World War, 1939-1945—New York (State)—New York—Fiction.
3. New York (N.Y.)—Fiction.   I. Title.
PS3569.C586T48 2005
813'.54—dc22   2004046242

Printed in the United States of America on acid-free paper

www.ballantinebooks.com

2   4   6   8   9   7   5   3   1

First Edition

Text design by Susan Turner

For Steven L. Prenzlauer

ACKNOWLEDGMENTS

Many thanks to Susan Caggiano, Beverly Maher, Marijane Meaker, and especially to Linda Crawford.

THIS DAME *for* HIRE

New York City—1943

A t ten-fifteen in the P.M. I was walking along Bleecker Street near Thompson, going home after putting on the feedbag with my friend Jeanne Darnell. It was snowing big wet flakes. Snow never brought nasty cold with it, so I was warm enough in my blue cloth coat. I didn't own a fur anyway, not even muskrat. Since there'd been no tip-off on the weather, I wasn't wearing galoshes and my feet were getting the full winter-weather treatment.

When it snowed in the city, it was always quiet, and I could almost con myself into thinking I heard the flakes land.

Then in the next second, I tripped over something on the sidewalk and flew through the air, landed on my hands, then fell to my knees. My coat and skirt hiked themselves up around my keister, and I was glad there was no one else on the street at this most embarrassing of moments.

My knees were chilled but the snow cushioned my fall, and I was sure the only thing hurt was my pride. There's nothing like a fall to make you feel stupid. Even alone on a Greenwich Village street.

I pushed myself up and stayed kneeling for a moment, then, with the help of a stoop railing, rose to my feet. I almost went down again cause I had broken the heel on one of my pumps.

Now what? I stood there in the wet while I got my wind back and took stock of the pickle I was in.

I knew I'd freeze my tootsies, but I had to take off my shoes if I was to make any headway. And what had I tripped over?

A few feet behind me I saw what looked like a pile of rags. Why would anyone put those there? I wondered. And almost at once my heart did a tumble and I knew that these weren't rags at all, but something alarming, something sinister.

In my stocking feet (the last of my hoarded hose) I inched my way closer to the heap on the sidewalk. My throat felt tight, and my eyes did an owl.

The moment I was closer I saw what I'd suspected. These weren't rags. This was a person. Was it someone else who'd fallen and got knocked out?

I bent down and right off took in that the white snow had a dark patch near the person's head. And I knew. Not because I was a detective, which I was, but because it was so clear.

This was blood, and the side of the victim's head was bashed in so that I couldn't see a profile, but the length of the hair and the clothing told me I was looking at a woman. A very dead woman.

ONE

I didn't start out to be a private eye. I thought I was gonna be a secretary—get my boss his java in the morning, take letters, and so on. Hell, I didn't get my degree in steno to put my life on the line. It was true I wanted an interesting job, but that I'd end up a PI myself . . . it never entered my mind.

Back in 1940 when I went for my interview, one look at Woody Mason and I thought for sure it was gonna be a bust.

There he was, brogans up on the wobbly wooden table he called his desk, wearing dark cheaters in the middle of the day, his trilby pulled down so low on his head it was a week before I knew he had straw-blond hair. A butt hung from his thin lips, smoke curled up past his rosy nose. I wondered if he was a boozehound.

"I'm Faye Quick," I said.

"Good for you."

"Mr. Mason, I came for the job. You wanna good secretary or not?" That got his attention.

Mason slid his legs off the desk, pushed down the sunglasses, and over the rims eyeballed my gams, while he stubbed out his Old Gold and lit a new one. So what did I expect from a gumshoe?

My friends told me I was a crackpot trying for a job with a shamus. But I thought it could be interesting. I didn't want to be in some nine-to-five pushing papers that had to do with mergers, business agreements, or the like. I wanted to be where whatever I was typing or listening to had some meat to it.

"Are ya?" Mason asked.

"Am I what?"

"Quick."

To myself I thought, *Hardy, har, har,* but I didn't say it. I gave him a look instead.

"Sorry. Guess ya get that a lot."

"Yeah."

"Sometimes I open my big yap too much. So Miss Quick, you wanna work for me?"

"That's the general idea," I said, and thought maybe he was a little slow or something. But Woody Mason was anything but slow, I was to find out.

We went through some Q and A's, then he hired me on the spot. I was slaphappy getting a job my first day looking.

That was how it was then.

But in '41 the Japs hit Pearl Harbor, and by January of '42, Woody Mason was in the army and I was running A Detective Agency. The *A* didn't stand for anything. He named it that so it would be first in the phone book. By the time I took over I knew almost as much as Woody, but in the beginning it was a scary idea.

"I'm not sure, boss."

"Ah, Quick, you can do it. I got complete confidence in ya."

"Yeah, but *I* don't."

"Listen, when I come back from this clambake I wanna have a business to come home to. You gotta keep the home fires burning, like they say."

"That's not what it means: a girl like me packin a heater and chasin the bad guys. Keepin the home fires burnin means sittin in the nest waitin for your man."

"Ain't I your man, Quick?" Woody smiled, the dimples making their mark in his cheeks, and my heart slipped a notch.

I wasn't in love with Woody, but he was a looker when he gave ya *the* smile. Mostly he reserved it for female clients. But on that day he brought it out for me.

"You're my boss, Mason, not my man."

"Ah, hell. Ya know what I mean."

"Even still. I can't be a PI."

"Why not?"

I wanted to tell him I didn't know how, but he knew that was a lie. So I said, "I'm afraid."

"Hell you are, Quick. I never saw the likes of you when it comes to guts."

I had been on a few stakeouts with him and never showed any fear even when we got into close shaves.

"If you're thinkin of some of those cases we did together, well, I had *you* with me, Mason."

"Ah, you coulda handled them alone."

"How'd ya know?"

"I know ya, Quick. I knew it from the first day I laid my headlights on ya."

"You were hungover and ya woulda hired King Kong."

"But I didn't. I hired you, and now I gotta get my rump overseas and knock off some Nips. Ya gotta take over."

"What if I'm so lousy at this I lose the agency."

"Ya won't."

And so far I hadn't.

I'm not what you'd call a raving beauty, but some even call me pretty, and I agree I'll pass. Take today. I was wearing a short-sleeved cream-colored dress that was covered with bright blue intersecting circles, cinched below my bosom and belted at the waist. My hair was black, the long sides ending in a fringe of manufactured curls, and every hair in my pompadour was in place. But I was getting sick of this style, and I'd been thinking of changing. Maybe I'd get it cut short, shock the pants off my pals. Rolling and pinning were getting to be a pain in the derriere.

My mouth was small but full; my nose had a little bump, but it was okay. So the point was that even though I *looked* like any twenty-six-year-old gal ankling round New York City in '43, there was one main difference between me and the rest of the broads. Show me another Jane who did my job and I'd eat my hat. And I wouldn't relish that cause my brown felt chapeau had a bright red feather sticking up from the left side of the brim, and I knew the feather would tickle going down.

Once or twice I had some numbskull who thought a dame couldn't handle his so-called important case, but most people didn't care that I was a girl, and they knew any self-respecting male private dick was fighting to keep us safe.

So I wasn't hurting for things to do when my secretary, Birdie, showed the Wests into my office. But I was surprised, even though it was no mystery why they'd come to me as I was the one who'd discovered their daughter's body and no one had been arrested so far. I lit a Camel and listened while they talked.

The man and woman who sat on the other side of my desk were in their late forties to early fifties and looked fifteen years older. Having yer child murdered will do that to you.

Porter West was a big man, but he slumped in his chair like a hunchback. His thinning blond hair was turning the color of old corn. And his brown eyes were dull and defeated.

His wife, Myrna, was a brunette, spear-thin with skin that looked like tracing paper and eyes too sad to look into.

"Will you take the case, Miss Quick?"

"Yeah, I'll take it," I said. "But starting this late after the murder will make it harder."

"Well, the police haven't done anything," Mrs. West said. Her voice was shrill.

I knew the coppers had probably done plenty. Still, this was what people who were connected to unsolved murders believed. I didn't say this to Mrs. West. I nodded in a way I hoped would give her the idea that I agreed with her and was sympathetic, which I was.

"You have to understand that chances are slim that I'll find the killer."

West said, "We have no other choice."

"Well, my fee is—"

"We don't care what the fee is."

He was a lawyer with an important firm, and the Wests were in clover.

"I have to tell ya anyway."

When that was settled, West gave me a picture of his dead daughter, a folder that included a history of Claudette West's short life, and all the newspaper clippings about the case. The murder, as I well knew, had taken place four months before.

"You don't have police reports, do ya?"

He snorted. "What do you think?"

"They wouldn't give us anything," she said.

"Not even the names of possible suspects?" I asked.

"There was only one. Her ex-boyfriend, Richard Cotten." She wrinkled her small nose like she was smelling Limburger.

"He was never charged," West said.

"But he *was* a suspect?" I knew he was.

"For a time."

"I guess neither of ya liked him much." I stubbed out my butt in the overflowing glass ashtray.

"Liked him? Cotten is a despicable bastard," he said.

"Tell me why ya say that?"

"He didn't love her. He was only interested in her money."

I'd heard this before, but mostly from wives hiring me to follow husbands they think are stepping out on them.

Mrs. West said, "He was from a poor family and was raised by a working mother. Not that there's anything wrong with a mother working, but she was never there and Richard ran wild."

I could tell Myrna West didn't think a mother should work no matter what.

"Father?"

"Shot in a bar fight when Cotten was four," West said.

"Richard is a very angry person."

"Did he hit your daughter?"

He said, "Oh, no. But he showed it in other ways."

"How?"

"It was the way he talked to her. He always acted as if she was dumb, said hurtful things. That's what we observed the three or four times we saw them together."

"Claudette would have told us if he'd hurt her physically," Myrna said.

I wasn't sure that was true.

"You ever talk to her about the things he said to her?"

"Yes. She said that it was just his way." West shook his head in disgust.

"You said *ex*-boyfriend. How long before the murder had they split up?"

"Only a few weeks."

"Do you have a picture of him?" I'd seen his picture in the paper, but I hadn't kept it.

"You'll find one in the clippings."

"Did he go to NYU, too?" I already knew the answer.

"Yes. And he's still there. They were juniors when it happened. Didn't you read the papers, Miss Quick? Weren't you interested, considering?"

"Yeah, sure. But I didn't keep a file."

The expression on Porter West's pale pinched face looked as though he didn't approve. I ignored it.

"Being a suspect didn't change his life; it made him a kind of hero."

I also knew this, but I wanted to get the straight skinny from the father.

Anger flashed in West's eyes, a small sign of life. "Some of the students got behind him, saying he was being picked on because he was poor."

"That he was a wonderful, kind boy," she said.

"The boy is a C student."

In my book this didn't make him a murderer.

"I guess he had a lot of friends," I said.

"But he didn't. Not until this happened. There are always those people looking for a martyr. Finding injustice wherever they can," West said.

"And there were no other suspects?"

"None that we knew about."

That didn't mean there weren't any. I'd have to have a meet with a dick named Marty Mitchum. He'd been Woody's connection, and he'd passed Mitchum on to me. Or maybe it was me to him.

"So, you suspect Cotten because he said mean things to your daughter and Claudette dumped him?"

West looked at me as though I was his enemy.

"I'm not crossin you, Mr. West. I'm just tryin to get things in place."

"Yes. Those actions and the fact that he was after her money. When she broke it off with him, he knew that the pot of gold was out of reach, and it made him furious."

This last was speculation, but I'd keep it in mind when I met with Cotten.

"Is there anything else I should know?" I lit another cig.

They looked at each other. Almost invisibly West shook his head at Myrna like a warning.

"No," he said.

"Okay. That's all for now. I'll need your phone number."

I took the number down, and West handed me a check.

"You'll call us every day?"

"That's not how I usually operate," I said.

"That's how *I* expect you to operate."

"What I normally do is call the client if I have somethin to tell."

"I don't care what you normally do. I want you to call us daily."

This was getting my goat, but I held back. "How about once a week unless I have somethin to tell you?"

"Every day."

I didn't like this arrangement, but I wanted this case. "Okay."

"We'll hear from you tonight," he said.

"Mr. West, I have to go through this material. I'll have nothin to say by tonight."

He weighed this information. "Tomorrow night then."

I nodded.

West put a hand on his wife and guided her toward the door. They went out and didn't look back.

Charming people, I thought. Then I brought to mind what they'd been through, who they'd lost, and I gave them some slack.

I thought about when West shook his head at his wife and knew it could've meant a simple no to my question, but I felt it meant something else.

I didn't know what it was.

But I knew I'd find out.

TWO

After the Wests left there was a tap on the pebbled glass in my door, and I told Birdie to come in. I never thought I'd have a secretary of my own when I was learning typing and shorthand.

"Were they who I think they are?"

"Yep."

"Jeez, Louise, they hire you?"

"They did."

Birdie Ritter was what you'd call a tomato. She was tall, five feet eight inches, unlike me, who measured just under five feet four inches. Her blonde hair was parted on the right and fell to her shoulders. There it flipped up in a Bette Davis style that framed a heart-shaped face. Bee-stung lips were painted scarlet, and Birdie's big eyes were the color of Milk Duds. She wore a pink blouse, wide collar with pearls at her throat, and a gray skirt.

"Guess it makes sense," she said. "I'm goin to lunch if it's okay by you."

"Sure, take a long one if you want."

"You're the best boss, Faye."

I lit up a Camel. "Where ya goin?"

"I'm meetin Pete over at the Automat."

"Thought you weren't gonna see him anymore."

"Ah, Faye, he's better than nobody. Pickins are slim these days."

I guess that was one way of looking at it, but I wouldn't want Pete McGill on my dance card if he was the last guy in town. And he practically was. McGill was 4F.

"Have a slice of apple pie for me," I said. There's nothing I liked better than Horn and Hardart apple pie with a slice of cheddar.

"I'll do that," Birdie said, and gave me a jaunty three-fingered salute.

After she left I recalled the last boyfriend I'd had. It was a year ago. I liked Private Don McCallister a lot; he had a hooper-dooper southern accent, and he was a nice kid. But I hardly knew him. Then he'd been sent overseas, and we wrote lots of letters saying a lot of stuff we probably wouldn't have said if there hadn't been a war on.

When the letters stopped coming, I had my fears, but I couldn't find out anything. Then a letter came from South Carolina. It was from Don's brother telling me Don had been killed and had received the purple heart. He asked me if I wanted my letters back. I didn't.

I swore I wouldn't get stuck on anyone again until this war was over, and I hadn't. Sometimes I'd volunteer at the USO Canteen, dance with some of the boys, talk a little, keep it light, but that was as far as it went.

Enough of that.

I took a long drag on my cig and remembered what a shock it'd been finding Claudette West that night. It had taken me days to perk up.

I glanced at the blank paper in my Underwood then began to make a list of names. Marlene Hayworth, the woman who came my way seconds after I'd found the body and who I sent to call the coppers; the first ones on the scene, Ryan and Conte; the detectives who followed it up, Clark and Hodiak. I might not have to talk to them, but they belonged on the list.

From the clippings in the folder the Wests had left I found names of Claudette's friends and teachers, all of which I added. And, of course, Richard Cotten's name.

I pulled the paper from the roller, folded it twice, and slipped it into my pocketbook. Time to do some legwork. That was what it was all about, this PI game, hitting the sidewalk and gabbing with everyone ya could.

But first I dialed Marty Mitchum, my personal friend at the NYPD, to set up a drink date later on.

In the bathroom mirror I stared at myself. A girl had to look her best when she was on a case and dealing with John Q. Public.

I pulled my lip case apart and twisted the end. Crazy Crimson was my choice. I used a different color every week just to keep it interesting. I put on the lipstick, then blotted hard on a piece of toilet paper, which showed my lips with all their creases and crimps like fingerprints.

I didn't use mascara or eyelash gunk. But I could hold up three wooden matchsticks with my eyelashes, not as many as my mother could. But I didn't want to think about her now. Or most of the time. I didn't like thinking about my family at all.

I decided, not for the first time, it was a damn nuisance getting ready to take on the world. At work I had always worn heels and hose, but it'd been a while since I'd had a pair of silk stockings cause they were making parachutes from the stuff. Once in a blue moon I got a pair of nylons. Usually, same as a lotta other girls, I wore leg makeup and used my eyebrow pencil to draw a seam down the back of my legs.

I got out the tortoiseshell compact that held my powder and a matching case that housed my rouge. Then I lightly powdered my face, and dabbed my cheeks to make me look healthy. After a final drag and one smoke ring, I threw the cig down the toilet, flushed, and left the WC.

From the little table next to the door I got my book and purse, grabbed my tan spring coat and my brown felt hat off the rack, and left the office.

The weather was getting nice, so I didn't button my coat. Next to my office building on Forty-third Street there was a cigar store run by a guy named Sam the Stork, so called cause he was tall and thin and bent his long neck in a way that made you think of his moniker. When I opened the door, I heard the strains of "Old Black Magic" coming from the radio.

"Stork," I said, "how goes it?"

He was behind his marble-topped counter and bobbed his neck to say everything was copacetic.

"Ya wanna pack a cigs, Faye?"

I said I did, and paid for the cigs as well as the two papers I'd be taking on my way out.

I happened to know, as well as owning the store, Sam ran a crap game in his back room, and there were always a few guys hanging around, waiting to get in on the action. Today Larry the Loser, Blackshirt Bob, and Fat Freddy took up space. They all greeted me with a touch to the brim of their hats, although it was Blackshirt Bob, with a face like a bag of screwdrivers, who spoke.

"How're ya doin, Faye?"

He asked me this whenever he saw me as he couldn't get over that a twist ran a detective agency. And cause when Woody left they made book on how long I'd last. The bet stood until Mason came back or I folded. They had no idea I knew about this, but Stork, who bet on me making good, had a leaky mouth and told me right away.

"I'm doin fine, Bob, just fine." I threw him a stunning smile.

The boys were smoking and flipping through magazines while they waited. I saw that Loser, leaning against the counter, was wearing his checkered jacket and eyeballing a racing form. He was famous for his love of the ponies and also for how often he lost, which was almost every day.

"Got any cases?" Fat Freddy asked me as he nonchalantly peered over the top of *Life* magazine.

I tried not to laugh. Fat Freddy was always short and regularly tried to tap me for a fin, which I never gave him. He wanted to win the bet more than the others.

He was getting fatter by the day. Folds now hid his neck altogether, and his belly spilled over his belt like a sack of flour.

"I have quite a few cases, Freddy, thank you. Matter of fact, I just got a new one which is prime."

Fat Freddy forced a smile, making him look like an egg had broken across his face. "Good for you, Faye."

I picked up my two papers from the shelf. "See ya, boys," I said as I went for the door, and as I was leaving I heard "Praise the Lord and Pass the Ammunition" starting and was glad I was getting out of there cause this song drove me to distraction.

I loved living in New York City. There was always a feeling of life going on no matter what time of day or night. I ankled over to the subway at Broadway and Forty-second Street and descended. Once down there I dropped a nickel in the slot, went through the turnstile, and waited on the platform for my train. First on my docket was Richard Cotten.

Even though I'd been in New York for five years, I still found eyeballing the citizens a pleasing pastime. Of course it *was* part of my job, taking in the clothes, colors, features of almost everyone I came across. So I guess I should've called it a habit.

There were only three people this time of day, two sailors and an older civilian of the male persuasion. Each was different. That's what made the human race so interesting to me. Two eyes, one nose, one mouth, but all different. Every joker was unique.

My train whooshed in, and one of the sailors and me got on. There were plenty of seats. After I cased the car I was in, mentally noting where each citizen was sitting, I opened *The Valley of Decision* to page 74 and read my way to my stop at West Eighty-sixth.

Cotten's building was on West Eighty-eighth. I saw by the buzzer that he was on the fifth floor. I didn't bother to ring, preferring the surprise of my arrival at his door.

In the hallway I smelled onions, garlic, tomato sauce, fish, and maybe a touch of liver. My schnoz was a great detector.

This was an older building, and the walls needed paint. Most walls needed paint these days, and they'd stay that way until the war was over, I thought. These walls still showed shades of green, though they were greasy and filmed over from years gone by.

I heard snippets of talk and radio music that wafted through doors as I made my way up the four flights. Cotten lived in 5C. I knocked.

In moments he opened the door and gave me a fast once-over. "Who are you and what do you want?"

The friendly type. I took my PI license from my pocketbook and flipped it open. Then I handed it to him.

He studied it. "So?"

"I have a few questions."

"About what?"

"I'll tell ya when I come in."

"I have nothing to say." He started to shut the door, but my foot was in place. I hated this part because it always hurt.

"Ya got nothin to say, ya can say no to my questions."

He stared at me. Finally he opened the door, and I went in. He knew why I was there, but pretended not to.

Richard Cotten was taller than me by about five inches and had a full head of dark curly hair. He had coffin-cold blue eyes and a short straight nose. His complexion was pink, and his lips were thin. He wore dungarees and a white shirt, sleeves rolled up. His feet were bare.

"What kind of questions?"

"About Claudette West."

"Is this never going to end?"

"Not until the killer is found."

"I'm not the killer."

"I know you're not," I said. I didn't know this at all, but I needed to make nice with him. "I wanna learn more about her so I can find the killer."

"Sit down."

We both sat. Me on a clumpy chair, him on a sagging faded flow-ered sofa. The place was neat for a college student. No week-old plates of food littering the room. But books and papers lay scattered around.

Cotten reached for a coffee cup on the table and took a slug. He didn't offer me anything to drink.

"How long did you date Claudette?"

"I didn't just date her. We were engaged."

This was news to me. "So how long?"

"Two years, four months, seven days."

I noted this display of caring. "She have other boyfriends?"

"I told you we were engaged."

"So why'd ya split?"

"Things end."

"She break up with you?"

He waited a second. "Yeah. No. I mean, it was sort of mutual."

"I didn't have that impression."

"Impression? Who from, the Wests? Did they hire you?"

I ignored all his questions. "Did you like Claudette's parents?"

"Hated their guts."

"Why?"

"They treated me like dirt."

This didn't surprise me. "How so?"

"It was like I didn't exist when they were around. Neither of them ever said anything to me except hello and goodbye. I always knew why."

"Why?"

"Because I'm not of their class."

"Claudette was a rich girl, wasn't she?"

"I guess. Yes."

"How'd you feel about that?"

"Feel? I didn't feel anything about it."

"You didn't care if she was rich or not?"

"It got in the way sometimes."

I asked him what he meant by that.

"I don't have an extra dime. So sometimes she'd pay."

"Sometimes?"

"A lot of times."

"You didn't like that?"

"No. It was awkward. But, hell. She wanted to do stuff all the time and knew I couldn't afford to. So that way we didn't have to sit home."

"So ya *did* have some feelins about it." I didn't wait for an answer. "And you were gonna marry her?"

"I thought so until near the end. We started to get tired of each other, I guess. Thing was, I was sick of the money thing."

"The inequality of your bankbooks?"

"Yeah."

"And was she sick of it, too?"

"She never said."

"I heard that you didn't accept the breakup."

"Did the Wests tell you that?"

I stood up. I hadn't expected to get a confession or anything much out of him. I'd wanted to see what he was like and now I'd seen.

"Where are you going?"

"To see a man about a dog." My pop had said that to me when I was a kid, and when he didn't come home with the dog, I cried for days.

"That's all you want to know? That's it?"

"That's it."

I left.

On the street I made a few notes. I didn't particularly like Cotten, but I didn't despise him either. He was a zero. I suppose he could've killed his girlfriend in a fit of jealousy, but he didn't seem to me to have real passion.

I wasn't persuaded that he was the killer.

THREE

After I left Cotten's I had a meat loaf sandwich at a favorite diner, then back to the office. Worked on some other small jobs and after that went to Smitty's on Forty-sixth, the watering hole where I met Marty Mitchum.

I knew Mitchum would be there first cause a dame going to a saloon alone wasn't duck soup. Most mugs got the wrong idea. Even here where I often met Mitchum.

Marty was sitting at the bar facing the door, the tail end of a cigar clenched between his choppers. He wore his hat perched on the back of his head, a thatch of straight brown hair hanging over his forehead like stubborn bangs.

He saw me, got up, and walked my way. Janes weren't allowed to sit at the bar even with an escort. You'd think this was some swank place or something.

"Faye, good to see ya." He pecked me on the cheek. "Let's get a table."

I followed him to the rear of the joint where we took our seats in a scrappy red leather booth.

Mitchum's brown eyes were red-rimmed like he was tired or hungover. His navy blue suit jacket had seen better days, and his wide patterned tie was pulled down, loose at the neck. The stogie in his mouth wasn't lit, but he kept it there when he talked, giving him a tight-lipped expression.

"Hey, I didn't ask. You want somethin to drink?"

"Sure. I'll take a manhattan."

"Right back," he said and slid out.

After I lit up I looked around. From where I sat I could see most of the place. There was sawdust on the floor, and the bar itself was long and curved, the customers two deep, noisy and boozy. From other times I knew they were mostly cops, but even if I hadn't been told I would've known. There was something about bulls that reeked of the law no matter where they were or how they dressed.

"Here ya go, Faye," Marty said, and put the cocktail glass in front of me. "So how's tricks? Ya hear from Woody?"

"Yeah. A letter came last week. He's in the thick of it, and ya could say he isn't exactly a happy boy. You wanna write to him?"

"Nah. I ain't good at that sort a thing, Faye. You write and tell him I said hello."

"Sure." I took the first sip of my manhattan and felt the warm alcohol go down my gullet. Tasty. "How's Bridgett?" She was Marty's wife.

"Bridgett's Bridgett." He looked away from me, and I knew it was cause he had a chippy on the side. Marty, like all the rest, thought nobody knew. Everybody did.

I didn't want to torture him, but the natural next question was to ask about his kids, so I did.

"Marty Jr. is gettin to be a big guy, and Catherine's smart as a whip. Takes after her mother, I guess." He chuckled, took another swig of beer. "How about you? Any big lugs knockin on your door?"

"Not lately. Anyway, I don't have time for romance."

"Oh, come on, Faye. You can tell me. A skirt like you ain't gonna be alone for long."

"In case ya haven't noticed, Marty, most of the guys my age are over there."

"Yeah, I guess."

"Why so glum?"

"Ah, I just wish I was younger so I could give them Krauts and Nips a piece a my mind."

Marty was about forty, I guessed. "Be glad you didn't have to go. It's no picnic over there, says Woody."

"You wouldn't understand, Faye." The bags under his eyes seemed to get darker.

"Yeah, maybe." He was right. There was something about men that made them want to fight this war. Me? I was glad I was a girl so I didn't hafta go. But guys felt differently about it.

We both worked on our drinks. I stubbed out my cig.

To break the silence I said, "I got a new case, thought ya might be able to gimme some dope on it."

"Ya know I will if I can." He looked relieved that I was changing the subject. "What's the deal?"

"Claudette West. Remember?"

"Sure thing. Wasn't on it myself, but I know guys who were. You been hired by who? The parents?"

I could tell Marty cause he was my friend. Any other law I'd keep my trap shut.

"I need to know if there were any other suspects beside the boyfriend, Cotten. And I wouldn't mind anything else you might come up with."

He leaned across the table to light my cig, but didn't torch his cigar. "Ya want the autopsy?"

"Might as well."

"Sure thing." He slapped his forehead with a meaty hand. "Hey, I'm just rememberin, you found the body, didn't ya?"

"That's right."

"So, this is like a personal thing with you, right?"

"I didn't think so, but maybe it'll turn out that way. I mean, I hadn't thought much about it the last couple a months till the parents walked in my office. At first it was all I could think about. It's not somethin that happens to a gal every day."

"Yeah, that must've been lousy for ya."

"No picnic. I usually don't have anything to do with dead bodies. People come to me for other things. Even if it's a murder case, it's after the fact."

"Yeah."

"So when do ya think you'll be able to get some dope on this?"

"I'll get on it first thing tomorrow. Good enough?"

"You betcha," I said.

My flop is a two-room apartment on Grove and Bleecker Streets in Greenwich Village. This was another reason why the case had piqued my interest. I'm close to Seventh Avenue, and I'd found her body on the other side of town near Seventh.

We don't have a lot of murders in the Village since prohibition was lifted, although we still have a rep for other nutty goings-on. Even during these war years, the Village was a haven for bohemians of all types. And the notion of free love lingered like a fading fragrance.

I liked living down here cause of the attitudes most people had. No judgments. And you didn't have to wear your glad rags all the time. Most weekends, when I did my chores, I wore a sweater or blouse with my gray gabardine slacks. I figured if Katharine Hepburn could wear them, so could I. But I wouldn't dream of going uptown decked out that way.

When I got off the subway at Christopher and Seventh Avenue, I walked to Bleecker, where the pushcarts lined the street. They were filled with the freshest vegetables, meats, fish, everything you'd want. So I shopped daily cause it was so close to where I lived. Between the carts and people it took some skill to move along the street.

I felt like having a nice piece of fish, so I made my way to Dom's cart near Jones.

"Hello, lady," Dom said. "You lookin good."

"Hey, Dom, thanks."

"You want some flounder? Sole?"

"Flounder."

"For you and your boyfriend or justa you?"

He always asked this even though I'd told him I had no boyfriend.

"Just me."

"Okay. I pick a good piece for you."

And he did, as always. I handed him my ration book.

"How's the family?"

"I hear from my boy overseas who fights the war." He beamed. "The others good, too." He pulled the stamps from the book.

Dom was proud of Thomas, who was serving his country, America. The *others* were five more and his wife. Neither Yolanda nor Dom were citizens, but all the kids had been born here. He handed me the wrapped fish in a paper bag and gave me back my book.

I thanked him and went down the street to Herman's to get my vegetables, string beans and a fresh cuke to add to my lettuce at home. I tried hard not to go into the pastry shop, but something sucked me in like magic. I bought a charlotte russe. When I was little, I would always get one on Saturdays. I still couldn't believe I could have one any time I wanted. And I wanted one a lot of times. So I was set.

I made my way along Bleecker till I came to Grove, where near the corner I climbed the stone steps to the big front door. They say Hart Crane, the poet, lived here. He killed himself in '32. Most people think he did a Brodie from the Brooklyn Bridge cause he wrote about it, but it was from a steamer ship on his way back from Mexico. Truth is, most people didn't think about Hart Crane at all.

In the foyer I opened my mailbox. I had some bills and a copy of *The New Yorker*. It was the only magazine I subscribed to. I confess once in a while I'd pick up a copy of *Photoplay* or *Movie Mirror* at Stork's, but I couldn't afford to subscribe to more than one magazine. So I'd spend my evening reading *The New Yorker* and listening to the Red Skelton show.

I opened the second door and went to my apartment, which was on the first floor. I could hear the phone ringing, so I juggled my packages and shoved in the key.

I got to it on the fourth ring.

"Miss Quick?"

I couldn't believe it. "Hold on," I said.

I wanted to get the fish in the fridge. When that was done, I picked up the receiver again.

"Yeah?"

"This is Porter West."

I knew who it was, and I was already boiling. "How'd ya get this number, Mr. West?"

"The phone book."

Well, sure. There weren't too many Faye Quicks in there; in fact, there was only me. "What can I do for ya?"

"I wanted to know what you thought of Cotten?"

"We made an agreement that *I'd* call *you* tomorrow night." As I was saying this, it dawned on me he *knew* I'd seen the guy. Was he following me?

"When we made that agreement, you said you'd have nothing to report by tonight. That's changed," West said.

"What's changed?" I reached into my pocketbook and pulled out my pack of Camels and matches.

"Well, you . . . I mean . . . I didn't know then that you were going to meet with Cotten."

"And how do ya know now?" I stuffed a cig in my mouth, lit it, and pictured myself like a cartoon with steam coming out of my ears.

West was silent.

"Well?" I took a healthy drag of my cig, and right away felt better. Calmer.

"I happen to know you saw him today."

"How do ya *happen* to know that?" I sat down on my chair next to the telephone table.

"I saw you go into his building."

"Mr. West," I said, "are you followin me?"

"No."

"Then how do ya explain that ya saw me go into Cotten's buildin?" I blew smoke through my nostrils like Joan Crawford.

"I was . . . I . . . was watching his building."

My place had once been the parlor floor of a town house. I looked up at my high ceiling and admired the carved cherubs in the corners of the molding. Then took in my red velvet draperies on either side of the two huge windows that faced Grove. I was waiting for West to explain. So I looked around some more. It was a big room with two sofas and three chairs. Also a folded table that I dragged out when I had company to dinner. Bookcases stuffed from top to bottom lined one wall. And the right-hand front corner was empty. Waiting. As soon as I had enough money saved I was gonna buy a piano. I loved to tickle the ivories. And I wasn't a bad canary either. No June Christy, but I could do a good rendition of "As Time Goes By" if requested. Even if it wasn't. The silence on the line finally got my goat.

"So you wanna tell me why you were watchin Cotten's buildin?"

"I always watch it," he said.

I didn't know what to make of that. "What do ya mean, *always*?"

His voice got stronger as though he was affirming his rights. "I go there and sit in my car, and when Cotten comes out I follow him."

"You have to stop that, Mr. West."

"Why?"

"For one thing, if Cotten catches ya, he can sue for harassment. For another, ya got *me* now. Ya have to back off. Anyway, what do ya think you're gonna gain by spyin on the kid?"

"I don't like how you said that."

"Said what?"

"The kid. As if you think he's some poor maligned person."

I tried not to sigh into the phone. I wasn't sure I could work with this guy. "Mr. West, I don't think anything of the kind. Now if you want me on this case you're gonna have to leave things like surveillance up to me."

"How will I know you're doing your job?"

"Ya won't. Ya'll have to trust me. *You* hired me, Mr. West. I didn't come to you."

"All right. But tell me, what did you think of Cotten?"

"I don't have a real feel for him yet."

"But you could see that he's guilty, couldn't you?"

This couldn't go on. "We'll stick to the agreement and I'll call ya tomorrow night."

"Can't you tell me that one thing?"

"No. Do ya still want me on this case?"

There was a long pause. "Yes."

"Fine. I'm gonna hang up now, Mr. West. Good night." I gently replaced the receiver.

I sat there staring at the spot where my piano was gonna go. This case was gonna be hell. I had to do something to get Porter West out of my way. It was too much to think about now. I needed to eat my nice piece of fish so I could get to my charlotte russe.

FOUR

The next morning I decided to skip the office and interview the next person on my list. I'd given her a jingle the night before, so she was expecting me at ten. I'm an early riser, so I had to cool my heels till it was time to go. But I didn't mind. I'd gone to my downtown news dealer, and the wait gave me a chance to enjoy two cups of joe while I read the *Daily News* and the *Herald Tribune*.

At nine-fifteen I figured I could leave to get to the Murray Hill area on the East Side in the Thirties by ten.

My neighbor across the hall, Dolores, was sweeping the floor in front of her door. Even though we had a janitor, Dolores did this every day. She was about seventy-five—no one knew for sure—and she wore a blonde wig. We could only guess why. It wasn't a good one and was always slipping down over her forehead, making her look wacky. Well, that's what she was. Wacky but nice.

Her face was long, and she had drooping brown eyes underscored by folds of skin the size of tea bags. And her mouth was always lipsticked above the line of her thin upper lip. She was wearing an emerald green blouse and a flame red rayon crepe A-line skirt. For Dolores this was subtle.

We exchanged greetings, and then I recklessly asked her how she was.

"Oy," she said, and leaned on her broom handle.

I knew I was in for it.

"Between the aches and the pains I don't know which is worse. One ache goes then comes a pain. Pain goes, ache comes back."

"Have you seen a doctor?"

"Have I seen a doctor? she asks. Is the Pope Catholic? You want I should name them for you?"

"No, that's okay."

"Wasserman, Mayer, Jessel, Ca—"

"Dolores, I believe you." Stopping her this way, I felt I had to ask the obvious next question. "What was the diagnosis?"

"From which one?"

"The one ya liked best."

"I hated them all. Age, they said. Decrepitude. It should be expected. Why I want to know? Do they give me a sensible explanation? No. So I'll live with the pain, the aches. What can a girl do?"

"I'm sorry you feel so bad."

"Eh, it's nothing."

I felt like saying my own "oy." "I gotta go, got an appointment."

"You got a big case, maybe?"

"Maybe," I said, opening the front door. "You take care, Dolores."

"Zay gezundt," she said.

Now I was gonna be late, so I walked to Seventh Avenue and hailed a hack I couldn't afford.

There was an alley called Sniffen Court off East Thirty-sixth between Lexington and Third. About ten brick carriage houses were sheltered behind a locked iron gate. They'd been converted into residences some time in the late 1920s. I'd never gotten past that gate, and I was all keyed up about finally going inside one of the houses. Marlene Hayworth, the dame who appeared after I found Claudette West's body, called one of them home.

She buzzed me through the gate. There were horsemen sculpted into the rear wall of the alley as though they were plaques. The other plugs who lived in the court had all put some type of plant or bush by their doors. The street itself was made up of different-sized stone blocks that had cracks in them here and there.

Miss Hayworth lived halfway down the alley in a two-story building with a rounded door and mullioned windows. I used the brass knocker, and about thirty seconds later she opened up.

I hadn't taken her in on the night of the murder, so I was surprised by her looks. She was a stunner. Exactly like the other Miss Hayworth, she had red locks flowing round an oval face with big brown eyes, long lashes, and a slash of burgundy mouth. She wore a colorful silk kimono and black fabric open-toed slippers.

"Hello, Miss Quick. Come in."

I did.

The living room was all white, which incidentally set off the owner's hair, from sofa to chairs to plush carpet, and I didn't like to walk across it. Miss Hayworth sensed this.

"I presume you wiped your feet."

Now that I reflected on the subject I realized I had, which I told her. "But should you want, I'll remove my shoes."

"Not necessary. Take a seat. Can I offer you something to drink? Coffee? Tea?"

"No thanks."

Her kimono swished sweetly as she sashayed to the couch. I settled for a wing chair.

She said, "I presume you want the details about my being where I was at the time I was there."

I secretly hoped she wouldn't keep saying "presume." "That would be helpful." I had wondered what a broad of this caliber was doing alone on Bleecker and Thompson streets at about eleven that night.

She took a cigarette from her white case, put it into an ivory holder, then lit it with a Zippo. A jarring combination. She offered me one, but I declined, got my own out of my pocketbook, lit it with a match.

Hayworth blew out a long smoke stream and said in her melodious voice, "I've been through this with the police, of course."

"Yeah, but I'm not workin for them."

"Who're you working for?" She crossed her legs in a splash of silk.

"Can't say. So, tell me, Miss Hayworth, how did you happen to be there?"

"I was coming from a friend's apartment, and I practically fell over you."

"A friend's apartment?"

"Yes. My friend lives on Thompson in a walk-up," she said, and pursed her lips in distaste.

"This man is your boyfriend?"

"Who said it was a man?"

"Wasn't it?" I realized then that this little fact hadn't been in the papers.

"Is that important?"

"Might be."

"Why?"

"You might need an alibi."

"For what?"

"Don't tell me you haven't thought about this."

"Thought about what? I'm not sure I like your implication."

I wasn't sure I liked *her.* "You bein the second to come across her body, well, you could be a suspect."

"But I'm not. No one has ever thought that. The police certainly didn't."

"Yet. It's all new from here, Miss Hayworth. See, I gotta look at everythin again, and take a new perspective. So I might have to talk to your boyfriend."

"Mr. Flynn is not my boyfriend. We're just good friends."

"Mr. Flynn?"

"The man I was visiting. Gregory Flynn."

"Not much of a gentleman, is he?"

"Why do you say that?"

"Lettin a lady leave by herself. Not gettin a taxi for ya."

After only smoking it halfway down, Marlene stubbed out her butt in a black Stork Club ashtray. I said, "I *presume* you lifted that from the club?"

"Mr. Billingsley gave it to me."

I happened to know that this was a lie as Sherman Billingsley was notoriously cheap and everyone stole his ashtrays. I heard he bought them by the carload knowing what he knew. But I could understand that a high muckety-muck like her didn't wanna be lumped in with the hoi polloi.

"You're good friends with Sherm?" I asked.

"Are you?"

I smiled. I didn't know why I was pushing this; I didn't care if she had light fingers. I let it go. "What about Mr. Flynn?"

"Mr. Flynn is very much a gentleman. It so happens I told him not to walk me to a cab. I pride myself on being independent. Don't you?"

She got me there. "I suppose I can understand that. So, you left his apartment a few minutes before you bumped into me and the body of Claudette West?"

"That's correct. As you may remember I screamed into the night."

I did remember, but I thought that was a dramatic way of putting it.

"So then I asked ya to call the coppers and ya did. Where did ya call from?"

She put a new cigarette in her holder and fired up again.

"I ran back up to Mr. Flynn's apartment, and we phoned the police. That was it. As you know they met you and me on the street five minutes later."

"Guess I'll have to see Mr. Flynn, too."

"Why? He can tell you less than I."

"That right?" I put out my cig in an ashtray near me.

"There's no need to interview Mr. Flynn."

"You have a reason to be scared of that?"

"That depends."

"On what?"

"What you're going to do with the information, Miss Quick."

"You can call me Faye. What I do with the info? I don't tell anybody about it, that's what ya mean."

"I suppose it is."

"Mr. Flynn has a wife?"

"He does."

"Ya tellin me the coppers kept their mouths shut, didn't inform Mrs. Flynn?"

"That's right."

I started to question this, but then I realized what was what and why it hadn't been in the papers. "So Mr. Flynn has friends in high places."

"You could say that."

"I just did."

"Mr. Flynn is an important man."

"And his home isn't really that apartment on Thompson Street, correct?"

"Correct. It's what he calls his home away from home."

So the married Mr. Flynn kept a setup in the Village. I wondered if Hayworth was his only guest or if from time to time he saw another skirt or two. Idle musings.

"How often do you see Mr. Flynn at that address?"

"What bearing could that possibly have on the murder?"

"Did you know Claudette West?"

"No. Of course not. Why would I know such a girl?"

Now that got my interest. "What kind of girl is that, Miss Hayworth?"

"I would think that would be obvious."

"It's not."

"Well . . . a girl who gets herself murdered, of course."

I almost laughed. So it was already becoming Claudette's fault she got herself killed. But I didn't say anything. I needed info from this dame, so best keep my opinions to myself.

I took out my pad and pencil. "What's Flynn's address?"

She clutched the neck of her kimono. "You wouldn't go to his house, would you?"

"How else am I gonna question him?"

"Can't you see him at the apartment?"

"But he doesn't live there, ya said."

"I can arrange for you to see him there."

"Okay. When?" I was a little let down that I wasn't gonna see where Flynn officially parked his slippers. But a girl had to take what she could get.

"I'll call him later."

"How about ya call him now." I raised one eyebrow, which always got people moving.

"All right," she said.

Hayworth rose and swished her way from the room. I noticed there was a phone on a table near the door, but knew she didn't want to talk in front of me.

I lit another cig while I waited. I wanted to get up and poke around, but it didn't seem worth it cause she could be back in a few secs. And she was.

"All right, Miss Quick, he'll be there tonight at eight."

"Thanks."

"Anything else?"

"Nope. I got what I need . . . for now."

"What does that mean?"

"Ya never know what might turn up, Miss Hayworth, ya never know. I'll find my own way out. S'long."

FIVE

When I hit the bricks again, I found a phone booth and gave my pal Anne Fontaine a jingle. I had a feeling she might be helpful on this case. She was home and said she'd meet me downtown at a used-book store on Fourth Avenue. This time I took the subway.

I loved Fourth cause it had lots of different kinds of bookstores. The books were all used, but some stores specialized in rare books, some art books, some popular fiction, and some everything all jammed together. We'd picked an everything called The Bookman to meet.

Inside, the smell was pure mold. But that was jake with me cause most of the books on the shelves weren't moldy. I'm not sure where the smell came from; maybe it was the general aroma of used-book stores.

The Bookman was owned and run by one Elisha Raft. He was a little palooka who didn't seem to have any help. The shelves sagged with the weight of the books, and I wondered how he could handle it all.

Raft came from the back room cause he heard the bell when I entered.

"Hello, Faye," he said.

I greeted him back. Raft was an oddball, to say the least. First time I clapped my eyes on him I almost jumped out of my pumps.

He had beady dark blinkers and bushy eyebrows. His black hair was busy with tufts, and he never smiled. The sunken cheeks didn't help the picture. As far as his body went, he looked like the ninety-seven-pound weakling in the Charles Atlas ad. He always wore dungarees and a crisp white shirt kept neat with a shabby leather belt, the buckle almost as big as him. But as strange as he looked, he was a very nice guy. And he knew his books.

"You lookin for anything special, Faye?"

"Just browsin today."

"Browse away then." He nodded his head once, which is what passed for a smile, and walked toward the back of the store.

While I waited for Anne I went over to the fiction and started at *A*. Even if I found something, I wouldn't let myself buy more than one book cause, not only couldn't my change purse let me, I was running out of book space in my apartment.

Anne had her own sense of time, so I knew I could be waiting here anywhere from ten minutes to an hour.

Books have always been my pals. I guess I turned to them in my childhood cause I didn't have any brothers or sisters. I almost had a brother, but he died of influenza when I was a baby. That's when my ma went off the deep end, my aunt Dolly told me. My ma couldn't get over little Frank dying like that. And I guess me staying alive. So that's why I spent the first four years of my life living with Aunt Dolly and Uncle Dan in Lancaster, Pennsylvania. When I came back to Newark, my ma was supposed to be better, but I don't think she was. By then she was already pretty well hooked on morphine.

My pop was around as much as he could be, and I loved him like crazy. He was nuts about me, too. He always read to me, and that's where I got my love of books. I had my own library card by the time I was six. So I brought home five, six books a week instead of five, six buddies. Books were safe and loyal and wouldn't dump me if my ma was nodding out in the living room or saying wacky things.

I read all kinds of stuff from Agatha Christie to Thomas Mann. But I'm not much of a nonfiction reader. I feel like ya can learn a lot by reading novels. I've learned a lot of what I know about humans that way.

I'd been browsing about fifteen minutes and was holding a Lloyd Douglas book when I heard the bell and saw Anne walking toward me. As eye-catching as ever, she wore a long colorful garment, which she'd folded and draped so that it hung on her frame perfectly, like Dorothy Lamour, though you couldn't call it a sarong. A cream crepe jacket cloaked her shoulders. She had her own sense of style, too. Like they say, she marched to a different drummer.

"Faye," she said.

We kissed each other's cheek.

"How are ya, Anne?"

"Fine," she said.

I didn't believe her. She was never fine. There were the usual dark circles beneath her brilliant blue eyes. And although she wore her blonde hair neat and short in its wavy way and her makeup was perfectly applied, I could tell. Being psychic took a lot out of her. It had always been like that.

Just walking around and seeing or knowing things didn't weaken her too much, but when she was doing her clairvoyant stuff for someone it was different. Anne would sometimes get sick to her stomach or get dizzy or both. But she felt since she had this gift it was her duty to help people.

Anne came from an upper-class family who lived on a gated block in the swankiest part of Newark, New Jersey. She was the oldest of four sisters and brothers. Her parents, especially her mother, had high hopes for her. She'd wanted Anne to be a college professor or maybe a doctor, even though it would be hard for a girl to do that. Anne'd gone to Vassar, but after she graduated she didn't want to go on with the halls of ivy. By then she felt she could do more good in the world if she plugged away at her clairvoyant knack. And she had a trust from her grandmother so she didn't have to worry about do re mi.

Her family was dead set against this, but Anne went for broke and she moved to New York and got her own place. She didn't advertise or anything, but word got around and soon she was finding lost things and sometimes lost people, and, although it made her sick, it also made her happy.

Anyway, I'd become aware of her psychic abilities the first day she spoke to me in the hall of Newark High. We were both sophomores. She stopped me and said, "How's Paul?"

I gave her the old jaw-dropping routine. Paul was a boy I was smitten with, but I hadn't told anyone and had never gone out with him.

"How'd ya know?" I said.

"It's written on your forehead in green."

I slapped a hand over where she said it was.

She laughed. "Don't worry. I'm the only one who can see it."

"What are ya, some freak or somethin?" I asked. Subtle as always. And kind, too.

"Yes," she said, and walked away.

Cause I didn't wanna ask anybody about her I didn't find her for two days. And when I did she was sitting alone under a tree, eating an apple.

I stood over her. "I'm sorry I said what I did."

"That's okay."

"You're used to it, huh?"

She stared at me, then patted the ground next to her.

I sat.

"Have you been asking people about me?" she said.

I told her I hadn't cause I didn't think she'd like that.

"Are you a psychic, too?"

"No. I just had a sneakin suspicion. Is that what you are? A psychic?"

"I guess. It's been happening all my life. I know things. I see things, like the name on your forehead. I don't usually say anything, don't know why I did with you."

"Cause you knew I was special?"

"Are you?"

I shrugged. "So you've been havin this stuff happen to you forever?"

"Yes, and it makes me sick. Physically sick."

"Then why do it?"

"I can't control it. I wish I could."

And that was the beginning. We became best friends.

Now I said, "Wanna go have some coffee?"

"Sure, there's a diner over on Third."

I knew she meant Earl's. I put back the copy of *Magnificent Obsession,* and we headed toward the door.

Elisha had come out when he'd heard the bell and was standing behind his wooden counter. "You gals leavin?"

"I'll be back," I said.

"I know you will," he said, and gave us the nod of his head.

Outside I asked Anne if she thought Raft was weird.

"Lonely," she said. "Since his parents died he's been living alone in an apartment that's much too big for him."

"I didn't know ya knew him that well."

"I don't," she said. "I don't know him at all."

"Oh." I didn't need to ask her how she knew.

At Third Avenue we crossed under the El. Earl's Diner was in the middle of the block. It was your usual dirt-cheap hash house in a chrome building set up to look like a dining car. Earl's name was on the roof, and at night it was lit up in red neon.

Inside there was a long counter and booths. The floor was a black-and-white-checkered linoleum. It being fairly empty, we took a booth near the back.

Before we could start jawing the waitress mooched over and slung a menu in front of each of us, then asked if we wanted coffee. Anne said tea.

Our soup jockey put a squint on her before she slouched away.

Personally, I didn't know how Anne could drink that swill, but it was none of my beeswax. We opened our menus and took a gander. I knew right away I'd have bread pudding. If that's all I had for lunch, I figured it wouldn't count. I asked Anne what she was having.

"I'm not hungry," she said.

She was never hungry. At first I thought it might be a problem of too little scratch, even with the trust, but when she came to my crib she never wanted anything either. I once made her a dinner of roast chicken, creamed spinach, and a baked potato. She picked at it, but I wouldn't say she ate it. I didn't do that again. The thing was she didn't look scrawny, she looked just right.

But I always wondered how a person could live without sweets, which Anne did. When I'd asked her about it in our teens, she'd told me she didn't care for them. I never got her to say more. I guess there wasn't a whole lot to say about it.

Our bubbly waitress returned with my cup of joe and Anne's tea.

"So youse know whatcha want?" She held her order pad in one chunky hand, a pencil in the other.

"I'd like the bread puddin. She doesn't want anything else."

She sighed so loud I thought the whole place could hear her, forgetting it was almost empty. But not even the two mugs at the counter looked our way.

"So what's up?" Anne asked.

"You remember that murdered student, Claudette West?"

"The one you found?"

"Yeah. Her parents came to see me yesterday."

"To hire you?"

I nodded. "Father was a pain in the derriere, but after what he's been through, well I gave him some room. He kept harpin on the ex-boyfriend, said he was the only suspect. Joker by the name Richard Cotten."

"Nothing about Brian Wayne?"

"No. Who's he?"

"He was her literature professor." She sipped her tea.

"I didn't see anything about him in the clippins the Wests gave me."

"He was never a suspect. They questioned him, of course. They questioned all her professors and friends."

"So why do you mention *him*?"

She bit her top lip, took a deep breath. "I have a feeling."

"You've met him?"

"No."

It didn't matter. I took this seriously. "How do you know about him?"

"In some article there was a brief mention of people in Claudette's life. He was listed. When I read his name, I started to feel dizzy and queasy, the way I do."

Had I missed Wayne's name in the clippings? Or did West leave out that report cause he was so fixed on Cotten? I took out my notebook and wrote down Wayne's name and what he taught.

"Anything or anybody else interest ya?"

She closed her eyes. "No. Not now."

The waitress threw my bread pudding in front of me. "Anything else?"

"No," I said.

"Why do I ask?" She scribbled on the pad, tore it off, and sailed it to me.

I eyeballed my dessert. It sure had the look. Bread pudding wasn't the ordinary dish that some people thought it was. There are all kinds of variations, which I won't go into, but this thing here, this beauty in front of me, looked like the real McCoy. I picked up my spoon and slipped it into the confection. It had the feel. And when I put it in my mouth, it had the taste.

"Good?"

"Perfect."

Anne smiled cause she was familiar with my sweet tooth.

"I'm glad," she said. And I knew she was.

I said, "Anne, will you work with me on this case? It's so cold I might need help." I hated to ask her cause I knew she'd go through hell if she helped. I also knew she always wanted to do good things.

"Of course I will, Faye."

"I don't know exactly what I want ya to do yet."

"That's all right. Get me something Claudette West used or wore."

"I will. I don't want to ask the Wests right away because . . ."

"They'll think you're a crackpot," Anne said.

"I . . . I guess they would."

"Don't feel bad. If I didn't know that by now, I'd be in big trouble."

True. She had no illusions about how anything to do with her being psychic affected most people.

"I feel like a crumb bum askin ya."

"Why?"

"Because it takes so much out of ya."

"So what?" She smiled the kind of smile that made men turn to mush. "It happens to me whether I'm concentrating on something specific or not. You know that, Faye."

"Sure. But isn't it worse when you're tryin to do something specific?"

"A little, maybe."

"But you're willin to help, anyway?"

"What's a psychic for?"

SIX

When I got to the office, Birdie handed me a bunch of pink memo slips with phone calls on them.

"Suddenly you're a very popular gal," she said.

"Yeah, I'm a regular June Allyson."

"Ya haven't been here much," Birdie said.

"Is that a knock?"

"Just sayin." She took out her compact and powdered her face. Something she did when she thought she hit a snag in a conversation.

"For your info I've been poundin the pavement."

"Any luck?"

I reached into my pocketbook and took out all my notes. "Would ya type these up?" I asked, handing them to her.

"You bet," she said. Birdie rolled a piece of paper into her Underwood.

"Before ya do that would ya look up a guy named Brian Wayne?"

"Sure thing, Boss Lady."

"It ain't funny, McGee."

"What ain't, Faye?" She batted her brown eyes at me all innocence. Birdie knew damn well what I meant. She knew her onions better than the next guy.

"You can drop the 'Boss Lady.' "

"Why? You ain't my boss anymore?"

"Can it, Birdie."

I opened my office door, and before I closed it behind me I heard her flipping through the phone book. Birdie could be irritating sometimes, but basically she was a good kid.

I sat behind my desk, threw the pink slips in front of me, and started going through them. There was one from my friend Jeanne, one from Anne, one from Marlene Hayworth, ten from Porter West, and none from Marty, which meant he hadn't been able to get the info yet.

I picked up West's, fanned them out like a poker hand, and felt myself starting to steam. I looked at Birdie's scratching of the times and saw that they'd come in fifteen-minute intervals.

I went out to talk to her. We didn't have an intercom, something I kept meaning to get.

"Birdie, tell me why ya didn't put all of West's calls on one sheet?"

"Well *you* got up on the wrong side of the bed, dincha?"

"Give it a rest. Why didn't ya do it?"

"Ya never told me to do it that way, Faye."

Her eyes were filling, and I knew I couldn't take that. Besides, I *was* being a grouse. "Okay, okay."

"Who ya really got a beef with, Faye?"

"Porter West for one. I didn't mean to take it out on you. What did he say when he called?"

"Just asked for you, and when I told him ya wasn't in he'd ask me the time."

"And?"

"And I'd tell him." She shrugged her padded shoulders.

"Then what?"

"Then he'd make a snortin sound and hang up."

"Every time?"

"Yup."

"Didn't say what he wanted?"

"I'd tell ya if he said something else, Faye."

"Yeah. Sure you would. I know that."

She took out a lace handkerchief and dabbed her eyes. I felt like a brute.

"My makeup mussed?" she asked.

"No. It's perfect. I'm sorry I yelled."

"That's okay."

"Nah. It's not okay. You're the best secretary a girl could have, and I don't wanna lose ya."

"Ah, Faye. I'm in for the long haul. Don't worry."

"Still and all, Bird, I had no call to treat ya that way."

She smiled and nodded, and I smiled, then started toward my office.

"Faye? I got a phone number for Brian Wayne. In fact, eight of them."

"Eight?"

"That's how many was in the directory."

"You write them down?"

"Yeah. Here."

"Thanks, kid. And the next time West calls tell me."

Back at my desk I lit a Camel and went over the addresses and phone numbers of the Brian Waynes. A wild guess told me he didn't live on Sutton Place, but I didn't scratch it out . . . just put a question mark next to it. I did the same with the one in Harlem. I settled on one in the Village. I knew I didn't have to do it this way cause I could go to the college and ask to see him. But I wanted to stake him out a couple a days before I met him.

I heard the phone ring, and Birdie picked it up. Then I heard the *click-clack* of her heels on the floor as she came toward my office. She rapped once and opened the door.

"It's him," she said.

I nodded my thanks and picked up the horn. "Hello," I said, like I didn't know who it was.

"It's about time," West said.

"Beg your pardon?"

"I've been calling you all day and you're never there."

I stubbed out my cig and lit another.

"Are you there?" West asked.

"I'm here and I'm tryin to cool down."

"What is that supposed to mean?"

"Mr. West, first ya shouldn't even be callin me, unless ya got a hot tip. Do ya?"

There was silence at the other end. Then he coughed.

"Well, do ya?"

"No. But why haven't you been in your office?"

"I don't solve crimes in my office, Mr. West. This is not a job where I come in nine to five. I'm out on the streets, gettin the poop, trackin down leads, doin interviews. Get it?"

"Who have you interviewed besides Cotten?"

"This isn't the deal we cut, Mr. West. I agreed to call ya once a day . . . at the end of my day startin tonight. But you've called me ten times already today. Not to mention last night. Now either we stick to that plan or you get another PI, and I can tell ya right now, nobody's gonna agree to your terms."

Silence.

I waited.

Finally, he said, "You have no idea what this is like."

He sounded so pitiful my heart went out to him. I softened my tone. "No, I don't know what it's like. But it must be terrible."

"Yes."

"Mr. West, I couldn't possibly know what you're feelin cause I don't have kids. But I can imagine. It's one of the reasons I took your case. Even so, we gotta have ground rules, and you gotta stick to them and let me do my job."

"Yes."

"I promise to call ya every night and like I told ya, that's not somethin I usually do. And I'll add this. If somethin bowls me over I'll let ya know right away. How's that seem?"

"That . . . that seems fair."

"Good. Now listen, I've been out there talkin and gettin leads, but I don't have anything to tell ya yet. And even if nothin else happens today, I'll phone ya tonight like we agreed."

"All right. I'll wait for your call then."

"Fine. I better go now."

"All right."

"Goodbye, Mr. West."

He mumbled a goodbye, and I hung up. I took a drag of my butt, then squashed it in my ashtray. I felt sorry for the guy, but I hoped I'd gotten through to him.

I went back to the Brian Waynes and dialed the one in the Village. A woman answered.

"Hello," I said. "Is this the residence of the Brian Wayne who teaches at NYU?"

"Who's calling?"

I made up a name.

"And who are you?" she asked.

"I'm an old friend. We went to the same high school. Haven't seen each other in a dog's age. So is he there?"

Silence.

"Is this Mrs. Wayne?"

"Yes, it is."

"Do I have the right phone number?"

"You do."

I smiled. Got it on the first try. Hardly ever happened. "Is your husband there, Mrs. Wayne?"

"No."

"You know where I can find him?"

"He's probably at the university."

"Probably?"

"Brian doesn't live here anymore."

"I see."

"I doubt that," she said.

I didn't tumble to her cue. "How long has he been livin elsewhere?"

"I don't have to talk to you, so I'm hanging up now."

"Wait. It's true ya don't have to talk to me, but could ya tell me where he's livin now?"

She didn't answer, and I thought she was gonna hang up, but after a few seconds she said, "I have no idea." Then she *did* hang up.

No two ways about it, I'd have to go to the school on Washington Square. Since he was a literature professor that was the branch where he was most likely to be found.

I returned my friend Janice's call, and we made our usual plans to meet at Chumley's in the Village. Anne wasn't home and neither was Marlene Hayworth. I hoped she wasn't gonna cancel my meeting with Gregory Flynn that night.

I heard the phone ring again, and Birdie shouted: "Faye, it's Marty Mitchum." Who needed an intercom when Birdie had a voice like Betty Hutton?

I picked up.

Marty said, "I got some dope, Faye."

"Shoot."

"Funny the Wests didn't tell ya about it."

"Tell me about what?"

"What was in the autopsy report."

He was getting under my skin. "What was in it?"

"Claudette West was three months pregnant."

The image of the Wests in my office came back to me. Especially the way he almost imperceptibly shook his head at his wife when I asked if there was anything else I should know.

"Marty, ya sure the Wests knew about this?"

"Oh, they knew, all right. That guy, Mr. West, leaned on Glenn Madison to tell him the whole thing."

Madison was an assistant to the coroner. It wasn't anything he'd make up.

Marty said, "I wish we had a way to know who the father was."

"Yeah. That might give us our killer. Well, there isn't a way. Did ya find out anything else?"

"There was this other monkey they liked for a few secs."

"Brian Wayne?"

"Yeah, how'd ya know?"

"I got other sources, Marty."

"Yeah? Like who?"

I shouldn't have said that. It made him jealous, and I didn't want to push him away. I quickly tried to fix it up. "Like the papers."

"Oh." He sounded relieved. "So ya know he was her teacher then?"

"Yeah. I know."

"Ya gonna have a sit-down with him?"

"Soon as I can. You got anything else?"

"Ain't Claudette havin a bun in the oven enough?"

"It's a doozy all right."

"Okay, then. I get anything else I'll phone ya."

"Right. And thanks, Marty."

"Yeah," he said and hung up.

Claudette West pregnant. And the parents knowing all along and not telling me. These were significant things. I supposed that Cotten was the father, but ya never knew. Maybe there was a mystery man in the cast of characters. Did the Wests know who the father was? That would have to wait till later. Right now I wanted to talk to Brian Wayne. The hell with staking him out.

After looking in the phone book I picked up the horn and dialed the university. I got an operator.

"Brian Wayne," I said.

"I'll ring him. Hold on, please."

I didn't. But now I knew for sure where to find him.

SEVEN

*N*ew York University's buildings were on the north side of Washington Square Park in Greenwich Village. At the bottom of Fifth Avenue was the so-called entrance to the park, where the Washington Arch stood. It was a copy of Paris's Arc de Triomphe.

Sometimes on Sundays, when I wasn't on a case, I'd go to the park with the *New York Times* and sit on the grass or a bench and peruse the paper.

I wouldna minded taking a load off right then so I could watch the citizens making their way to and fro, but I had work to do.

An information desk was right inside the main building, and a gal with cantaloupe-colored hair and a pair of horn-rims sat behind it. If there hadn't been a war on, a guy woulda been sitting there. I wondered what would happen to all these gals when the boys came home.

"Help you?" she said.

"Yeah. I'd like to see a teacher here, name of Brian Wayne."

"What department?"

"He teaches literature."

"That would be the English department," she said.

"Yeah. Right."

She rustled through some pages in a binder. "Is Dr. Wayne expecting you?"

The "doctor" didn't escape me. "No."

"Can I ask what this is about?"

"No."

She looked up. Her baby blues behind the glasses were all aflutter. "Well, you can't expect me to let you see him without knowing the nature of your call, can you?"

I didn't like doing this, but I could see I didn't have a choice. I reached in my bag, pulled out my wallet, and showed her my PI license.

"What's that?"

I told her.

"You're the police?"

"No. I'm a private investigator. I need to see Wayne to discuss a student of his."

"*Dr.* Wayne," she said, her mouth going into a prissy pout.

"Yeah. Him."

"Well, I suppose since you're official you can see him without an appointment."

"Thanks," I said.

After she rummaged through another binder she told me he wasn't teaching at the moment and gave me the floor and room number where I could find him.

The elevator man was about a hundred years old. He'd lose his job, too, when the boys came back. He had a face like a beat-up Buster Brown shoe, with eyebrows like John L. Lewis, and his blue uniform draped his frame like he was a human hanger.

I told him which floor, and we were off. He drove that thing like it was a hot rod. When we stopped at my floor, he jolted it so much that I'm pretty sure I left the ground for a second.

He opened the doors and we were about two feet above the floor. I cracked a smile, but he didn't move to close the doors and try for a better landing.

"You expect me to jump?" I asked.

"Do as you please," he said.

"I'm not jumpin."

He shrugged. "You want to go back downstairs?"

"No. I want you to get this thing even with the floor."

"I suppose I can try."

If he hadn't been so old I woulda popped my cork. "Yeah. Try, please."

He shut the doors, heaved a huge sigh, and grabbed the stick that made it go.

I don't know how many times we bounced, but when we finally made our landing and the doors opened, the space between elevator and floor was about six inches.

"Good enough for you?" he asked.

I wanted out, so I stepped up to the floor. I turned back to face him. "I just want ya to know that was the worst elevator ride I've ever had and I consider the whole thing a hijackin."

"Good for you," he said and closed the doors in my face.

I guess he knew he had his employers by the short and curlies and if I reported him nothing would happen. The hell with it.

I looked both ways to see how the numbers were going and took a left. When I got to Room 504, I put my ear against the wooden door and listened. There was muffled sound, but I couldn't make it out. So I knocked. The sounds from inside stopped. I knocked again.

"Yes, who is it?" said a male voice I took to be Wayne's.

I told him who I was.

Another silence.

"Dr. Wayne?"

"Yes?"

"I'd like to talk to you."

"I'm with a student now."

"I'll wait," I said.

"Well . . . well, all right. We'll just be a moment."

"That's okay. I got all day." I wanted to be accommodating so he'd be more willing to answer some questions.

I couldn't help hearing some strange sounds from inside, like they were rushing around or something. I wanted to believe it was the gathering of books and papers.

Not too much time passed before the door was unlocked (that it was locked struck me as strange) and the good doctor and his student stood in front of the closed door.

She was a babe in the woods and had what they called a pert little nose. Her hair was blonde, and her lips were cherry-colored. She wore a red-and-white-checked dress with a scalloped collar. In her arms, crossed in front of her, she balanced a large black notebook with two other books stacked on top. Her pretty face had a rosy hue, and she never once looked at me.

"Thanks for your help, Dr. Wayne."

"You're welcome, Miss Bergman."

With that, Miss Bergman quickly made her way down the hall.

Brian Wayne watched her go. The guy was a walking cliché of a college professor. He had the full head of dark hair, graying at the temples, a handsome craggy face, and he wore a white shirt, green-

and-white four-in-hand, a brown gabardine jacket, tan trousers, and brown oxfords.

He turned back and gave a smarmy smile that I knew he thought dripped with charm. It didn't do the trick for me.

"She sorta looks like Claudette West, don't ya think?" I said.

He didn't blink or move a muscle. "Now that you mention it, I suppose she does in a negligible way. If it's Miss West you want to talk to me about, I've told the police all that I know, which isn't much."

"Can we go into your office?"

"What for?"

He seemed uncomfortable for the first time.

"I want to talk to ya."

"Let's go to the cafeteria. I need a cup of coffee." He turned and locked the door.

I got the idea Dr. Wayne didn't want me to see the inside of his office, but I didn't know why. Too messy?

"It's only one flight down," he said. "Let's take the stairs."

"Yeah. I'd rather not have another elevator trip right now."

He laughed. "Oh, you've experienced our Mr. Gable's ride, hmmm?"

"You got it."

He opened the door to the stairs and motioned me through. I couldn't help feeling a little uneasy about taking this lonely route even though it was only one flight. There was something about Wayne that gave me the willies.

But nothing happened, and soon we were entering the cafeteria, which was loaded with people. We found a table near a wall.

"What would you like, Miss Quick?"

"You're havin java, I'll have the same."

"Fine. I'll be right back."

I lit up and looked around the place, which was jumping with students. There were a few older types, and I guessed they were teachers exempt from the war. I wondered when this thing would be over. It wasn't just that I had a personal interest with Woody doing his bit, it was the whole damn thing. I couldn't read Ernie Pyle's column without getting the snuffles. The way he wrote about the GIs gave me a pretty damn good picture of what it was like to be over there. I couldn't imagine myself in a foxhole for days on end or waiting for the enemy to attack. I guess at heart I was a coward.

Wayne came back and put the cup and saucer in front of me, pulled out his chair, placed his java at his spot, and sat down.

"Now," he said, "what exactly can I do for you?" He took out a silver cigarette case, delicately picked one out, snapped the case shut. He didn't offer me one cause I was already smoking.

"What were ya doin with Miss Bergman upstairs?"

"I beg your pardon?"

I didn't really think the rustling around in his office was book gathering. "The cutie who looks like Claudette West. Why were ya locked in with her?"

He lit his cigarette with a good-looking lighter. "You make it sound prurient, Miss Quick."

I knew he thought I wouldn't know what the word meant, so I played along. Always better to let them think they're smarter than you are. "Prurient?"

"Concupiscent. Amorous."

Concupiscent. I mean. "You talking lecherous?" I didn't smile.

His mouth twitched. "You make it sound that way."

"Yeah. That's because it seemed that way to me. Locked in and all."

"We weren't locked in."

"You weren't? I heard ya unlock the door."

"Yes, I did. I meant, we weren't locked in in the way you're implying. I always lock my door when I'm with a student so no one can barge in with some stupid question."

"Ya do that with Claudette West?"

He took a belt of his java and gave me a look-see over the cup brim, then set it back in the saucer. "I just told you I do that with all my students."

"So ya locked yourself in with Claudette."

"You're a very irritating girl," he said.

"So I've been told. Could ya answer the question?"

"Yes. Of course I did. Why would I treat her any differently from other students?"

"You tell me." I blew a plume of smoke past his head.

"There's nothing to tell. I *didn't* treat her differently."

"So, ya have affairs with *all* your female students?"

He started to get up, and I put a hand on his arm. "Sorry," I said. "That was uncalled for."

"You're right. Tell me about your relationship with Claudette."

"My *professional* relationship was professor and student. Nothing more."

"Dr. Wayne, I've been led to believe it was somethin more."

"Then you've been led astray."

"So why don't you level with me and tell me about you and Claudette."

"There's nothing to tell. I was her professor in comparative literature. She chose to do a paper on Henry James. I was her adviser."

"So she'd see ya outside of class?"

"In my office, yes."

"Ya never saw her anywhere else?" I noticed that he was chewing the inside of his right cheek.

"No."

"Tell me about her."

He looked at me blankly. "What do you mean?"

The question seemed easy as pie to me, so I didn't know what his dilemma was.

"I want ya to tell me what she was like, what your ideas, impressions of Claudette were."

Wayne seemed to be twisting in the wind. He stubbed out his cigarette and lit another. "She was a nice girl. I thought very highly of her."

"Was she smart?"

"Yes. And diligent about her work."

"Did ya think she was a looker?"

He pursed his lips, annoyed by the question.

"She was attractive. Well groomed," he said.

"She confide in ya about personal things?"

"Such as?"

"That's what I wanna know."

"She spoke of her boyfriend, Richard Cotten."

"What'd she have to say about him?"

"She wanted to end the relationship."

"Why?"

"He was too possessive."

"Sounds like she spoke to ya about pretty intimate things."

"No. Not really. Only about Cotten."

"Did she tell ya she was pregnant?"

His head flipped back as though I'd slapped him. "No. She didn't."

"Be honest, Dr. Wayne. You ever pitch woo with Claudette?"

"Pitch woo?" he said, his nostrils flaring.

"Yeah. Make love."

"Never."

Since there was no way to prove a negative I didn't pursue this.

"She ever mention any other guy?"

"No."

"Well, I guess that's all for now," I said and stood up. "Thanks for talkin to me."

Standing, he said, "You're welcome. Miss Quick? Are you certain Claudette was pregnant?"

"Yeah, that's what the autopsy showed."

"I see."

He seemed a little down in the dumps.

"Well, I'll be seein ya."

He nodded and sat again while I walked away.

I wasn't sure what it meant in the grander scheme of the case, but I knew for sure that he'd been sleeping with Claudette West.

EIGHT

J was pretty hot under the collar about the Wests not telling me about Claudette being pregnant, and I wanted to know their reasons. If Porter West could call me anytime he wanted, I figured I could drop in on him anytime *I* wanted.

I caught an uptown subway and settled in for the ride. I started to open my book when I noticed a guy sitting across from me who looked a lot like my old man. Same brown eyes, same full head of hair with a widow's peak. A good-looking gent. Coulda been my pop twenty years ago when I was just a kid. That's when I loved him like crazy. I was too young to know the ins and outs of one Frank Quick.

What I *did* know was that we were always moving and that I'd had a brother who died of influenza in 1918 and there was something strange about my old lady. But I didn't understand any of these things then.

I looked over at the man across from me, and he gave me what you might call a suggestive smile. I didn't wanna inflame Casanova, so I turned to my book. But I couldn't read. Now that Frank and Helen had invaded my mind I was done for.

When I was a kid, before dinner I played Casino with my old man, and he didn't like losing. Same as with any game he played, and he played them all. Frank was a gambler, and that's why we always kept moving.

One time he scored big and he bought us a cute little house in a nice neighborhood and I had my own bedroom, but within six months he lost the place. I don't know whether that was the straw for my old lady or if my brother's death had done it, but she started on the morphine heavy around then. She'd had the flu as well as Frank Jr., and often cried and screamed at God, who she said shoulda taken her instead of my brother.

Not that she believed in God. She didn't believe in anything and always said to me I should expect the worst from life and then I'd never be disappointed.

These days she was pretty much in her morphine fog all the time, and my father had a job at the downtown Newark Paradise, taking tickets. When I first heard this, I figured he'd fallen pretty far.

I knew what the lay of the land was through my aunt Dolly, who I'd lived with those four years. Anyway, nowadays my aunt gave me the skinny about my parents when I asked, but never brought them up unless I did. I asked a few months back, and that's when I learned what they were doing, how things were.

One time I put on a disguise, blonde wig, dark glasses, and went to the Paradise in Newark when the old man was working. I almost started bawling right there in the big lobby with the marble stairways and sculpture, velvet draperies, and crystal chandeliers.

There was my pop in his scarlet tunic piped in gold and looped across the front with more gold and tassels. He looked older than his forty-eight years, but he also looked happy. Especially when a kid would come up holding out his ticket. Frank Quick never failed to say something to them, though I couldn't hear what it was. The kid always laughed, and my old man patted whoever it was on their little shoulder.

I had to leave after a while cause he kept looking at me, and I was afraid he might come over and ask if I was okay or something. I sure as hell didn't want him to know it was me.

After that I wasn't ashamed of him cause I could see he wasn't. He liked the job much as he could like any job. I think he felt special in his uniform. All that gold. That would be like Frank Quick.

I almost missed my stop, but got up just in time before the doors closed.

Out on Eighty-sixth Street I packed away my family thoughts and crossed Broadway to walk over to Central Park West. In the middle of the street there was an island with benches, and some old folks sat there, watching the world go by. I wondered what it was like to be that old and if every night ya wondered if you'd see another day.

The weather was good, and I unbuttoned my coat, let it flap around me. I was a fast walker, so I made it to CPW in no time at all.

In minutes I found the Wests' swanky building, awning and doorman in place. I wasn't worried about getting in cause West would wanna see me. And then I realized what a dummy I was. He wouldn't be there; he'd be at work. I'd been so fit to be tied about feeling I'd been hoodwinked by the Wests that I'd forgotten. Then I thought maybe it was okay after all. I might do better with the missus alone.

The doorman made me think of Ebenezer Scrooge.

"May I help you?" he asked.

"Yeah. I'm here to see Mrs. Porter West."

"Who should I say is calling?"

I told him, and he picked up the receiver end of a black contraption and pushed a button.

"A Miss Faye Quick is here to see Madam. Yes, I'll wait."

I figured some maid was tellin the missus. It felt like a long wait, but I knew it wasn't when the doorman spoke into the blower again.

"All right, I'll send her up."

He directed me to the elevator but not before he gave me the once-over and showed me a kisser that said I didn't pass muster.

The elevator operator was another ancient jobbie, and I hoped he'd be a smoother driver than the one at NYU. He was. He pulled in tight at the tenth.

This was one of those deals that had only two apartments to a floor. And I didn't know which one it was. But then the door on the left side opened, and there stood a girl in a gray maid's outfit right down to the white apron and starched white headdress.

"Miss Quick?"

"That's me."

"Madam is waiting for you."

She stepped aside as I entered. We were in a foyer with a marble floor, a couple a mean-looking chairs, and some potted plants. I waited until she closed the door, then followed her as she led me to a large living room.

I suppose it was Louis somebody furniture, but I wasn't up to snuff on my antiques. All I knew was that it looked uncomfortable. I also knew that the intricate patterned rugs were probably Oriental. Put it all together and it spelled plenty of lettuce. Everything was in its place except for Madam, who was nowhere in sight.

"Please take a seat, and Madam will be right in."

"Thanks."

I looked around trying to figure which would be the most comfy seat, sorta a losing battle in this case. Before I could decide, Myrna West was entering with a man who was not Porter.

"Hello, Miss Quick. This is my brother, Cornell Walker."

We greeted each other. Walker was obviously a younger brother. He had brown hair and blue eyes like his sister's and was wearing a Marine uniform. Perfect features made him a looker if ya liked that type. He even had a cleft chin.

"I'm sorry to barge in on ya this way," I said.

"That's all right. I presume you have a good reason."

I didn't answer.

Myrna motioned to the stiffest-looking chair in the place, so there was no way out of taking it, which I did.

They both sat on the couch.

"Cornell is home on leave," the missus said.

This I could see. "And where's home, Captain Walker?" I knew my ranks.

"When on leave I live here with my sister." He smiled crookedly. "And her husband."

"Of course," he said.

This wasn't that unusual an arrangement. But I wondered why he didn't live with his parents if he wasn't married, and I assumed he wasn't. Or why he didn't have a place of his own.

"You never told me where your parents live, Mrs. West."

"No, I didn't. They live in Connecticut. Madison."

This meant nothing to me. Except to say Walker would rather stay in New York than Connecticut. Me, too. But it was possible he didn't get along with the old folks at home.

Myrna bent toward a silver box on the glass coffee table, opened it, and took out a cigarette. By the time she leaned back, Walker held out a light for her.

I took my cigs from my pocketbook.

"Forgive me," Myrna said. "My manners. I should have offered you one."

"That's okay. I like my own."

Walker was up and giving me a light before I knew what was happening.

"Thanks."

When he returned to his seat, Myrna said, "Do you have some news for us, Miss Quick?"

"Call me Faye." I didn't know how much to say in front of the brother. I glanced his way purposely.

"You can say anything in front of Cornell."

"You're sure?"

"Of course."

"I was thinkin your husband would be here, but then I realized he's probably at work."

"Yes." She took a deep draw on her cigarette and let the smoke dribble out.

"It's not so much that I have any news, it's more that I wanna ask you some questions."

"We told you everything we know."

"Did you?"

"Is that an accusation?"

"It's a question."

Cornell took his sister's hand. "Now Myrna, don't get upset."

"I just don't know what she means." She sounded whiny.

"Miss Quick is making sure you haven't forgotten anything, isn't that right?"

"Ya could put it that way."

He eyed me real close. "What other way could you put it?"

I ignored his question and said, "Mrs. West, why didn't you tell me your daughter was pregnant?"

She sucked in her breath like I'd punched her. "How dare you suggest such a thing."

"I'm not suggestin it, it's a fact. She was three months pregnant."

Angry color rose in Cornell's cheeks. "I presume you have something to back that up."

These people were always presuming. "Yeah, I do. It's in the autopsy report."

Myrna stubbed out her cig like she wanted to destroy it. I didn't expect that much fury from her. She was a lot different without Porter.

"That's a lie," she said.

Cornell said, "Wait a minute, Myrna. Did you see the report?"

Her bosom was heaving as she tried to catch her breath. "Porter did."

"You didn't?" I asked.

"No. I couldn't bear to."

"Did he tell you what was in it?"

"He said . . . he said there was nothing I needed to know."

"Damn him," Cornell said.

"You don't like your brother-in-law, Captain Walker?"

"No, it's not that. I *do* like him. I don't like it when he treats Myrna like she's not part of the picture. If Claudette was pregnant, Myrna had a right to know. I'm sure he thought he was protecting her, but . . ."

"Porter's always been that way," she said.

"And it's time he stopped," Walker said.

"Mrs. West, when you were at my office, I asked ya if there was anything else and your husband gave ya a tiny shake of his head, as if there *was* somethin. Somethin he didn't want me to know. What was that about?"

"I don't remember that."

"I think ya do. And if ya want my help finding your daughter's killer, ya gotta come clean with me, completely honest."

"Do you know who was the father of Claudette's child?" she asked.

Just like I hadn't said anything about her being honest. "No, I don't."

"Myrna, is there something you're keeping from Miss Quick?"

"Porter will kill me," she said.

"Seems like since he didn't tell you an important thing ya have some leverage here."

"She's right," Cornell said.

"You're absolutely sure that Claudette was pregnant?"

"The coroner is absolutely sure, Mrs. West."

After a few moments, she went for the silver box and Cornell once again lit her cigarette. She inhaled and let it out. "Porter hates Richard Cotten, you know that."

I nodded.

"No matter what the evidence said, he wanted the killer to be Cotten. But . . . there was this other boy. Claudette had just begun to see him. Only two weeks before she was killed. He was the kind of boy Porter wanted for her. He comes from a very prominent family. They're in the Social Register. Porter said there was no point in dragging that family into this because he knew Alec couldn't have had anything to do with it."

"And how did he know that?"

"He said people with Alec's breeding simply didn't do things like that."

"Is that right?" I said. "Amazin deduction."

"That's why Porter looked at me that way. He was afraid I might give you Alec's name."

"Will ya give it to me now?"

"He couldn't be the father of the child," she said.

"I still need his name."

"Oh, Porter will have my head."

"I won't tell him if you don't," I said.

"Really?"

"Really."

"I just can't believe my little girl was pregnant." She started to cry.

I gave Cornell a pleading look.

He put his arm around her and squeezed gently. "Myrna, tell Miss Quick what she wants to know."

"If ya got some info and you're not tellin me, you're impedin this investigation," I said.

"Even if you don't tell Porter about where you got the boy's name, he'll know it was me."

"Ya mean nobody else knew who he was?"

"Well, yes, people did. They went out in public. And that's another reason Porter thinks Richard killed her. He thinks he saw them someplace together."

"Did Claudette say that happened?" Walker asked.

"No. Oh, you people don't know how angry Porter can get."

"How angry?" I asked. I felt a little alarmed.

"He rages," Myrna said.

"Ya mean he yells? Nothin else?"

"What do you mean?"

"He doesn't hit ya or anything like that?"

She sat up straight. "Of course not. What kind of people do you think we are?"

I thought I'd let that one pass. No time to explain it happened in the best of families.

"Myrna," Walker said. "You have to tell Miss Quick whatever you know."

There was a long silence while she thought it over and then she said, "Are you going to tell the police?"

"That depends on what I find out."

"Oh, what's the difference? His name is Alec Rockefeller."

NINE

*M*yrna told me that the Rockefeller kid lived on Park Avenue. Where else? Armed with his address I took a bus across Eighty-sixth Street through the park and another one down Fifth Avenue. I wasn't in a big hurry, and sometimes I didn't feel like being underground.

Sitting by the window I watched people rushing to somewhere. Every once in a while I'd see a person, usually a woman, in a coat or jacket, and I'd think: *That person actually went to a store and picked out that item.* It boggled my mind. What could she have been thinking? She paid a lot of filthy lucre for that ugly thing. Why?

And that speculation always led me to taste. A very individual thing. The woman I was passing now was wearing a coat with big green and yellow squares like a checkerboard gone crazy. She must've thought she looked swell in it or she wouldn't have bought it. But how could she see it like that? It was a futile game I played with myself, cause I never came up with satisfying answers.

I quit my rubbernecking and settled down to thinking about Alec Rockefeller. Myrna told me he was in his early twenties, very good-looking, courteous, and charming. He'd come to the funeral and had visited the Wests once a week for about a month and then he stopped. She figured it was too painful for him. She also said he was a second cousin of a more famous Rockefeller but couldn't remember which one.

My stop came at Sixtieth Street. When I got off, I walked east toward Madison. There were a lotta town houses on this block, and I knew you had to be rolling in dough to live in one of them. And there were trees. Small, but still they were there.

I crossed Madison and walked the final block to Park. The building I was looking for was on the corner of Sixtieth across the avenue.

It was tall and brown except the top two floors, which were a tan color. Even from where I was standing I knew that under the eaves was a lot of decorative stonework. It could've been flowers or angels or anything, but I'd never know.

When the light changed, I crossed. Standing in the doorway was a doorman, of course. My life was getting to be nothing but these mugs. This one was wearing a green uniform with the usual generous gilt. I honestly didn't know how I was gonna get into a Rockefeller household, but I had to try.

"Good afternoon," I said.

This one looked like something you'd mount on a wall. He touched the shiny black bill of his cap and nodded politely. "How may I help you, miss?"

"I'm not sure I have the right address, but I'm supposed to meet with an Alec Rockefeller."

"Rockefeller?"

"Yeah, Alec."

"I'm afraid we don't have any Rockefellers in this building."

"No Alec Rockefeller?"

"No *any* Rockefeller. Believe me, I'd know."

Dopily I handed him the piece of paper that I'd written on when Myrna read it to me from her address book.

He stared at it a long time as though the numbers might change. "Well, that's this building, but no one by that name lives here."

"Is there a young man who has the first name Alec?"

"No one."

"You didn't even think about it."

He took a step back from me and looked stern. "Miss, I don't have to think about it. I know the name of everyone who lives here."

"Of course ya do, sorry. Ya wouldn't be doin your job if ya didn't, right?"

"That's precisely right. Good day, miss." He walked quickly to the door and opened it for an older woman in a dark fur coat, her cheeks rouged so she looked like a puppet.

"May I get you a cab, Mrs. Skeffington?"

"No thank you, Chester. I'm going to walk. It's such a lovely day."

"Yes, madam." He touched the bill of his cap as she turned and started down Park.

Should I or shouldn't I? I decided I would do it, but I had to make it look good for old Chester. I turned and peered uptown, then east, and when I saw the light was in my favor, I scurried across the avenue and started downtown, the whole time with my eyes on Mrs. Skeffington.

At Fifty-seventh she crossed to my side and headed down the block. I followed.

There were a lot of people on Fifty-seventh, so I didn't have to be too careful shadowing her. We crossed Madison and about two yards in she went into a store. Only I saw it wasn't a store when I got there. It was a gallery, and it was up some stairs. The glass in the door was clear, and I waited until she'd disappeared at the first landing before I went in.

By the time I reached the landing she was going in another door. There was a sign on it that said: GEORGE BAILEY, FINE ART. I'd never been in one of these galleries, so I didn't know what to expect. I went to the Met when I wanted to look at pictures. Fact was I went to it a lot. I guess I could say afternoons at the Met had saved my bacon more than once. Being there in the quiet, looking at paintings guys did a long time ago, calmed me down and got my mind going in a straight line instead of all over the lot.

I waited a minute and then I opened the door of the Bailey Gallery. Inside, the walls were white and hung with pictures the likes of which I'd never seen. Every one of them looked like a blank canvas. But the name of the show was above the so-called paintings. *White on White.*

There was a girl at a desk with sleek black hair who gave me the once-over, and Mrs. Skeffington seemed to be the only customer. Her back was to me as she stared at a picture that I could now see had white paint on the canvas. I didn't get it.

But I sauntered over to stand next to her, not too close, but it wasn't a very big room, so I was close enough. I was looking at the picture next to the one she was looking at. But I could've been looking at any picture cause far as I could tell they were all the same.

From the corner of my eye I saw Mrs. S. turn and look at me, so I turned to look at her. She smiled and was starting to turn away when I said, "Mrs. Skeffington, what a surprise." I put out my hand, which she took in the tips of her soft gloved fingers. Carefully, I said, "How are you?"

I could see she was flummoxed, but she wasn't letting on. She was a fine-boned lady with eyes that had a sparkle, like Christmas tree lights.

She said, "I'm fine and how are you?"

"Just fine, thanks. Mrs. Skeffington, I can see you aren't sure you remember me."

"Oh, no. Of course I do. I'm simply at a loss as to where we last saw one another."

"It was the Rockefeller party."

"Oh, of course, of course. How silly of me. The Rockefeller party."

"The last one."

"Yes, yes. I recall now." She fussed with the collar of her brown fur coat.

"That was some shindig, wasn't it?"

"Shindig?"

"I mean it was a lovely party." I almost blew it, and reminded myself that a Mrs. Skeffington wouldn't talk like me. I needed to tone up my chat.

"Shindig," she said again.

I smiled. "Oh, it's a word I picked up last week at the Mellons. The boy used it. I thought it had a nice ring to it."

"Yes, yes it does. Well, are you a devotee?" She held out her arm and swept her black-gloved hand, as though it was a wand, toward the pictures.

"First time," I said.

"How did you hear about him?"

Good thing I read the social notes in the paper. "Brooke," I said.

"Really? I didn't know she knew about Ronald. Did she say she knew him personally?"

Mrs. S. pressed her lips together, and I saw a muscle jump in her cheek.

A nifty wrinkle was creeping in here, and I couldn't resist.

"Yes. She said she was with him a few days ago."

"How very interesting."

"I thought so," I said. I whispered, "Brooke said she might take him on a cruise this year."

"A cruise?" She crinkled her brow and her eyes narrowed. Then she started giving me the fish-eye, so I thought I'd better clean things up. Maybe Brooke didn't go on cruises.

Trying to sound giddy, I said, "Back to the Rockefeller party."

"Hmmm?"

"I don't know them very well, do you?"

"Very."

"Oh, good. I was curious about one of them."

She looked skeptical and curious at the same time but didn't say anything like a normal person would. She just waited.

I could feel sweat starting under my arms and on my back. "A young man, maybe twenty or so. He was so nice to me. You see I felt a little faint, and he took me outside to get some air. When we came back in, I lost track of him and I so wanted to thank him. His name was Alec Rockefeller. Do you know him?"

"No, I don't."

"Oh, dear."

"Alec you say?"

"Yes. Quite good-looking. Blond. Maybe six feet tall."

"Miss . . . what did you say your name was?"

"I didn't, but it's Harriman."

"Harriman?"

"A cousin," I said.

"Distant?"

"Quite." I smiled. "At any rate, I was asking about Alec Rockefeller. I believe he, too, is a cousin. Perhaps distant."

"Yes. You were. And I was about to tell you that I know the Rockefellers very well . . . all of them. And I've never heard anyone mention an Alec."

"But surely you met him at the party."

"Surely I didn't. I'm not in the habit of running around with twenty-year-olds, Miss Harriman."

I couldn't believe it, but she actually sniffed at the end of her sentence.

"Oh, I wasn't running around with him, Mrs. Skeffington. He was simply courteous and helped me downstairs to get a breath of fresh air."

"Nevertheless, Miss Harriman, I've known the Rockefellers for decades and to my knowledge, which is sizable, there isn't now nor has there ever been anyone named Alec. Clearly he was making sport of you passing himself off as a Rockefeller."

"Oh, dear, oh, dear." I tried to look as though I might faint, but I didn't know how to fake that. I thought it was best to blow the joint. "I'm so upset, I must go."

"Yes, you look quite peaked, Miss *Harr-i-man*."

Definitely time to take a powder. I backed away, turned, and made for the door. As I was leaving I called over my shoulder, "Say hello to Mr. Skeffington for me; he's such a lovely man."

Before I closed the door I heard her reply.

"Yes, especially now that he's dead."

I ran down the stairs and out onto Fifty-seventh, where I took a right going east. Had to do it, didn't ya, Quick, I said to myself. Always that one final thing that really gives the game away. Oh, well. What could she do to me anyway?

When I got to Fifth, I started downtown and didn't stop until I got to Forty-third Street. I made my way to my office.

Birdie was doing her hunt and peck but looked up when I came in.

"What happened to you, Faye? Ya look like ya seen a ghost or somethin."

"Wish I had."

"Huh?"

"Never mind. I gotta think."

I went into my office and closed the door, threw my coat and hat on the client's chair, then sat down behind my desk.

My near catastrophe with Mrs. Skeffington made me feel a little shaky. Sometimes I didn't know where I got the nerve. Woody would've been proud of me.

I lit one up and sat back in my chair. Mrs. Skeffington was only one source, and I knew I'd have to check out others, but I had the nasty feeling that she was right.

There *was* no Alec Rockefeller. So *who* was this considerate, charming young man? And *where* was he? And *why* did he say he was a Rockefeller? And *how* in Hades was I going to find him? And most of all, did *he* kill Claudette West?

TEN

I was running low on ration stamps, so I made myself a big salad with everything but the you know what. I had my date with Mr. Flynn at eight o'clock, but my mind kept scooching back to Alec Rockefeller. Or whatever his name was.

I knew I'd have to find this kid, but I didn't have the vaguest of where to start. I had no address or phone number or the right name. I'd have to ask West if he remembered anything. I thought Myrna had given me all the info she knew. Still, sometimes there were things a person didn't know they knew until their mind was jogged. I could call Porter now with my report and ask him some questions. I wouldn't tell where I got the name.

I took my salad to the phone table and dialed.

Porter answered. He was naturally excited cause he hoped I had some hot news, but I told him right away I had a question instead.

"I'd like ya to tell me about Alec Rockefeller."

There was a moment of silence and then he said in a pinched voice, "Where did you get that name?"

"I don't reveal my sources even to my client."

"I never heard of such a thing."

"How many PIs have ya worked with?" I knew the answer and took a healthy helping of salad.

"That's not the point."

My mouth was still full, but I tried talking through the lettuce. "Stanner pwactith."

"What's that?"

I swallowed. "I said standard practice."

"Did my wife give you his name? And don't tell me you can't reveal that."

I decided on an outright lie. "No, she didn't. Now, can you tell me somethin about this guy?"

He made some grumping noises cause I wouldn't tell him how I got the guy's name. He gave me the same hogwash Myrna had dished out. So I put it to him that there was no such person.

"But I met him," West said.

"You met someone, but not Alec Rockefeller."

"How do you know?"

"It's my business to find out these things, Mr. West. The problem is that I don't have anythin to go on except a physical description of the boy. I need ya to remember somethin else about him. Anythin."

"Are you saying the lad I met was *not* a Rockefeller?"

I couldn't be sure if he was in a stew cause he'd been snookered or that it was a bitter pill to swallow that his dead daughter had been courted by a fraud. I thought the second reason would fit him best.

"Yeah, that's what I'm sayin. He wasn't who he said he was."

"But how can you be sure?"

Definitely the second reason. "You'll have to trust me on this. It's part of my job to find out these things. Now, do you remember anything special or revealin about sonny boy?"

He was silent, and I took the opportunity to shovel in more rabbit food.

Finally he said, "I'm so upset I can't think."

"So when ya get over the shock, can ya put on your thinkin cap and give it a whirl?"

"Yes, yes." He hung up.

I was caught off base with that one and replaced the phone. I hoped he wasn't gonna give Myrna the third degree cause I wasn't sure she'd be able to stand up under something like Porter West being high and mighty. I thought of calling back, disguising my voice, and asking for Myrna so I could warn her, but I didn't think that would wash.

I thought about Claudette. She was shaping up to be a mystery in herself. Her mother didn't know she was pregnant, and there were all of these men in her life. All different types. Brian Wayne, Richard Cotten, the so-called Rockefeller, and the father of her baby, who may or may not be another guy. Claudette, it seemed, kicked up her heels a lot, to say the least.

I finished my salad, dumped the dish and fork in the sink, made a quick rest stop, then grabbed my coat, hat, gloves, and pocketbook and was out the door.

While I was locking up, a newish neighbor from upstairs came down into the hallway, and I wasn't fast enough to escape. Not that there was anything really wrong with Jim Duryea, but I was in a hurry and not in the mood.

"How are you, Faye?"

"Just fine, Jim. You?"

"My mother's coming to visit."

"Oh, that's nice." He looked like he'd been beaten with a cat-o'-nine-tails. "Or is it?"

"She's a lovely woman."

"But?"

"I was wondering, Faye. Do you think you could meet her?"

This was coming from left field. Why would Jim Duryea want *me* to meet his mother? We'd never even been on a date. He was a man in his forties and not my type. And it wasn't only cause he combed his hair from the bottom of the right side over to the left to disguise his baldness. Although that didn't endear him to me.

I hardly knew what to say. "Are you havin a party or somethin?"

"No, it's not that. I just thought you'd like each other."

"Oh, I see." But I didn't.

He brightened up. "Then you'll do it?"

"When is she blowin in?"

"Tomorrow. But I thought the night after that you could come to dinner."

I wanted to give an outright no, but he looked so pathetic that I sashayed around.

"You know my work, Jim, so I can't make real firm plans. Somethin might come up, and I wouldn't want to disappoint ya."

"Could we say it's tentative then?"

"Sure."

He grinned like a baby getting his first taste of sugar.

"Oh, thank you, Faye. You don't know how much this means to me."

I felt like a heel cause I knew I was gonna get out of this.

"Jim, please don't count me in. I've got a big case and anythin could happen."

"I know, I know. But that you *might* be able to is so . . . so helpful. You'll never know."

"Okay. Good. I gotta run now."

"I'll walk out with you. I need to buy a pack of Luckies. Which direction are you going in?"

The call I'd gotten from Marlene Hayworth had changed my meeting with Flynn from his apartment to the Caffe Reggio on MacDougal Street.

"I'm goin to MacDougal," I said.

"I'll go to Seventh Avenue with you."

I thanked my lucky stars that wasn't far.

The Reggio was about halfway down MacDougal between Third and Bleecker streets. It was a small coffee place and real authentic. Italians ran it, and the espresso was the best in the Village. So were the cannolis.

Over the entrance it had a rounded green awning, like a hood, and the wood around the big windows was painted a brighter shade of green.

Inside the tables had marble tops and the café chairs were wrought iron with round leather seats. At the back was a huge brass espresso machine on the counter and a glass-front case featured the desserts.

It was always pretty crowded, but I found a table for two in the middle of the room. Our appointment was for eight, but I was fifteen minutes early as always. When I was meeting somebody I was interviewing, I liked to get there first.

I put my pocketbook on the table, shoved my gloves in my coat pocket, hung it and my hat on the wooden rack in the corner with everybody else's, then took my seat.

The people at surrounding tables weren't tourists cause out of towners didn't seem to know about the Reggio even though it had been on this very spot since 1927. Still, I knew one of these days the word would get out. For now I enjoyed the locals, and some of them seemed to live here. They were the ones I saw every time I dropped in, like a couple I knew by name, Veronica March and Charlie Peck. They were a happy duo. He was an artist and she kept trying to be an actress, but so far she'd only had one role as a vanilla ice-cream cone. We all went, and she did a good job.

I once went back to Charlie's studio with them so he could show me his pictures. I couldn't make head or tail of them. They weren't white on white, but they might as well have been for all they said to me. I liked people in my pictures, and his were abstract. I couldn't read the story in his paintings, but I said I liked them. Why not? I didn't see any reason to hit a person where they lived.

Veronica and Charlie were sitting across the room from me, and we waved back and forth.

And there were others I knew. A couple of the men wore berets, but the women in here were hatless. Another reason I knew none were tourists. Like me they took them off when they got inside. You'd never catch a tourist without her hat on, inside or out.

Maria, the waitress, came to my table. Over her blue skirt she wore a small white apron tied around her waist.

"Hello, Faye. What can I get you tonight?"

"I think I'll have a cappuccino. How's Oscar doin?" He was in the navy.

"He's okay, I guess. I haven't heard from him lately. About ten days, so I guess that isn't anything to get the jumps about."

"The mails are slow." I was thinking of my friend Jeanne, who heard from her boyfriend about once a month even though he wrote more often. Then sometimes she'd get ten letters all at once.

"Sure. I know that. Like I said I'm not jittery or anything. You meeting someone?"

"Yes. He should be here soon."

"*He,* huh?" She gave me a big smile.

"Business," I said.

"Aw, heck. I'll get your cap."

Seemed like everybody wanted me to have a boyfriend. Not that I'd mind, even though I swore I wouldn't until the war was over. But it sure wasn't gonna be Jim Duryea.

The door opened, and I knew right off it was Gregory Flynn. He looked like he belonged here the way I'd look like I belonged at the 21 Club.

He was a tall gent with a build that went with it, and he wore a gray topcoat and a gray fedora that he removed the second he was through the door. He had salt-and-pepper hair. Very distinguished.

I put my hand up, and he came over to the table.

"Miss Quick?"

"Yes."

"I realized as I entered that we hadn't made any arrangements on how to recognize each other."

"Yeah, that's right, but I figured it was you."

"Really?"

He unbuttoned his coat, and I pointed at the coatrack.

He eyed it like it was crawling with insects and said, "That's all right. I'll fold it over my lap."

I watched while he took it off then turned it inside out, showing a matching silk lining. He sat down and laid the coat on his lap folded in half, his fedora on top of that.

Flynn was a looker. Big brown eyes, straight nose, and a mustache above an ample mouth. I never liked mustaches myself, but some girls did.

"Do you want to order before we start talkin?"

"Yes. Do they make a good espresso?"

"The best." I guessed that although he had an apartment in the area he didn't go out much.

I waved a hand at Maria, who nodded, and when I looked back at Flynn I could see he was upset by something.

"What's wrong?"

"Nothing."

"Mr. Flynn, I can see somethin has upset you."

"Well, I'm not used to ladies calling for the waitress."

Off to a great start. "Sorry. It's just that I know Maria so well I didn't think." What I *did* think was that this Casanova was a stuffed shirt. I shoulda known.

He tried on a smile that looked like a broken rubber band. Then Maria was at our table.

Flynn ordered his espresso. "Quaint place," he said.

I'd never thought of the Reggio as quaint.

"Ya probably don't spend a whole lot of time in cafés like this, huh?"

"Not much."

I took a sip of my cap and offered him a cig.

"Thank you, I have my own." He put his hand inside his jacket and pulled out a gold case. I had no doubt that it was real gold.

After popping the thing open with one hand, taking out his smoke, snapping it shut, and putting it away, he lit mine and then his own with a gold lighter that had a flip-top arm. By this time Maria was back with his espresso. I noticed he didn't thank her. I guessed that the rich didn't find it proper to thank underlings.

"So, Miss Quick, what can I do for you?"

"I'd like to hear your account of what went on the night of the murder of Claudette West."

"I suppose it doesn't matter that I've told all of this to the police, does it?"

"No. The police aren't working with me on this case."

"Frankly I'm surprised to see a young woman like you working as a . . . a what do you call it?"

"A private investigator." I told him how my career came about.

"I see. Still, I imagine it could be dangerous work."

If I didn't know better I might think this was a threat. But I did know better. Didn't I?

"Sometimes," I said. "Mr. Flynn, if you'll just gimme your rundown of what happened that night, ya can be on yer way."

"What makes you think I *want* to be on my way?"

Oh, no. The man gave me a definite leer. I acted like I didn't notice. And I paid no attention to his smarmy remark. Instead, I urged him once more to tell me his tale.

ELEVEN

There was nothing remarkable in what Gregory Flynn had to say. He skidded around Marlene Hayworth's presence until he got to the cigarette part.

"Whoa," I said. "You went out to buy her cigs?"

"Yes."

"What time was that?"

"I didn't notice." He sipped his espresso.

"Did she have cigarettes when she arrived?"

"She smoked one before . . . yes."

I knew what the before was. "So it was *after* that she noticed she didn't have any."

"Yes." Then he coughed and blushed and moved around in his chair, catching the drift of what we'd both said.

"Actually, she smoked another and then was out of them."

"Was that when ya went out?"

"Shortly after she mentioned it."

"What time did Miss Hayworth get there?"

"About eight."

"Did ya have any dinner?"

"I'd bought some pâté and crackers."

"So what time do ya think ya went out for the cigs?"

"It must have been around nine-thirty."

"Where'd ya get them?"

"The cigarettes? I walked to Eighth Street. There's a tobacco store there."

"That's a pretty long walk in the snow."

"I don't mind snow. Besides, Miss Hayworth wanted a pack of Gauloises, and since the war, they're the only store that carries them."

I was getting a good picture of who was running the show here.

"Gauloises?"

"They're French."

"Ah. What time did ya get back to the apartment?"

"I'm not sure. But that particular walk to and fro usually takes about fifteen minutes."

"So ya got back before ten?"

"Oh, yes, definitely."

"And ya didn't see anybody?"

He sipped and acted like he was thinking this over. "No one was around. The inclement weather kept people at home, I suppose."

"Did ya know the deceased, Mr. Flynn?"

He looked at me with a shocked expression. "Certainly not."

"Miss Hayworth is the only woman ya see at that apartment?"

"Now look here, Miss Quick, I—"

"How many children do ya have?"

"Children? What does that have to do with anything?"

"Just curious." I was trying to upset his applecart.

"Forgive me, Miss Quick, but I'm not here to satisfy your curiosity. I met you out of my desire to help you find the killer of that poor girl."

His face was turning red.

"Ya met me because you're cheatin on your wife and ya were afraid I'd spill the beans. So don't go gettin high-hat with me, Mr. Flynn."

He continued to sputter, not words, but odd little noises as though he was gasping for air.

"Ya didn't answer if Miss Hayworth is the only dame ya see at that apartment."

"Yes. She is."

"And ya never knew Claudette West?"

I could see his prissy mouth starting to form the word *who*, but he quickly stopped, remembering.

"No, I never did. Now let me ask you something. Do you plan to tell anyone . . . about . . . our meeting?"

"Ya mean yer wife?"

"Anyone."

"No. This is confidential."

"Thank you." He began to fuss with his hat on his lap. "Is there anything else?"

"When ya came back from gettin the cigarettes, did ya look around outside or go right into yer buildin?"

"It was snowing. I had no reason to look anywhere."

"So the girl could've been there and you just didn't see her, is that right?"

"She was not in front of my building, so yes, I suppose she could've been there. There was no reason I would've noticed her."

What he said made sense. "Okay, I guess that's it."

He nodded, then raised his hand for Maria. She came right over.

"Check, please," he said.

"No, no," I said. "I'm stayin."

"Miss Quick, I intend to pay this check. What you do once I leave is your business."

Maria wrote out the check and put it on the table in front of him.

He reached inside his jacket and pulled out a long thin black leather billfold. He put a fin under the check. When he stood up and I realized he wasn't gonna wait for change, I was surprised cause a five spot was way too much.

He unfolded his coat, shrugged into it, and buttoned.

"I won't say it's been charming because it hasn't. But I suppose you're just doing your job."

"Ya got it right there, Mr. Flynn."

"And a very unsavory job for a woman, I might add."

"Ya might, but don't bother."

"Good night, Miss Quick."

I said good night and watched him make his way to the door. Once outside he looked both ways, then put on his hat, pulling it low over his forehead, and headed north.

Maria was at my side. "He didn't wait for his change."

"It's your tip."

"Gosh. Bring some more guys like that in here."

"I'd rather not. Bring me another cap, Maria." I wanted to get the bad taste outta my mouth.

My bedroom was big with a fireplace I never used. Two huge windows faced the back of another building, so I'd hung long white curtains. I kept a desk between the two windows, but I never used that either. Against the right wall was a mahogany highboy. And on the left was a matching chest of drawers with a mirror. I'd put some pictures on the walls. They were posters I'd bought and had framed. There was a Renoir, a Degas, and a Monet. I loved the colors, and I made up stories to go with the pictures.

I sat in bed, my hair bobby-pinned and rolled, two pillows behind me. I had my radio tuned to the news, which wasn't good any way ya sliced it. The Japs made a big fighter-plane effort to regain the Solomon Islands, and we shot down thirty-nine but we lost a bunch ourselves. I was glad Woody wasn't in the air force. I didn't want to hear any more so I turned the dial. Just in time for *Nick Carter Master Detective*. I didn't want to hear that either. It was a bunch of bunk. So I got a music station. And while Tex Beneke and The Modernaires sang "I've Got a Girl in Kalamazoo," I went over my notes.

I wasn't any closer to finding out who killed Claudette than I had been the day before. The first thing I had to do in the morning was to find out who this joker Alec Rockefeller really was. Gabbing with Claudette's pals might be my road in. I knew they'd probably bought the Rockefeller scam, too, but they might have an angle the Wests wouldn't have. I'd made a list of them I'd found in the newspaper clippings. And maybe it was time to use Anne. I wondered what Porter West would say if I asked for a piece of Claudette's clothing?

The Voice came on next singing "Night and Day." Even though we were hardly bobby-soxers, I'd gone with Jeanne to the Paramount the year before to hear Frankie sing. It was a night I'd never forget. We got way down close, and all around us girls were screaming and some even fainted, but Frank Sinatra was singing just for me. That's the way he made me feel.

When Frank finished his song, I turned off the radio and picked up my book. I knew I was gonna be asleep in minutes. Maybe if I was lucky I'd dream about Frankie taking me out on a date.

I started my day with a stop at Stork's. Larry the Loser was missing, but Fat Freddy and Blackshirt Bob were in place. They all greeted me.

I got my usual pack of cigs and my papers.

"How's that prime case comin, Faye?" Freddy asked.

"I'm movin along."

The little bell rang, and a young pup with slicked-back blond hair came in.

If the customer was a stranger to us, it was our habit to zip our lips and eyeball the transaction.

"Pack of Luckies, Stork."

So he was a known figure, at least to Stork. Money and cigs changed hands, and the kid left.

"Who was that?" I asked.

Blackshirt Bob said, "Ya know, Faye, you're one nosy dame."

"Thanks for gettin that off yer chest, Bob."

"Well, whaddaya care who that monkey was?"

"I care about everything, haven't ya noticed?"

"She's a gumshoe, Bob, whaddaya expect?"

Then they laughed like somebody said something funny.

Stork said, "Don't know his name, Faye. He's just a small-time grifter."

"What's his game?" I asked.

"There she goes," Bob said. "Whaddaya care?"

"Can it," Stork said. "He does the pigeon drop, Spanish prisoner, three-card monte, that kinda deal."

"Strictly penny ante," Freddy said.

You'd think Freddy was Ponzi or somebody. That gave me an idea.

"Hey, you guys ever come across a scammer who makes like he's from a famous family?"

They looked at me like I was speaking in a foreign language. "Ya know what I mean. Passes himself off as royalty or says he's a Rockefeller. One of those guys."

"Ah." Bob said. "Can't say I have. Why?"

I ignored his question. "How about you, Freddy?"

"I, a course, get your drift, Faye. But I haven't come across such a scammer lately."

"Whaddaya mean, lately?" I asked.

Fat Freddy puffed out his big chest and rolled his half-smoked cigar from one side of his mouth to the other.

"What I am gettin at, Faye, is that once upon a time I knew a shark who made a lotta cabbage by actin the part of a count. He was the darlin of a certain group of ladies in their autumn years, ya get my meanin."

"How long ago was this?"

"Maybe twenty."

"What was his con exactly?"

"He'd meet a lady accidentally on purpose in the lobby of some posh hotel in Europe or some big city over here. Havin researched the mark, he'd pretend to know her friends, the ones who were away, take her to tea, then lunch, dinner, the opera or whatnot, meet others of her group who were convinced they'd met him or knew his family, which they didn't, and then one thing led to another, and before ya knew it the lady in question would be puttin up moola to match his funds that would be arrivin any day. I guess I don't have to spell out the rest."

"It's an amazin thing that anybody would go for that," I said.

"Like the man said, 'There's a sucker born every minute.' "

"Yeah, I guess."

Blackshirt Bob said, "If that's the kinda tale ya want, Faye, I could regale ya for hours."

"Regale?" we said in unison.

Bob turned a shade of pink. "What's wrong with that?"

"Nothin," I said. "It's just we, well, it's . . ." I decided not to embarrass him any further. "It's a good word, 'regale.' Very good. We're just not used to hearin it much, right, fellas?"

They agreed.

"And I wish I had time to hear your regalin, Bob, but I gotta hightail it to work."

Freddy said, "That was a good story I tole ya, wasn't it, Faye?"

Uh-oh. I knew what he was after.

"It *was*, Fat Freddy. And I appreciate it. It gives me some perspective. Thank you."

I waved at the guys and made it out the door before Freddy could actually try to tap me for a fin or more.

So what this fake count did wasn't that different from the fake Alec Rockefeller's MO. He got everyone to believe him without a hitch. And he, too, was definitely after the pot of gold. Though I wasn't exactly sure how he planned to get it.

Birdie was hunting and pecking away when I got into the office. I gave her the list of Claudette's friends I'd jotted down.

"I need phone numbers and addresses on these, Bird."

"Sure thing."

As I hung up my hat and coat I heard her go back to the typewriter.

"Birdie, I need those pronto."

"Yeah. Okay."

"What're ya typin?"

I could tell by the expression on her face that she was doing something personal. I could also see she was thinking about fudging the truth.

"Ah, Faye. I'm writin a letter to Pete."

"A letter? Why? Ya see him every day."

"Yeah, but now I'm not."

"What happened?"

"A friend a mine saw him in a Fifty-second Street jazz joint with another dame."

"Some friend," I said.

"I'm glad she told me so I would know just what a two-timin louse he is."

I coulda told her that without seeing him with another gal.

"Maybe it was his sister, Bird."

"He don't have a sister."

"Cousin?"

"Nah. Stop tryin to make me feel better. He's a crumb bum, and it's time I faced it."

"I'm sorry, Birdie. I really am." And I was.

"Thanks. I'll get right on this list."

"Good." I went into my office and sat down at my desk. I was flipping through the mail when I heard the phone ring. Then Birdie yelled my name.

"Yeah?"

"Pick up. It's an Alec Rockefeller."

TWELVE

There was a moment when I thought I'd heard wrong and almost asked Birdie to repeat. But in my marrow I knew she really had said Alec Rockefeller.

I reached out to the phone like it was a snake. My hand hovered over the receiver, and I noticed a slight tremor in my fingers. Then I asked myself what the hell I was afraid of and that pushed me to pick up the phone.

"Faye Quick," I said.

Nothing.

"Hello." I lit up a Camel cause I couldn't talk on the phone without a cig.

Nothing.

"Hello."

"Faye Quick?"

"Yeah. Who's this?"

"Alec Rockefeller."

I didn't bother to tell him there was no such person cause I knew he knew this. He sounded muffled, like maybe he had a handkerchief over the mouthpiece.

"What can I do for ya, Mr. Rockefeller?"

"Isn't it more like what I can do for *you*?"

"Okay. I'll bite."

"I didn't kill Claudette West."

"Thanks for bein so honest, Mr. Rockefeller. What makes ya think I'm gonna believe that?" I tipped my head back and blew out a plume of smoke.

"Why shouldn't you believe it?"

"Let me count the ways."

"What?"

"Never mind."

"Isn't that what you want to know?"

I ignored the question. "I'd like to meet ya, Mr. Rockefeller."

"I bet you would."

I couldn't figure how he knew I was looking for him. I hadn't even begun.

"Mr. Rockefeller, ya want to tell me how ya knew to call me?"

"I have my sources."

"So do I. Why don't ya tell me yer real name?"

There was only the sound of static on the line.

"Alec?"

"Why are you calling me Alec if you don't think that's my name?"

"What should I call ya, Ishmael?"

"Why not?"

"Yeah, yer right. Ishmael is as good a name for ya as Alec is. Tell me yer real name."

"Now listen, Miss Quick. I want you to stop looking for me. I've told you what you need to know. There's no point in going any further."

"Just cause ya tell me ya didn't kill Claudette proves nothin."

"I'm afraid you'll have to take my word for it."

"Why are ya so scared to meet me?"

There was a silence, and then he spoke like he was clenching his teeth.

"I'm not scared, Miss Quick. I just choose not to."

I heard the click when he hung up like it was a clap of thunder.

I stubbed out my butt and lit another. I'm not a chain smoker, yet certain times called for it. How did this guy even know I was on the case?

Had that wormy-looking girl at the Bailey gallery overheard my conversation with Mrs. Skeffington? And what if she did? Mrs. S. knew there was no Alec Rockefeller, so the girl did, too. And what was I thinking . . . that the girl was in on this scam with whatever his name was?

So who was he? He didn't threaten me, but there was menace in his voice. If I didn't back off, I wondered if he'd come for me, punch my ticket? Most cons didn't get violent, but ya never knew. Somehow I had to find him before he got to me.

I went out to Birdie.

"What exactly did that guy say?"

She looked at me like I was crazy.

"I told ya, Faye."

"All of it."

"From when I picked up?"

"Yeah."

"I said, A Detective Agency, how can I help ya?"

"And he said?"

"Does a Miss Faye Quick work there?"

"Ha!"

"Ha?"

"Go on. What next?"

"I told him, yeah, ya worked here. Then he asked to speak to ya, and I asked him who was callin. Just like ya taught me, Faye. Did I do somethin wrong?"

"No, of course not, Bird. Go on."

"Well, he said it was Alec Rockefeller callin. I have to say I was a little surprised that a Rockefeller was callin here, but I didn't let on. I said one sec, and then I covered the mouthpiece and yelled out to ya. That was it. The whole thing. What's goin on?"

"He didn't say anythin else?"

"Yeah, he asked me out on a date."

"That's a real knee-slapper, Bird."

"Sorry. But what else *would* he say?"

"Did his voice sound disguised?"

"Disguised from what?"

"I mean did it sound to you like he was maybe talkin through a handkerchief?"

She gave it a second's thought. "No. It was nice and clear. And I could tell he was young. Funny how voices change as people get older. Gals, too. Ever notice that, Faye?"

"That's a very interestin observation, but it's for another day. I guess there was no way to tell where he was callin from, huh?"

"Well, there was a lot a noise in the background."

That was strange cause I didn't hear any noise. "What kinda noise?"

"Like a lotta people."

"So it was from a public phone then?"

"Yeah, I guess."

"Ya mean like in a saloon?" I asked.

"Nah. It was more than that."

"Whaddaya mean *more*?"

"It was noisier. More people and other noises."

"What kinda other noises?"

"I knew ya were gonna ask me that. I don't know, Faye. Just other noises."

"Street noises? Car horns and such?"

"Come to think of it, no. Didn't sound like he was on a street."

I said, "When I picked up, there wasn't any background noise at all. Seems like maybe when he was talkin to you he had the door open of a booth then closed it when he was talkin to me."

"Sounds right."

"But not on the street."

"So what, Faye? There's lots of phone booths that aren't on the street."

"Yeah, but they don't all have a lotta noise in the background. Ya know what, Birdie? I bet he was in Grand Central Station."

"Well, then ya shouldn't have no trouble findin him."

"Yeah. Yer right. What am I thinkin?"

"So which Rockefeller is he, Faye?"

"No Rockefeller. That's the point. He passes himself off as one." I told her what I knew.

"So how'd he know about you?" Birdie asked.

"That's what's got me bamboozled. I haven't asked anybody about him yet. The only people who've even mentioned him to me are the Wests and Myrna West's brother."

"So maybe it was one a them told somebody about ya."

"Even so, where's the connection to this phony Rockefeller?" Then I remembered Porter West's reaction when I told him the guy he knew as Rockefeller was an impostor.

"Ya may have somethin after all, Bird," I said as I rushed back into my office.

I dialed West's number.

"Porter West's office," said a very snooty-sounding girl.

"I'd like to speak to him. Tell him Faye Quick is callin." My cig had died in the ashtray so I lit up again.

"Faye who?"

"Quick, like in fast."

"May I ask what you're calling about?"

"No, you may not."

"I beg your pardon."

"That's quite all right. Now put me through." I woulda liked to give her one in the chops.

"I'm afraid I'll have to know—"

"Look, girlie, he'll be damn mad at you if ya don't put this call through. Tell him my name and see."

"Just a moment."

West came on the line before I could count to five.

"What is it, Miss Quick?"

"Are ya over yer shock about Alec Rockefeller yet?"

"I'm still not totally convinced."

"Yeah? Why is that?"

"I've made some inquiries of my own."

I had my answer before I had my answer.

"What kind of inquiries?"

"I checked with some of Claudette's friends."

I tried not to sound steamed. "Mr. West, I thought we agreed that I'd do the detectin."

"I have a right to speak to my dead daughter's friends, don't I?"

"Sure thing. But now you've given her friends a heads-up so they might be on their guard when I interview them."

"You intend to interrogate Claudette's friends?"

He was getting my dander up. "I intend to interview a lotta people, Claudette's friends included. So who did ya talk to and what did ya ask?"

"I spoke to Claudette's closest friend, June Landis. I asked her about Alec."

"What did she say?"

"Not too much. But she confirmed that he was who he said he was."

"And how did she do that? I mean, how did she confirm it?"

He cleared his throat. "She said she had no reason to doubt him."

"And that's why you're not sure he's an impostor?"

"Yes, June would never lie. I'm sure she wouldn't."

"I'm sure she wouldn't either. Did ya tell her you'd hired a private eye?"

"I don't recall."

"Would ya try to recall, please."

"Why is that important?"

Talk about getting hot under the collar, I was burning up. "Mr. West, when I ask ya a question, it's *because* it's important. I'm not makin idle chitchat here."

He was silent for a moment, and I thought maybe he was gonna hang up on me again. Then he said, "I'm sorry, Miss Quick, I simply don't remember. I know I told someone, but I'm not sure who it was."

Terrific. "Ya mean you called a lot of Claudette's friends and asked about Alec?"

"A few. Yes."

"Can I have their names, please?"

"Why?"

"I'm losin my patience here, Mr. West."

"I don't think you should bother these nice young people."

"Is that right?"

"Yes."

"Did ya ever think that maybe one of these *nice young people* murdered your daughter, or knows who did?"

"That's outrageous."

"I'll tell ya what's outrageous, Mr. West. Alec Rockefeller just gave me a jingle and told me to back off. Now how did this impostor know who I was and what I was doin?"

"But I don't even know where or who he is."

"I believe ya. *You* don't know, but somebody does. Maybe one of the nice young people ya called."

"I see."

He gave me their names, addresses, and phone numbers. After that we said our goodbyes. I dialed June Landis.

Her mother said she was sleeping, but I didn't take no for an answer. I told her I was investigating the murder of Claudette West, and that got her attention.

June got on the horn in a few minutes, and I made an appointment with her for later that morning. I'd find out from her who was the best candidate for me to see next. By the end of the day maybe I'd have some reliable info about Alec Rockefeller's real name and likely stomping grounds.

I left my office and spoke to Birdie.

"Ya don't have to work on that list anymore."

"But I have most of them done."

"Let's see."

She handed me the list. The five names West had given me were there along with phone numbers and addresses.

"Ya did a good job, Bird."

"So why don'tcha want it then?" She brushed back her blonde hair over her right shoulder.

I explained.

"So maybe you'll end up needin these other ones."

"If I do, there'll be time enough for you to work on them. Now it's more important for you to finish yer letter to Pete."

"Ah, I don't think I'm gonna send it."

"Why not?"

She looked up at me with those big brown peepers. "I think you were probably right. I mean, how do I know the dame he was with wasn't his sister?"

"I thought ya said he didn't have a sister."

"Yeah, that's right. So maybe it was his cousin like ya said. I mean he's innocent until proven guilty, right?"

"Right. Are ya at least gonna ask him?"

"Sure. Sure I'll ask him. Tonight."

I knew she wouldn't, but it was her life not mine, so I let it go at that. I gave her an encouraging smile, got my things together, and went off to keep my appointment with June Landis.

THIRTEEN

June Landis was definitely whistle bait. Blonde, tall and slinky, skin like marble, eyes so blue they looked salty, and a mouth that must've driven the guys wild. She was wearing a dark blue dress with buttons down the side and a collar that looked like a sailor suit.

The living room we sat in was snazzy but a long way from comfortable. What was it with these people who were in the bucks? Hadn't they ever heard of soft furniture?

A maid with skin the color of Hershey's milk chocolate served us coffee and little buns.

"Thank you, Hattie," June said. When the maid was gone, June allowed as how we could now begin the consultation, as she called it.

I'd already thanked her for seeing me, so I didn't have to go through that deal again. I put my cigarette out in a crystal ashtray, eyeballing those little buns. I wanted one, but didn't think a snatch and grab would go over big, so I waited for the Landis dame's cue.

"I've been told that you were a close friend of Claudette's," I said.

"Her *best* friend." She blinked back tears, puffing on her Chesterfield at the same time. A neat trick.

"Then ya probably knew more about her than anyone."

"I think I did." She produced a lace handkerchief and held it tight.

I've noticed how these broads with bucks can always come up with a hanky even though there was no place they could stash it.

"She told ya secrets?"

June smiled. "Certainly."

"She tell ya about Alec Rockefeller?"

"She did." June leaned forward and picked up the glass plate with the buns. "Would you care for one, Miss Quick?"

"Oh, all right. Yes, thanks." I reached out in a casual way, trying to give the impression I could take em or leave em.

But while my hand was still hanging in the air, she withdrew the plate, picked up a bun with something that looked like giant sterling silver tweezers, and transferred it to a smaller china plate.

She handed it, and a cloth napkin, to me.

"Thank you."

"Would you like sugar and cream?"

"I take it black."

When we were done with that rigamarole, I asked her if she knew Alec Rockefeller.

"I met him several times."

"What did ya think of him?"

I thought I saw a slight blush spreading across her creamy cheeks.

"In a word, he's a dreamboat."

I took a bite of my bun so I could chew over her description of Alec. The bun was a tasty little thing, but I had no idea what it was. I guess it was a rich people's bun. The coffee, on the other hand, tasted like a dreary day. Rich people's coffee.

"A dreamboat, hmmm?"

"Just heaven, Miss Quick."

"Call me Faye. Did ya have a sneaker for him?"

"I beg your pardon?"

"I mean, did ya want him for yourself?"

She sat straighter in her chair, looking like she was gonna give me the business. "He was Claudette's boyfriend."

"That's true. So what did Claudette tell ya about Alec?"

"She said that even though she'd known him only a short time, she was sure she was in love with him. Oh, poor Claudette."

"Did she think that he was in love with her?"

"Yes. And she hoped Richard wouldn't find out about them. She was afraid of Richard, you know."

"Why?"

"He has a terrible temper, and he was jealous of everyone. She couldn't even look at another boy when he was around."

"What would he do?"

"Oh, he'd drag her out of wherever they were. Sometimes he'd yell at her."

"Did ya ever see Richard hit her?"

"Oh, no. Nothing like that."

"Was she still afraid of him after they broke up?"

"Absolutely. She thought he might be angry that she had gotten involved again so soon."

"Let's get back to Alec. What else did Claudette say about him? When they got together, would they go to his place?"

June's head snapped back as though I'd socked her. "What are you implying, Miss Quick?"

"Nothing. I just wanna know how they spent time on their dates?"

"He took her to swell places like Twenty-one and the Latin Quarter, all the big nightclubs."

"Did she tell ya where he lived?"

A look passed across her face that I couldn't nail down.

"No. No, I don't think she ever did."

"Would ya say that they were serious about each other?"

"Well, she wouldn't have married him right away, if that's what you mean."

"Why not?"

"She very much wanted to finish school."

"To be what?"

"Not to *be* anything. She just wanted a college education. Then she'd get married like everyone else. But not before."

"Did Alec know her plans?"

"Yes. He was disappointed because he wanted to marry her right away."

"Pretty fast operator, wouldn't ya say?"

"I guess so. But some boys are like that, don't you find?"

"Some," I said. I took another bite of my bun, and it was gone. I put a quick squint on June's plate and flashed that she hadn't even touched hers.

I guess she took my look-see in cause she said, "Would you like another bun, Faye?"

I wanted one like crazy. "No thank you, June. Did Alec try to pressure Claudette?"

"A little, I think. But there's something you should know about Claudette. She fell in and out of love all the time."

"Even when she was with Richard?"

"Oh, yes. But she didn't do anything about it. She was prone to crushes."

"Was Alec a crush?"

"I think he was more than that."

"Have ya seen Alec lately?"

"Why would I see him?"

Her question told me that she had. When they ask a question back instead of a yes or no, they're usually lying.

"Why wouldn't ya?"

She took a long drag of her cigarette, shrugged, and put the butt out in a wine-colored ashtray the size of a birdbath.

"Mr. West told ya I was workin this case, right?"

"Well, yes, I guess he did. That is, he mentioned your name. He didn't go into a lot of detail."

"Did you mention my name to anyone?"

"I might have mentioned it to Peggy Ann."

"Peggy Ann Lanchester?"

"Yes. That's correct."

"So why'd ya mention me to her?"

"Oh, I don't know. We were just chatting on the telephone about this and that, and I told her about Mr. West's call."

"Did ya tell Alec?"

"I told you I haven't seen Alec."

"Since when?"

"Maybe a week before Claudette . . . Claudette . . . you know."

A lotta people had a hard time using the word "murdered" or even "died." So I supplied it for her.

"A week before she was murdered?"

"Yes."

"Did Mr. West ask you about Alec?"

"Yes. It was strange. He wanted to know if I thought Alec was really Alec? If he was who he said he was?"

"And do you?"

"Of course. I didn't even understand Mr. West's question. Why wouldn't Alec be Alec?"

"What if I told ya that Alec Rockefeller isn't his real name?"

"Why would you tell me that?"

"Because it isn't."

She jumped up from her chair and flounced around, lit another cigarette, and started pacing back and forth and puffing on her cig like she was Bette Davis.

"Why do you say that, Miss Quick?"

"There is no Alec Rockefeller. No Alec in that family."

"Then who is he?"

"I was hopin you'd tell me."

"How can *I* tell you? I know him as Alec Rockefeller."

"I'd like to meet the young man who calls himself Alec Rockefeller. Could you arrange that?"

"I told you—"

"Ya told me ya hadn't seen him. But maybe ya have an address or phone number for him."

Suddenly she stopped pacing and stared right at me. "No. No, I don't." There was that odd look on her face again.

"How about your friend, Peggy Ann? She know where he lives?"

"I don't know. We never discussed that."

"Yer findin it strange now, aren't ya? Strange that ya don't know where he lives or what his number is."

June dropped into her chair and wilted like a plant in the desert. "Why? Why would Alec lie about who he is?"

"How do ya get in touch with him, June?"

"He calls me," she said.

And there it was, the admission.

"So could we be honest about stuff now?"

She nodded.

"When'd ya talk to him last?"

"Yesterday."

"And did ya tell him about West's call and me?"

Sheepishly she said, "Yes, I did."

"Don't feel bad. How were ya supposed to know?"

"I feel like a fool."

I shoulda known she wasn't feeling bad about me. Dames like this were pretty swell-headed.

"Why did ya want to keep it a secret that you were seein him?"

"It didn't seem proper. I mean, he was Claudette's boyfriend."

"But that was months ago. When did he first get in touch with you?"

"About a month after she . . . died."

"And ya went out with him?"

"Well, yes."

"Ya didn't think it was strange that a boy who wanted to marry another girl a month before would now ask you out?"

"I did at first. But then Alec told me something very different from what Claudette had said."

"And what was that?"

"He said he didn't mean to be disrespectful of the dead, but Claudette had wanted to run away and get married and he hadn't."

"You believed him?"

"I did."

This didn't surprise me. Most people will believe what they want to hear.

"Since you didn't go to his place where'd you two go?"

"We didn't go anywhere public because we both felt it wasn't the proper thing to do so soon."

"So where'd ya see him?"

"I misspoke. We went to public places but not those our set would frequent. Not the places he'd taken Claudette. No one knew us where we went."

"Such as?"

"Places in Greenwich Village."

"Ah. Ya mean you were slummin?"

"Yes."

"So who picked the meetin places?"

"He did. I wouldn't know about places like that." She wrinkled her nose like she was smelling a dead fish.

"Ya have a date with him comin up?"

"No. He said he'd call."

"Was that before or after ya told him about Mr. West and me?"

I could see her thinking. "It was after."

"Your friend, Peggy Ann, do ya think she might know somethin about Alec that you don't know?"

"No. Peggy Ann only knows what I've told her."

"Are ya sure about that?" I knew how con men operated.

"What do you mean?"

Should I tell her? I thought I should. "June, dollars to doughnuts, the man who calls himself Alec Rockefeller is most likely a con artist."

"A what?"

Was it possible she was hearing this term for the first time? It was pretty clear that the big blue marble she lived in was like night and day from the one where I knocked around. So I explained.

"I see. And you think that's what Alec is?"

"Yup."

"So what's that got to do with Peggy Ann?"

"Well, Mr. Rockefeller might be seein her, too."

"But she'd tell me."

"Would she? It wouldn't be the first time two gals were seein the same guy and one of them kept zipped about it."

"Not in our set, Miss Quick."

I got the drift of that remark. "In any set, Miss Landis."

"I can't believe all this. Do you think Alec . . . or whoever he is . . . killed Claudette?"

"I don't know. But I need to rule him out."

"How will you do that?"

"I gotta meet him, talk to him."

"And you want me to make a date with him for that purpose?"

"You catch on fast. Either you or Peggy Ann."

"But we don't know if she's seeing him."

"That's why yer gonna call her now."

She lit another cigarette, her hands shaking. "But I don't think that's right. You want me to trick her into admitting that she's seeing him."

"I do? I didn't say anything about tricks. I want ya to tell her everything I told you and ask her nicely if she's seein him. Tell her ya won't be mad. Ya won't, will ya?"

Her eyes sparked like small gems. "I have to admit I'm not sure."

"Yeah, well, I can understand that." I wouldn't be over the moon if my friend Jeanne did that to me. "So ya don't have to say ya won't be mad."

"If I don't reassure her about that, she'll never tell me. It'll be a white lie."

White, black, I never did get a handle on that one. "Good. Whatever works best for you. Ya think ya could call her now? She'll be home?"

"I think so."

She crossed the room to the telephone and dialed. She said hello, and I knew it was Peggy Ann on the other end of the line cause she didn't ask for her.

I listened while June talked turkey. It took a while, but finally she gave me a high sign, making a circle with her thumb and forefinger.

Then she thanked Peggy Ann and told her she'd call her back. June looked like she'd been leveled and wasn't gonna get up for the count.

"She's meeting him at the Four Oaks for cocktails this evening."

"You upset?"

"I guess I feel betrayed."

"By Alec?"

"By Peggy Ann. I never thought she'd try to take a beau away from me."

"I guess it doesn't happen too often in your set." I couldn't help myself. "Sorry ya feel bad, June." And I was. "Ya did a first-rate job."

"Thanks."

"So Peggy Ann bought everything you told her and said she was willin to help me?"

"Yes."

"What time is she meetin Alec?"

"Six."

I'd have to move back my date with Jeanne, but she'd understand. "That spot's not far from where I live."

"You don't expect me to come with you, do you?" The lovely Miss Landis looked like she'd be lucky to crawl across the room by evening.

"No. I want ya to call Peggy Ann back and ask her what she'll be wearin so I'll know who she is."

She did. I thanked her, asked her to dummy up about what she knew, and then I left to get ready for a night in the slums.

FOURTEEN

I needed an escort to get into the Four Oaks, so I called on Marty Mitchum. I can't say he was floating on air when I told him he had to wear a tie.

He picked me up at five-forty, and I filled him in on the Alec

Rockefeller connection while we walked down Bleecker toward the restaurant.

"So yer thinkin this bozo might've knocked off the West gal?"

"I don't know. But he was after her money for sure, and maybe when she shot down his marriage plans he went bonkers in the conkus."

"What good would it do him to put her on ice?"

"We gotta remember she was pregnant."

"Yeah, but ya said she was only seein this guy for two weeks before she was rubbed out."

"That's what the Wests said."

"And June Landis?"

"She could've been datin this guy long before she let anyone know."

"Yeah. Sure."

At the door of the restaurant, Marty held it open for me, and I went in. There was a long staircase ya had to go down to get to the restaurant proper, a huge room with tables covered in enough white cloths and settings of sparkling silver to make me squint. At the back was a mahogany bar with padded stools.

The maître d' greeted us.

"Good evening. Do you have a reservation?"

Marty looked at me.

"No." I'd overlooked that little wrinkle. Of course, at this unfashionable hour all the tables were empty, and even the bar had only three customers.

"Well, let me see," he said.

He went over to a wooden stand where he kept his reservation book, staring at it like it was in code, muttering to himself. But when he finally looked up, he gave us a smile like we'd won a jackpot.

"You're in luck. I have one table for two over in that corner."

"Fine," I said.

"Perhaps you'd like to check your coat?"

"I'll hang on to it, thanks." I was wearing a light jacket, and Marty was in his suit.

Looking grumpy, he escorted us to the table, and before we even sat down I realized we were right next to the kitchen door. Well, we weren't there to make snappy conversation.

The maître d' pulled out my chair, and when I was seated he helped me drag it closer to the table.

"Your waiter will be with you in a moment."

Marty said, "This is some snooty place."

He took out his cigarettes and lit up both of us with a pack of Four Oaks matches. They weren't on the table, so he must've pocketed them as we came in. Mitchum was fast. He would've made a good clipper.

"So ya don't know what the guy looks like, but ya got a bead on the girl, is that right?"

"I know what she'll be wearin. It's funny they'd be meetin so early. I hope June got it right."

"It don't seem that early to me. I guess fancy people eat later, huh?"

"Yeah, I think they do. Maybe they're just havin drinks here."

Our waiter appeared at the table. He was an arrangement of skin and bones, hair plastered to his skull, face like a corkscrew.

"May I get you a cocktail?"

Marty looked at me. "Faye?"

"I'll have a manhattan."

"I'll have a beer. What kinda draft ya have?"

"No draft, sir. We carry only bottled brews." His nostrils flared.

"Oh. Then bring me a Rheingold."

"Certainly, sir." He seemed to disappear like a ghost.

"Ya ever hear of a place didn't have draft?"

"I guess swanky spots don't carry it, Marty."

"Yeah." He started to pull down his tie in discomfort, then caught himself.

"Hey," I said, "don't let this place get ya down in the dumps."

"I hate places that put on airs, ya know what I mean, Faye? That waiter looked at me like I was somethin he'd scraped off the bottom of his shoe."

"Pay no attention to him."

"Yeah. He's just a waiter, right?"

"Right."

"He's not the mayor or nothin."

"Right." I glanced at my watch. It was six. They should be arriving any second.

When the stuck-up waiter came back with our drinks and left, Marty said, "I guess I shouldn't drink outta the bottle, should I?"

"Probably better if ya don't."

"Yeah." He poured his beer into a pilsner glass.

It was then that they came in. I recognized the pale pink jacket and the matching chapeau that Peggy Ann Lanchester was wearing.

Whoever he was, he was something all right. A long drink of water in a tweed suit, resting on wide shoulders, narrowing slightly at the waist, looking like he'd been born in it. He wore a silvery gray tie and a gray trilby, which he lifted right away, revealing blond hair parted on the left. From where I was sitting, he looked every bit as good as he'd been advertised.

"They're here," I said to Marty, whose head was down. "Don't look yet. Talk to me like we're having fun."

"Ya mean we ain't havin fun?"

"Ha-ha."

"I don't know what to say."

"You've never been at a loss for words in yer life."

"Want me to talk more about this phony-baloney place?"

I watched as the maître d', holding what's-his-name's hat, led the couple to a table in a private corner far from the kitchen. Once they were seated I told Marty he could look at them.

"Holy hell," he said.

"What?"

"He looks like a pansy."

"Can it, Marty."

"He even has a pipe."

"Yeah, like half the men in America. It's fashionable to smoke a pipe."

"Not where I come from."

"Yeah, well, yer from the other half of America."

"And proud of it, too."

"Marty. Stuff it. We're not here to debate fashion." I lit another cigarette, then took a big sip of my manhattan.

After the waiter took their order, the guy placed his hand over Peggy Ann's, which was conveniently lying on the table. She batted her blinkers at him, all misty and adoring. I hated dames who played that game. On the other hand, maybe Peggy Ann was demonstrating

her thespian skills cause June had told her the truth about this monkey.

"So now what?" Marty asked.

"So pretty soon I go over there."

"And do what?" He had a slight mustache from the head on his
beer.

"Confront him."

"Ya crazy, Faye? What if he's got a gun?"

"He's a con, Marty." Cons hardly ever packed a piece.

Once they had their drinks I pushed back from our table in
Siberia. "Wish me luck," I whispered.

"I'm right here, ya get in trouble."

After one deep breath I walked straight to their table and sat
down in the empty chair facing Alec, not giving him a chance to rise.

"I thought it was you," I said to him.

"Yes, it's me," he said, being a gentleman. I thought the statement
was pretty funny under the circumstances.

"Aren't ya gonna introduce me?" I looked at Peggy Ann.

He was rattled. I could see doubts flickering in his deep brown
eyes. I waited.

He took a pull on his martini.

Peggy Ann asked, "What's wrong?"

"Nothing. I . . . I'm so sorry and terribly embarrassed, but I can't
bring your name to mind. Although your voice is familiar."

"That's a funny thing," I said, "cause your name has slipped my
mind, too, and yer voice is *very* familiar." I could see by his eyes that
he was beginning to get the picture. "I just know that we met at some
party."

"The Astors' perhaps?"

"Could be. Then again it might've been at the Rockefellers'."

A flush started creeping up his neck.

Peggy Ann laughed on cue. "Oh, tell her, Alec."

"I'm . . . I'm . . ."

"You silly," Peggy Ann said. "Alec is a Rockefeller."

"Really?"

He nodded.

I said, "Who are your parents, Alec?"

"I'm a distant cousin," he said. The rest of his martini disappeared in a flash.

"What branch of the family?"

"You know the family?"

"Oh, yes," I said. "Very well."

"What did you say your name was?" he asked softly.

I ignored his question. "It's the strangest thing. I thought I knew about *all* the family. But I've never heard anyone mention an Alec."

"And your name is," he said.

"Faye Skeffington."

"Skeffington? I don't remember any Faye?"

"No, you wouldn't. Because I'm a Skeffington just like you're a Rockefeller."

His eyes flashed anger, and I was sure he knew who I was. "I'm not certain I understand," he said.

"I think you do. What's your *real* name, bub?"

"I don't want to appear rude, Miss Skeffington, but I think it's time for you to leave this table."

"And I think it's time for you to come clean."

"I'll have to call the waiter," he said.

"Oh, I don't think you want to do that."

"Miss Skeffington—"

"Quick. That's my name. Miss Quick."

"I'm beginning to think we've never met before."

"You're right. We haven't. But we've talked on the phone. I'm that private eye you threatened, and you're an impostor."

"How dare you—"

"Take yer outrage somewhere else, and tell me yer name before I ask my cop friend over there to join us." I motioned toward Marty with a toss of my head.

"This is impossible," he said.

"Quit stallin. I've got some questions about the death of Claudette West."

"I had nothing to do with that," he said.

"Maybe, maybe not."

"Peggy Ann, I think I should escort you to a taxi," he said.

"She stays. She knows yer a fraud, mister."

He looked trapped.

"So who are ya? Ya might as well tell me cause the cat's outta the bag with the Rockefeller thing."

"I haven't done anything illegal," he said.

"Impersonation isn't exactly kosher."

"I wasn't impersonating anyone. I just used another name."

"But for what purpose?"

He glanced from me to Peggy Ann and back to me. I couldn't remember when I'd last seen anyone look so much like a dead duck. Maybe when Fat Freddy lost a bundle on Requested running at the Kentucky Derby the year before.

"I'd prefer it if you'd leave, Peggy Ann," he said.

I nodded to her that I agreed.

He said, "I'll walk you to a cab."

"No, ya won't," I said. I gave a signal to Marty.

"What's up, Faye?" he asked when he got to the table with our drinks.

"Would ya walk Miss Lanchester to a cab?"

"My pleasure," he said.

Peggy Ann rose, glomming on Alec before she left. "I think you're one of the most contemptible people I've ever met."

He said nothing, but he didn't lift his head either.

Marty and Peggy Ann shoved off.

"So," I said, "who are ya?"

"Nobody."

"I know that but what's your real moniker?"

"Leon Johnson."

"Where do ya hail from?"

"Ohio."

"But ya been in New York for a while, huh?"

"Yes."

"Do ya have an alibi for the time of Claudette West's murder?"

"Yes, I do. But I don't want to use it."

"Why not?"

Marty came back and joined us.

"This is Leon Johnson. Detective Mitchum."

"Hello," Leon said.

"Leon here was just tellin me he has an alibi for the night in question but he doesn't wanna use it."

"It involves a young lady, and I don't want to compromise her."

"Awww. Ain't that somethin," Marty said. "A real gent."

"Listen, Leon, if you don't cough up your alibi, Detective Mitchum is gonna have to take ya in. You're a prime suspect."

"That's what I've been afraid of."

"But not afraid enough to drop your con. How come ya didn't skip town?"

The mâitre d' materialized at the table. "May I know what your plans are, please?"

"Plans?"

"Are you and the gentleman joining this gentleman?"

"Yeah," I said.

"Then you won't be needing your table?"

"Right," Marty said.

"Thank you."

He slithered away.

"So where were we? Oh, yeah. Why'd ya hang around town after Claudette was killed?"

"You're not going to believe any of this."

"Try us."

"While I was dating Claudette, I fell in love."

Marty mimed playing a violin.

"But not with Claudette. Even so, I had to go on with the plan, so I asked her to marry me. It was the night before . . . you know . . . the night before she was murdered."

"What did she say when ya asked her to be yer blushin bride?"

"She said she couldn't because she was in love with someone else."

Another one? Or maybe it was Brian Wayne. "She tell ya who it was?"

"No. She said she couldn't."

"Because he was already hitched?" I asked.

"She didn't give me a reason, and I didn't push it because, frankly, I was relieved."

"How long had ya really been seein each other?"

"A few months."

"Why didn't she want her parents to know before those last two weeks when ya made it public?"

"I'm not sure, but now I think it must've been because of the man she was in love with."

"Did ya know she was pregnant?"

He looked like I'd thrown a glass a water in his face.

"No. No, I didn't know that."

"You the father?"

"Absolutely not."

"How can ya be so sure?" Marty asked. "Just between us guys, ya can't always be that sure."

As if I didn't know what he was talking about.

"We never . . . we never went that far."

"See, Faye. What'd I tell ya. The guy's a fruitcake."

Leon pulled himself up in his chair, looking indignant. "I am not."

Better to be thought of as a murderer than a homo, I guessed. Some people.

Marty said, "So how do ya know ya ain't the father?"

"I told you, we never went all the way."

"Why not?"

"She wouldn't."

"Well, she did with somebody."

"Not me. She said she was saving herself for marriage. Boy, she had me fooled."

He actually sounded like the injured party.

"Let's get back to yer alibi, Leon."

"Will you have to tell anyone else who I was with?"

"We'll have to check it out with her."

"Oh, God. This is awful."

"Spill it," Marty said.

"Her name is Gladys Wright."

"Who's that?" I asked.

"She's Myrna West's younger sister."

FIFTEEN

Chumley's, on Bedford Street, wasn't far from the Four Oaks. It'd been there since the Twenties and had once been a speakeasy. If ya didn't know where it was, it wasn't easy to find cause there was no sign outside the place. But if ya did know, ya recognized the wooden door with number 86 on it.

Inside, it was warm and cozy, the fireplace going, the picture frames on the walls holding book jackets. The tables were wooden with names scratched in them. I'd even found F. Scott Fitzgerald's one night.

For once I wasn't early, and Jeanne Darnell was waiting for me sipping a beer.

"I'm really sorry to be late, Jeanne."

She blew off the apology with a flick of her hand. I sat down, shrugged off my coat, and hung it over the back of the chair.

Jeanne was a good-looking dame without being a great beauty. Her hazel eyes were a little too close together, but her smile and loony laugh made ya forget that in a hurry. She was wearing a brown-and-blue plaid wool suit with three chocolate brown buttons diagonally across the front of the jacket. Her clothes always had some slight twist to them, never simple straight perfection, kinda like the eyes.

"So what's going on, Faye?"

I took out a cig and lit it. "Let me get a beer first." Chumley's didn't serve hard liquor.

When my beer arrived, I brought Jeanne up to date on the West case.

"The mother's sister?" she said.

"Yeah. I didn't even know she had a sister. No reason I should. I met their brother, too. Nice-lookin Marine. Anyway, Leon told me the sister is younger than Myrna West, but still a bit older than Leon, also known as Alec."

"How much older?"

"About ten years."

"So Gladys is around thirty?"

"Yeah. He thinks of her as an older woman."

"Well, she is to him."

"True. Hey, isn't that Ernest Hemingway over at that table behind ya? Don't look now."

"Not sure I'd know if I *did* look."

"Sure ya would. Okay, ya can look now."

Jeanne slowly turned and looked in the direction I'd indicated. Then she turned back to me.

"Sorry, Faye. I'm not sure."

"Well, I say it's him."

"You read him?"

"Sure. Don't you?"

"Tried one, but it was too violent for me."

"What a sissy you are."

She was anything but. Jeanne was a nurse, and I could never have done some of the things she'd told me about.

"So where were we? Oh, yes. Leon's alibi is that he was with Gladys," she said.

"Yeah."

"How did this come about, him with the sister?"

"Gladys was Claudette's favorite aunt. She confided in her and brought Alec to her apartment long before everybody met the so-called Rockefeller."

"When did the affair with Gladys start?"

"I don't know."

"You going to interview her?"

"After we have dinner. Sorry to do this, Jeanne, but we better order."

"Don't worry about it, Faye. Murder comes first."

"You're a pal."

Gladys Wright met me at the door in a silver satin dressing gown that brushed her matching slippers and had a split up the right side showing a nicely turned ankle. Her almond-shaped eyes were azure. She wore her bleached blonde hair in a chignon, and her makeup was dead on, not too much, not too little. Obviously Gladys and Cornell had gotten the looks in the family, though for all I knew there were more brothers and sisters. I wondered why Gladys bothered to bleach her hair, but it wasn't something I could ask her.

Her apartment was in the Village on Eleventh Street, a four-story walk-up, which took me by surprise. I expected to find anyone related to Myrna West in a swankier building. At least one with an elevator.

"Miss Quick? Come in."

Her voice was throaty, like she'd been yelling all night. I followed her down a long hall to a large living room. The walls were painted white and three large windows were partially covered by yellow checked curtains. The furniture was mismatched, as if she'd thrown it all together in a hurry.

"Sit down," she said, motioning to a comfortable-looking tan sofa. At last, a piece a normal furniture.

I sat. She took a blue club chair across from me and lit a cigarette.

"You said you wanted to talk to me about Leon."

"Have ya always known him by that name?"

"No. When my niece introduced him to me, he was Alec Rockefeller."

"When did ya find out he was Leon Johnson?"

"The first time we were alone together."

"And when was that?" I lit a cig of my own.

"About a week after I'd first met him. He phoned to say he wanted to talk to me about something important. Naturally, I thought it had to do with Claudette, so I agreed."

"Ya didn't think ya needed to check with Claudette first."

"I was planning to tell her after I met with him."

"And did ya?"

She flicked some ash from her cig into a green ashtray. Ugly thing.

"No. I didn't."

"Why not?"

"Because Leon and I began an affair that night."

"Ya didn't feel you were betrayin your niece?"

"I didn't think about it."

"When did ya think about it?"

"Never."

This was one cold cookie.

"So was it that first night Leon confessed to you who he really was?"

"That's right."

"Ya didn't think he was a con artist?"

"Oh, I knew he was."

This dame was driving me bananas.

"So how come ya got involved with a con?" I asked.

She laughed, low like a vamp. "I've been *married* to worse," she said and lazily stubbed out her cigarette.

"Married. So that's why your name is Wright instead of Walker?"

"Give this girl a cigar."

I wanted to give *her* an uppercut. It was hard to believe that she was the sister of Myrna West.

"In case you're wondering, I'm the black sheep," she said, like she was reading my mind.

"How old were ya when ya got married?"

"Which time?"

"How many times were there?"

"Three."

"Three?"

"Yes. Three dismal failures. Want their names?"

"Not really. So how old were ya the first time ya got hitched?"

"Seventeen. He was sixty. A fur trapper."

"Your parents must have liked that a lot."

"We eloped," she said.

"But they knew about it?"

"Only afterward. Then they had it annulled."

"How about hubby number two?"

"I was twenty-two, and he was seventy. A mafia don. Didn't need to elope that time. It lasted eight months."

"Number three?"

"I was twenty-eight, and he was eighteen. A high school senior."

"Annulled?"

"Yes. *His* parents this time. But I kept his last name."

"Why?"

"Why not? Besides, everything was already monogrammed."

"So why didn't you go back to Walker?"

"Why would I do that?"

"It was yer maiden name."

"Hard to believe I was ever a maiden. Anyway, maybe I don't like being related to Cornell."

"Your own brother?"

"Half brother."

"So, what's wrong with Cornell?"

"Everything."

"Meanin?"

"Let's just say I find him incredibly boring."

"That's all ya want to say about him?"

"Miss Quick, a person can be stupid, arrogant, cruel, or prejudiced, but if he's boring that's it for me. Thinking about him makes me want to have a drink. Would you like one?"

"Sure."

"What would you like? I have everything."

Her smile was seductive. I thought she was one of those gals who flirted with everyone. This was the only way she knew how to smile.

"What are you havin?"

"Scotch."

"Sounds good to me."

I watched her leg it over to a wooden cabinet that had seen better days and open the door. There was quite a stash in there. She took out a bottle and turned to me.

"Ice?"

"Yeah, if ya don't mind."

"No trouble."

She disappeared with the glass into what I assumed was the kitchen. There weren't any nearby drawers to open, so I stayed on the sofa. Good thing, cause she was back in seconds.

"Here you are," she said.

She gave me my drink on the rocks, but her own was neat. Usually I have a little seltzer with my Scotch, but I knew I'd have no trouble getting this down. I'd long since stopped thinking of Scotch as tasting medicinal.

Gladys took a healthy sip from her drink then oozed back into her chair, crossing her legs so that the dressing gown revealed a lot of leg.

"So what else would you like to know?"

"I guess I'm wonderin why ya didn't let anyone know that Leon was a phony."

"You mean why I didn't tell Claudette?"

"Yeah."

"How would I explain my knowledge?" she said.

"I can think of a few ways."

"Well, I couldn't. Besides, if Leon got Claudette to marry him, we'd all be in the money."

That knocked me for a loop.

"Ya wanna explain that?"

"I think it's fairly clear."

"Ya mean ya would've let him marry her for her money? Yer favorite niece?"

"When did I say she was my favorite niece?"

"I thought you were her favorite aunt."

"Two and two don't always make four. I won't deny being fond of Claudette, but fondness never trumps money. And, as you can see, I'm in need of some." She swept her arm from right to left, taking in the living room.

This was colder than a well-digger's behind, and I was caught flat-footed for a moment.

"So are you sayin yer a con yerself?"

"Aren't we all, Miss Quick? In one way or another."

"No. I don't think so."

"I *know* so, and you can stop looking at me that way."

I wasn't aware I was looking at her in any particular way. "What way?"

"As though you'd just stumbled across the Hope diamond. You know, stunned."

I took a swig of my drink and lit another cig.

"Look, Miss Wright, this is a shockin development. I think what yer tellin me is that you and Leon were partners in separatin Claudette from her money."

"Yes, that *is* what I'm telling you. It's done all the time, Miss Quick. I don't see what the drama is."

And I believed her. She didn't see.

"I don't think it *is* done all the time. Not by people like you."

"And just what kind of person is that?"

"Ya got me there. I guess I meant the person I thought ya were. Let's not get sidetracked here. Claudette refused Leon's marriage proposal, didn't she?"

"She did indeed."

"So what was the plan then?"

"June Landis."

"What were ya gonna do, go through the whole set until he snagged one of them?"

"Something like that."

This was too much for me. I'd been on plenty of cases that were down and dirty, but this was a winner.

"So Leon was with you when Claudette was murdered, is that right?"

"He was. Right in there." She pointed to a door which I took to be the bedroom. "From seven in the evening . . . you want to know what we had for dinner?"

"No, thanks."

"After dinner we listened to some music, Vivaldi. Do you know who that is?"

She was beginning to irk me, looking down her nose on top of everything else.

"Yeah, I know who Antonio Vivaldi is. Go on."

The look she shot me was supposed to reflect respect, I guessed. I wanted to tell her to stuff it.

"After listening to the music we played a game of chess."

"I know what that is, too."

"Then we repaired to the bedroom. Want to know what we did in there?"

"No. He was with ya all night?"

"All night." She smiled.

"What time did he leave here?"

"About nine the next morning. Right after I got the call from Myrna about Claudette."

"Why should I believe ya about him bein here? Yer a con, which means yer a liar."

She shrugged. "Don't believe me then."

But I did. She hadn't pulled any punches about anything else. Besides, there was no reason for Leon to kill Claudette unless she'd caught on to their scheme. I put that idea forward.

"Even if she had, Leon was here all night."

"So you say."

"That's the best I can do, Miss Quick."

It was time for me to scram. I stood up.

"Are you leaving so soon?"

"I think I got everything I need."

"I'll walk you to the door."

We made our way down the long hall again, and she opened the door for me. Just before I went through it, I turned and looked at her.

"I got to tell ya, Gladys, I've met a lot of cold customers in my line of work, but you take the cake."

"What kind?"

"What?"

"I like cake. What kind?"

I left.

SIXTEEN

I couldn't cross Leon off my list cause there was still the possibility that Claudette had wised up and was gonna expose him. It was a long shot, but he was still in my sights. And I now knew where he lived.

It was time for me to get a piece of Claudette's clothing from the Wests. I was in my pjs and my hair was still in pins and rolled up. I wondered if someday they'd have something like phoneavision? I'd hate that cause I'd never be able to make a call unless I was dolled up.

Myrna answered.

"I'd like to come up and see ya, Mrs. West."

"Do you have some news?"

"Yes, I do, and I want to ask ya for a favor which I'd rather not go into on the phone."

"A favor?"

"It's no big deal."

"All right. When do you wish to come?"

I looked at my clock. "In about an hour."

"Porter wasn't happy about our last meeting. What I mean is, he didn't like me seeing you without him."

"So what do you want to do?"

"I'll call him at the office and see if he can come home."

"If that's not convenient for him, we could meet some other place."

"May I call you back?"

"Sure."

I put off taking a shower so I wouldn't miss her call, staying at the telephone table and sipping my cup of joe.

I hoped Porter would arrange to come home cause if he agreed to give me a piece of his daughter's clothing we'd have to go back to their place anyway. Meeting elsewhere could be a real time waster.

Hashing over my visit with Gladys the night before, I thought: Who says Claudette West's killer has to be a man? Dames didn't top my list of murder suspects, but that didn't mean there weren't any. What about Ruth Snyder or Lizzie Borden or Belle Gunness or . . . that was all I could come up with off the top of my head, but I knew there were more than those three.

So maybe Gladys knocked off her niece. But why? Cause Claudette wouldn't marry Leon? That didn't wash. I was still searching for a solid motive when the phone rang. I picked it up right away.

"Porter said he'd come home. He doesn't think meeting in a public place is a good idea."

"Okay." I was glad, but wondered why West nixed seeing me in the open.

"You can still come in an hour if you'd like to."

"Right."

I finished off my java and put the cup in the sink. My bathroom was small, but I told myself that meant less cleaning. I liked bubble baths and listening to the radio and taking my time. Sometimes I even had a drink while lying in the tub. No baths when I was in a hurry.

I turned on the water and when it was warm enough, put on my bathing cap, stepped in, picked up my rubber hose with the spray head on it, and started my shower.

When I left my apartment, Jim Duryea was in the hallway. He tried to act casual, like he just happened to be there, but I knew different.

"Hello, Faye."

"Hi, Jim. I'm runnin late as usual."

"I hope you won't be late tonight."

"No, I won't," I said. Uh-oh. I'd forgotten and wasn't paying attention. "I mean—"

"Oh, Mother is going to be so pleased. I've told her all about you."

All about me? That'd be one short conversation. "I told ya I was on a case that might make it tough for me to show, Jim."

"But you just said you wouldn't be late."

"I wasn't thinkin."

The look on his face was so down in the mouth that I couldn't take it. "What time?"

"How would seven be?"

"Ya have to understand that somethin might come up which would make it impossible."

He moved closer, and his breath smelled of sardines. "Faye, this would mean so much to me. You have no idea."

"I'm *gettin* the idea."

"I'm a wonderful cook."

"It isn't that, Jim. It's my work."

"Surely you could take a couple of hours away from your work."

"What I do isn't like that. If an important person in a case can only see me at seven tonight, then I gotta see that person then."

"Well, do you think that's going to happen?" He was actually wringing his hands.

"I have no way of knowin, Jim. That's what I'm tryin to tell ya."

"I'm making sweetbreads with baby asparagus for an appetizer and braised rabbit for the entrée. And, of course, Zito's bread. Then for dessert a hot chocolate mousse that—"

"Where'd ya get the rations for all that?"

His face flushed. "I've been saving them up for this occasion. And Frank at Ottomanelli's helped me."

How Jim's destiny landed in my mitts was beyond me, but that's how he made me feel. "Jim, I'll do everything in my power to get to dinner on time."

"If you're a little late, it won't matter."

"Okay. I gotta go now."

"See you later, Faye." He waved as I made for the outer door. I wiggled my fingers in the air without looking back.

Out on the street I tried to focus cause I had work to do. But I couldn't get Jim's face outta my mind. When I said I'd be there, he looked like a little boy who'd just found his long-lost puppy. Even if something did come up, unless it was the murderer wanting to confess, I was gonna get to that dinner.

Porter, Myrna, and Cornell were all in the living room when I arrived. Kinda like finding a firing squad waiting for me.

"What news do you have?" Porter asked.

"Alec Rockefeller is a con man named Leon Johnson."

Pursing his mouth, Porter said, "I don't see how that's possible."

I was dealing with a character who couldn't stand being wrong.

"Mr. West, it *is* possible. I've met with Johnson."

"He admitted pretending to be a Rockefeller?"

"Yeah, he did."

"Outrageous. Have you had him arrested?"

"On what charge?"

"Impersonation. False representation. Fraud."

"The fact is, Mr. West, he wasn't impersonating anyone cause there *isn't* an Alec Rockefeller. Anyway, he didn't do anything criminal."

"What do you mean? He might have killed Claudette."

"But he didn't."

"How do you know?"

"He has an alibi."

"How do you know it's real?"

"It's been confirmed." The last thing I wanted to do was bring in Gladys Wright as the alibi witness.

"By whom?"

"I'm sorry, but right now that's privileged information."

Porter's face looked like it might explode. "I'm paying you, Miss Quick."

Myrna put a hand lightly on his leg, and he shook it off. She whispered, "Porter, please."

"I know yer paying me, Mr. West, but I've told ya before there are certain things, sources, that I can't reveal. It would compromise me for work in the future and in some cases compromise you."

"Me?"

"Yeah. We don't want everybody knowin that you hired me, do we?"

"I'm not ashamed of it."

"That's not the point. It's best to keep these things as hush-hush as possible. You'll have to take my word for it. Leon Johnson has an alibi."

"Outrageous," he said again.

Cornell Walker said, "Porter, why don't we give Miss Quick a chance to explain things to us."

"Us? Frankly, Cornell, I don't even know why you're in on this meeting."

Walker flinched like he'd been slapped. I thought about Gladys telling me Cornell was boring. I'd have to keep an ear out for that.

Myrna, sitting between the two men, was looking kinda peaky.

"I'm in on this meeting because Claudette was my niece, Porter. You think I don't care who killed her?"

Porter ignored him. "Then we're back to Richard Cotten, aren't we?"

"Not necessarily. Another reason I came up here was to ask you for a favor." I expected Porter to say "outrageous" again, but he didn't. "I know this is gonna sound odd, and I'll understand if ya don't wanna go down this avenue, but I have to ask."

"Get to the point, please," West said, checking his watch.

"I know someone who specializes . . . there's somethin I'd like to try. A colleague of mine uses a technique that's a little unusual, but I respect her, and it's worked before."

"What is she, a clairvoyant?" Cornell asked.

"Not exactly."

"Not *exactly*?" Porter said. "Are you thinking of suggesting a séance?"

"No." I could see how this was gonna go over. "My colleague is psychic and—"

Porter bounded up and started pacing. "Miss Quick, is this why you've gotten me here, to waste my time?"

"I know how this sounds, Mr. West. Hear me out."

"I'm curious, Porter," Myrna said.

He glared at her as if he hoped the look would clam her up forever. I wouldn't put money on it.

"Go on," Cornell said.

"I told you to stay out of this," Porter said.

Cornell squeezed his fists at his sides. "And I told you that I care about what happened to Claudette. I think we should listen to what Miss Quick has to say. What have we got to lose?"

I didn't find him so boring!

"Well, I'm beginning to think I should fire Miss Quick," Porter said.

I stood up. "If ya wanna do that, feel free."

"No," Myrna said.

Porter said, "What did you say?"

"I said no. We're not firing her." She stood up.

With everybody standing I didn't know what to do next. I was glad to see Myrna was bucking Porter and not just cause I wanted to stay on the case.

"I think we should all calm down," Cornell said.

Porter looked like he wanted to deck him, but he turned his back to all of us instead. I could tell that he was breathing hard.

The rest of us stared at his back, silent, waiting for his next move. I watched his breathing slow and then he turned back to us.

"Let's all sit down," he said. The picture of reason, at least for now.

"What exactly is it that you're proposing, Miss Quick?"

"My colleague—"

"Who is named?"

Oh, no. Anne didn't like people knowing about her. "I don't see what her name has to do with it," I said.

"I suppose that's confidential, too."

"Let's just leave her nameless for now, okay?"

"*Her.* Another female." Porter said.

I ignored him. "My colleague works by touchin clothin of the deceased."

Myrna said, "Oh, I've heard about that."

"From where?" Porter asked.

"I've . . . I've read it, I guess."

"In some ridiculous woman's magazine, I suppose."

Myrna looked down at her hands, and I knew her emancipation was over.

I went on quickly. "If ya have a piece of clothin that Claudette wore, I'd like to take it to my colleague."

"We have all her clothing," Myrna said. "We haven't been able to part with it yet."

"*You* haven't," Porter said.

"Will anything do?" she asked me.

"Yes."

"I'll go get something." She hurried from the room.

Porter said, "You're giving her false hope."

"There's a chance we'll get some help from this. As Mr. Walker said, what've ya got to lose?"

The two men glared at each other.

"Mr. Walker, is it just you two?"

"Two what?"

"Sorry. Brother and sister. Are there any others in your family?"

"Myrna's my half sister. Her father married twice. Myrna's mother died when she was small. Her father married my mother, who already had a daughter, Gladys, my other half sister, and then together they had me."

So Cornell and Myrna had the same father, and Cornell and Gladys had the same mother.

"And where is she now?"

"Who?"

"Gladys."

"God knows," Porter said.

"Why do you say that, Mr. West?"

"She's a wild thing. Married three times before she was thirty."

Myrna came back in the room carrying something pink clutched against her breast.

"It's a sweater," she said.

"That's fine." I stood up and held out my hand, but Myrna hesitated.

She said, "I *will* get this back, won't I?"

"Sure," I said.

"What does it matter now, Myrna?"

"Please, Porter." She handed me the sweater.

"Thank you. I'll take good care of it."

"I know you will."

"When is this miracle going to take place?" Porter asked.

"Within the next twenty-four hours."

He sneered. "Does it happen at midnight?"

"Not usually." I wasn't gonna let him get to me. "I guess I'll be goin now. Thanks for cooperatin."

"When will we hear from you?"

"I won't call tonight cause we've just seen each other. But tomorrow night per usual."

"What if you know something before tomorrow night?"

I almost laughed cause I knew he was referring to what the sweater might reveal. He wanted to believe the psychic contact would work. "Then I'll call ya right away. I can see myself out."

At the door Cornell stopped me.

"Miss Quick. Please don't let my brother-in-law put you off."

"Oh, he doesn't."

"Good. He's a lot of hot air, you know."

"You don't like each other much, do ya?"

"I think that's safe to say." He smiled. Him I could go for, cleft chin and all.

"Any special reason ya don't like him?"

"I don't like the way he treats Myrna, for one thing."

"When we first met, ya said ya liked him."

"I know. I didn't want to indicate my real feelings in front of Myrna."

"How did he treat Claudette?"

"That's complicated. He adored her, but she was more his possession than his daughter. He acted as if he owned her."

"But he didn't treat her like he treats his wife?"

"Oh, no."

"Would ya say he loved his daughter?"

"Yes. But when Porter loves someone it's not pure. It's laced with a kind of quid pro quo. He gave her anything she wanted, and she gave him total loyalty."

"In what way?"

"I hate to say this, but she and Porter were lined up against Myrna. Claudette always took her father's side, and sometimes they'd make fun of Myrna."

"How did Myrna take that?"

"Well, she was never sure what they were up to because they joked about her in French."

"Nice," I said.

"I don't want to give you the wrong idea about Claudette, Miss Quick. She was a wonderful girl. And if she defied Porter, like she did with that Cotten boy, he'd get very nasty."

"Let me ask ya somethin, Mr. Walker. Do you think Porter West was capable of killin his own daughter?"

"I think Porter West is capable of anything."

SEVENTEEN

Anne Fontaine's apartment was on the East Side in a tenement on Avenue A overlooking Tompkins Square Park. She shared her building and the area with immigrants from Germany, Poland, and Russia. Anne liked it cause most of them didn't speak English, so she didn't have to talk to anybody.

Her place was a third-floor walk-up in a small building with only two apartments to a floor. Hers was at the head of the stairs.

Anne opened the door as I hit the second to last step. I'd called ahead but hadn't said exactly when I'd be there.

"How's tricks?" I said.

"Not a good way to greet a psychic," she said, smiling. We went inside.

It was a one bedroom. In the kitchen, next to one wall, was a bathtub on curved legs and clawed feet. The WC was off the living room, where it was always like night cause Anne didn't open the heavy curtains on the two windows.

She had a bamboo sofa that was colorfully covered in a striped pattern, ditto for the two bamboo armchairs. Between the living room and the bedroom hung ceiling-to-floor strings of colored glass beads instead of a door. All the walls had bookcases crammed with books she'd read. I think she had more books than I did. But her taste and mine weren't quite the same. She read about philosophy, explorations of the occult, traveling on inner journeys, what I might've called hocus-pocus if I hadn't known Anne.

"I made us some tea," she said.

Uh-oh. I knew what this meant. Green tea. Bitter and nasty-tasting. No sugar allowed.

When she went into the kitchen, I sat in one of the chairs with my pocketbook and the Lord & Taylor bag in my lap. I eyeballed the room to see if there was anything new, but it seemed like the only additions were books and more books. They were stacked everywhere, some on a kinda angle that made yer heart pound a little faster.

"Here you are, Faye." She handed me a white mug with CHILD'S RESTAURANT printed on it. Steam rose from the mug as I put it on a small, wobbly table next to my chair. Anne sat across from me on the sofa.

"So," she said. "You brought me a piece of Claudette's clothing."

I hadn't told her this on the phone. I'd just said I wanted to see her. But it didn't bowl me over or anything, cause I was pretty used to this kinda thing from Anne.

"Yeah." I picked up the L & T bag from my lap.

"Not yours," she said.

"How very psychic of you."

"Toss it."

I did, and she caught it one-handed.

I watched while she reached in and pulled out the pink sweater.

"You know for certain that this was Claudette's?"

"Yeah."

"Did you say what it was for?"

"I did . . . without usin your name . . . and it was touch-and-go for a while with Daddy, but I finally got him to agree."

"Did he choose this?" She held the sweater in both hands as if it were a baby.

"No, the mother."

"I wanted to make sure because some people like to see if they can fool me."

"She wouldn't. He might."

Anne took a sip of her tea, something I'd yet to do. This didn't escape her, so I lifted my mug and knocked back a little.

"It doesn't matter if you hate it, Faye. It's good for you. You need it for energy. And you'll need plenty of that tonight."

"Okay, what does that mean?"

"Your dinner date with that guy and his mother."

"I didn't know I told ya . . ." And of course I *hadn't* told her. "I'm really havin dinner with them, huh?"

"About seven-thirty."

"Seven," I said.

"You won't get there until seven-thirty."

"Why not?"

"How should I know? Drink your tea."

I took another swig and tried to look happy about it. "Mmmm . . . yummy for the tummy," I said.

She ignored me, and I couldn't blame her. She put down her mug and ran her hands over the sweater, which lay across her lap. I knew that soon she'd close her eyes and feel the sweater like she was kneading dough.

But the God-Love-You lady started before that happened. The back of Anne's building, along with three others, created a well. In one of those buildings the God-Love-You lady had an apartment.

"Oh, no," Anne said. "I was hoping we'd be spared."

"It's sort of early for her to start, isn't it?" I'd never heard her in the daytime.

"God love you," the woman yelled.

It was a terrible sound, like a talking crow with a small vocabulary.

"What'll we do?" I asked.

"Wait her out, I guess. What else can we do?"

No one we knew of had ever seen the God-Love-You lady. Everyone living in the apartments had heard her. Even when somebody called the cops they hadn't found her.

"God love you."

Anne said, "I think that's the last one."

I started to ask her how she knew but caught myself. Still, I did have a nagging question.

"Anne, how come *you* can't figure out where she lives?"

"Too frivolous," she said.

"The woman drives everybody crazy. This was small potatoes today, but I've been here when it goes on for hours."

"Faye, it's not my job to find out where she lives. Anyway, she has a right to yell anything she wants."

"She does?"

"She never does it after eleven at night. People have rights."

I guessed she had a point, but I didn't think I could've lived there with that going on two or three times a week.

"Since when has she been givin matinees?"

"Oh, for a few months now. But it doesn't happen often, and it doesn't last too long. She's done now."

Anne went back to the sweater, and within moments she closed her eyes. I waited. It felt like hours were slipping by.

Finally, Anne said, "A man has touched this sweater. Did the father touch it when it was given to you?"

"No."

"Rough."

I waited.

Her face got all screwed up like she was in pain. It was tough to keep my trap shut, but I knew the drill.

"Oh, God. No. Very rough."

She was swinging her head back and forth.

"Stop it, stop it," she said.

Anne was moving around on the sofa and then she jumped up. With one hand she swung at the air. "Don't. Don't do that. Oh, no. Oh, God." She crumpled to the floor, and her eyes opened.

I stayed still, asking only if she was okay.

She nodded and stood up very slowly, the sweater still in her hands as she went back to the sofa. She put it next to her on a cushion and took a long swig of the tea.

My patience, not my long suit, caved in. "What happened, Anne?"

She put up a hand, palm out, signaling me to wait. Her eyes looked funny, as flat as slate. After a sec, when some light came back into them, she focused on me and I knew she was okay.

"Was she wearing this sweater the night she was killed?"

"I don't know. I don't think so. I can't believe they'd keep those clothes."

"We need to be sure."

"Okay, let me make a call."

She nodded.

I crossed my fingers that Myrna would be home. She was, and I asked her. She told me that Claudette hadn't been wearing her pink sweater the night I stumbled over her. Myrna hadn't even wanted those clothes back from the police. I thanked her and hung up.

"There was a man," Anne said. "He was trying to hurt me. But I don't think he wanted to kill me."

"What did the man look like?"

"I don't know. His face was blurry."

"Could ya see anything? Like the color of his hair maybe?"

"No. He was in the shadows."

"How'd ya know it was a man?"

"His hands. I could see them because they were pulling at me, then grabbing me hard. He hurt my arms. This man was strong." She shuddered. "And then it turned into what it always does lately."

"What?"

"There's a battlefield."

"Whaddaya mean?"

"No matter what images I start with they devolve into a battlefield or a foxhole or something to do with war."

"Don't ya think that's because ya hear so much about it on the radio and read it in the papers?"

"I don't have a radio, Faye, and I never read the papers. You know that."

"I forgot." This was hard for me to keep in mind cause I couldn't live without my papers and radio. But I understood that Anne didn't want the interference. She'd explained it all to me once, but I kept forgetting.

"So what do ya make of it?"

"I don't know. Not everything needs clarification."

We sure differed there. For me, not only did everything *need* reasons, everything *had* reasons. But Anne and I lived in different worlds, even though we sometimes found common ground.

"Okay, ya don't have an answer . . . but ya must have an idea about the battlefield, what it is, where it comes from. Like that Dr. Freud said, ya get stuff from dreams."

"I don't agree with Dr. Freud. I believe dreams tell us the future, and he believes it tells us the past or present."

"Okay, forget Freud. Do ya have any idea what these visions of war mean?"

"That would be a clarification, Faye."

"No, it wouldn't."

"Tell me the difference."

"A clarification is tellin the facts, an explanation. Ideas are more like opinions."

"So you're asking for my opinion of these war visions?"

"Yeah. Why not?"

"It's not going to be very edifying, but if that's what you want I'll tell you. I *do* know there is a war going on, and along the road of my life I've seen images of war in books, images I'd rather not have seen. And for some reason I'm incorporating them into my visions."

"That makes sense. Does it happen every time ya try to do somethin like ya did today?"

"No. Not all the time."

"What about when it does happen? Anythin in common? Are there certain visions that connect to war themes?"

"I don't know. I haven't thought about that and you're trying to get me to clarify this." She smiled.

"Yeah. Guess I am. Okay, so what do ya make out of the stuff ya saw before the war scenes?"

"That's pretty clear. Someone, some man, was trying to hurt Claudette. Or make her do something she didn't want to do."

It could be her killer or it could be Leon or Richard or Brian Wayne. Or some guy I didn't even know about yet. Maybe the one she said she was in love with.

"Ya got any idea what he was tryin to make her do?"

"Something she definitely didn't want to do. Or have any part of."

"Yeah, I think so, too."

"I know why I think that," Anne said. "But why do you?"

"No. Why do *you*?"

"A sense. A feeling. Different feelings go with different images. Even though he hurt me . . . her . . . it wasn't pain he wanted to inflict. He wanted his will to overcome hers. That has a different feel to it. And then, of course, colors."

She'd told me before that different feelings had different colors that went with them.

"What color did ya see?"

"Red. A very deep red."

"And that means?"

"Domination. So why do *you* think it was some kind of power struggle?"

"I think this case has to be about sex and money, and they usually add up to a power struggle. Claudette was pregnant, and she had tons of money. Or at least her family did. Sex and money. Murder's almost always about one or the other or both. Everythin is. Everythin except the God-Love-You lady."

"Don't be so sure."

"What are you talkin about?"

"Just a theory of mine. Nothing I've experienced."

"Spill."

"She's obviously deranged, and her disturbance seems to be located in the religious area . . . or it's manifested itself in religious terms."

"Agreed."

"How does something like that happen? Many ways. But I think the God-Love-You lady had some bad sexual experiences when she was a child and she hid out in religion. That just made her crazier though because she went into it very deeply, and a certain kind of piety can turn highly toxic."

"It made her go round the bend?"

"Why not?"

"What religion?"

"Who knows? And it wasn't the religion's fault. It's what she did with it."

"Because of some bad sexual stuff in her past?"

"It's just a theory, Faye. Not much different from your theory about Claudette West."

"Which you corroborated."

"I simply didn't say you were wrong. More tea?"

EIGHTEEN

As I knocked on Jim Duryea's door I gave my watch a look-see. It was seven-thirty on the dot. I smiled, thinking of Anne's prediction. Porter West had kept me on the phone longer than I'd expected. He wanted to hear about every moment of Anne's experience with Claudette's sweater. I told him what had happened and asked if it meant anything to him. It didn't. But he raved on about Richard Cotten again, saying he must have roughed up Claudette without their knowing. I told him it was possible and that I'd check Cotten again.

The door opened, and there was Jim in a red smoking jacket with lapels, cuffs, and belt of black velvet. His trousers were gray gabardine.

"Welcome, Faye."

I'd brought a bottle of Chianti, and I held it out in front of me, speechless.

He took the bottle. "Thank you. Come in, come in."

When I stepped across the threshold, I felt like I was gonna suffocate. Every square inch, as far as I could see, was taken up, filled, decorated, covered. It was like being in a museum, except museums left space between items. There were figurines, tiny boxes, glass objects, pottery, china cups, and geegaws on every available surface.

The walls got the same treatment with mirrors, paintings, drawings, and other hanging objects I didn't wanna even guess at.

"You look lovely," he said.

I'd worn a dress I'd had for several years, but it was in good shape.

"Thanks."

"Come, meet Mother."

Mother, I could see, was seated in a thronelike chair near one of the large windows (in my apartment that was where the piano was gonna go).

"Mother, this is Faye Quick. Faye, my mother."

"Howdayado, Mrs. Duryea." I held out my hand.

She took it and squeezed hard. Mrs. Duryea was a large woman with a big head, and she wore a black hat with a wide brim over curls of gray hair peeking from beneath.

"Pleasure," she said. But her brown eyes said otherwise.

It was hard not to stare at the perfectly round circles of rouge on each heavily powdered cheek, like the red rings ya might see on a wooden soldier. Her mouth was lipsticked scarlet, and she coulda used a palette knife to put it on.

She was wearing a navy dress that must've come from the Thirties. It buttoned at the neck, had long sleeves and no particular style that I could put the squint on. Her shoes were black with matching laces tied in neat bows. I noticed she wore silk stockings and wondered where she'd got em, before deciding they were something she hoarded. Could even be her original pair. Nothing to it to imagine that.

"Look, Mother, Faye brought us wine."

She flashed a fake smile.

I rattled my noggin for an excuse to get outta there, but nothing came to me.

"Sit down, Faye." He pointed to a red velvet sofa. "Would you like a sherry?"

Mother, I saw, had her glass on a table next to her chair.

"Sure," I said.

Jim went into the little kitchen while Mother and I laid our glims on each other. I broke first. To one side of the room Jim had set up a table and chairs. I could see that each place had swanky silver and what looked like linen napkins.

"Jimmy's father went to the corner store for milk and never came back," she said.

What do you say to that? I nodded and smiled.

"You think it's funny? Nothing funny about it."

"No, I don't think it's funny. It's sad."

"That's right. Jimmy tells me you're a private investigator. Think you can find him?"

"Your husband?"

"Well, who else are we talking about?" She reached for her glass and drained it. "Jimmy, I need to be filled up again."

"Coming, Mother."

I felt like I was in the middle of a bizarre version of the Henry Aldrich show.

Mother held out her glass. Jim took it from her without a word and went back into the kitchen.

"So," she said. "You think you can find Mr. Duryea?"

"When did he disappear?"

"I know exactly. That's not something you forget."

"No. I'm sure it isn't."

"It was May twenty-seventh, nineteen aught one."

"Mrs. Duryea, that's forty-two years ago."

"That's correct. Jimmy was just a baby. I was about your age. Mr. Duryea was an older man. He was forty-five."

"Then he'd be . . . he'd be eighty-six now."

"Good at math, aren't you?"

"Here you are, Mother." Jim handed her the sherry. "And one for you, Faye. I'll just go get mine."

"The reason I mentioned his age," I said, "is because he might be dead by now."

"That's what you can find out."

Jim came back and sat on the opposite end of the sofa. I wondered if he knew just how much he clashed with it.

"So what are you two talking about, hmmm?" he asked.

I started to answer, but Mrs. Duryea cut me off with a firm "Nothing."

"I heard your voices. It must have been something."

My lips stayed zipped.

"We were just making pleasantries, Jimmy, that's all."

"Oh, I see."

Mrs. Duryea said, "How do you feel about Mr. Roosevelt, Faye?"

I wondered if this was a trick question and gave Jim a gander, but he was no help cause he was staring at Mother. I decided to tell the truth. Who was she, anyway?

"I like the president very much," I said.

"Good. Think he'll win this war?"

"Yeah, I do."

"So glad Jimmy was too old to go."

"I'm sure ya are." I looked at Jim, who seemed uncomfortable and was squirming in his seat. Maybe he thought I didn't know his age.

"Anybody getting hungry?" he asked.

"We're having cocktail hour, Jimmy."

"Yes, Mother."

"Now, Faye," she said. "I hope you're not going to hurt my Jimmy."

"Mother, please."

"That last one did."

I felt for him. I was sure he didn't wanna be talking about this. "Do *you* think the president will help us win the war?" I asked, trying to change the subject of Jim's love life or whatever it was.

"We're finished with that topic, Faye. Pay attention."

I looked to Jim for some help, but he wasn't about to give me any.

"Jimmy's a sensitive boy, and a girl like you has to take special care not to hurt his feelings. That last one just did him in. What was her name, Jimmy?"

"Mother, I told you, she wasn't a girlfriend."

"I know you said she was a customer, but that didn't fool me."

I realized then that I had no idea what Jim did for a living. So I asked.

"I have an antique shop."

"And that's where you met her, but she was more than a customer. I could tell when you talked about her. You had a twinkle in your eye. Can't fool a mother, you know. Now what was her name?"

"Oh, Mother."

"Come on, tell me."

"Claudette," he said.

That gave me a turn to say the least. "Claudette?"

"A snooty name if you ask me," Mrs. Duryea said.

"She couldn't help what her name was, Mother."

"Well, whatever her name was, she broke your heart."

"That's not true. Don't listen to her, Faye. I hardly knew the girl. And as I said, she was a customer."

I had to get the full skinny on this. "What was her last name, Jim?"

"West," he said. "I think she must have moved away because I haven't seen her in months."

How many Claudette Wests could there be? And was Jim ignorant of what had happened to her? How could he be? It was plastered all over the papers. I had to start easy.

"I'm afraid she stopped caring for you, Jimmy."

"Mother, our association was strictly business. I'm sure Faye doesn't want to hear about this." He turned and looked at me.

"I'd be tickled pink to hear about Claudette," I said.

"There's not much to hear. She was quite young. Very refined. You could tell she came from good stock. Anyway, she was a customer."

"What did she buy?"

"Jewelry. A bracelet, cuff links, a pendant. Small things. No furniture."

"Cuff links?"

"Yes. She said they were for someone special."

"That should have been a signal right then," Mrs. Duryea said.

"Mother, please. They could've been for a family member for all I knew."

Did Porter or Wayne wear cuff links? I knew Cotten didn't, but maybe Leon did.

"One day I asked her to have lunch with me. It was that hour. And she did."

"Where'd you go?" I asked.

"To the Algonquin. It was a pleasant two hours, and that's all there was to it. I never saw her again, actually." He looked as though this was the first time he'd made that connection.

"You must've been *some* lunch companion," Mrs. Duryea said.

Jim blushed, clashing with both his jacket and the sofa. "We had a perfectly nice time. I'm going to put the finishing touches on dinner," he said.

I grabbed his arm. "Jim, don't ya know what happened to Claudette West?"

"What do you mean, *happened*?"

"Don't ya read the newspapers?"

"As a matter of fact, I don't."

"Listen to the radio?"

"Music," he said. "The opera on Saturdays with Milton Cross."

"No news?"

"I hate news. It's never good."

"He barely knows who Mr. Roosevelt is," Mrs. Duryea said.

"That's how you raised me, Mother. You always said nothing good could come from reading newspapers or listening to news."

I couldn't believe I'd found another one who didn't read papers or listen to the radio.

"And I believe it to this day," she said.

"Jim, when did Claudette West stop coming to your store?"

He closed his eyes while he noodled the question around.

"As if he doesn't know the exact day and minute," Mrs. D. said.

His eyes flew open, and the look he turned on Mother was burned up. I hadn't seen this side of him before. He was way past simmer, but not a muscle moved. He coulda been set in concrete.

I wanted to break this up. "Jim, ya remember when ya took her to lunch?"

"It was in January. There was snow on the ground." He kept staring at his mother.

"I hate to be the one to tell ya this, but Claudette is dead, Jim."

"What?"

"She was murdered."

Jim popped up as though the sofa spring beneath him had sprung. "Murdered?"

"You do it, Jimmy?" Mother asked.

"Murdered." He brought his hands to his face, one on each cheek. It made me think of Cuddles Sakall.

"Fraid so," I said.

"It's impossible," he said.

"It happened in January. Probably around the time ya last saw her. Would ya describe her to me so we can be sure?"

In a wistful voice he said, "She was beautiful. Her skin was so soft. Looked soft. Her eyes were a cinnamon brown. She was tall for a girl, maybe five seven, and she couldn't have weighed more than a hundred pounds or so."

"I think it's the same one, Jim."

"Who would hurt her? Who did it?"

"We don't know yet."

"We?"

"I'm investigatin this case."

"That's too much, Faye."

"Whaddaya mean?"

"How could we both be involved with Claudette?"

"Thought you weren't *involved* with the girl, Jimmy?"

"We live in the same building," he said, ignoring his mother. "It's all so strange."

"I have to admit it's a coincidence, which I basically don't believe in. Coincidences, that is." Could he have done it? I wondered. "But there's one big difference. You knew her before she died, and I got involved after she died."

"After she died," Jim said.

"So she didn't jilt you, after all, Jimmy."

A goofy smile creased his face. "No. No, she didn't."

It wasn't surprising that Jim was a queer duck, I'd already known that. And now that I'd gotten a load of Mother, let's just say my impression was confirmed. But it was as plain as his smoking jacket that all Jim's thoughts of Claudette had not been platonic.

"You cared for her, didn't ya, Jim?"

"She was very kind to me. And always so polite, refined, a lady. She was interested in the arts, opera, dance, you know. I'd planned to ask her to go with me to the opera the next time she came into the store. But I never saw her again."

"You didn't have her phone number or address?"

"Oh, no. I thought it was too forward to ask, and she never offered. I was sure I'd see her again. But now I never will."

I wasn't gonna ask him if he killed her cause what murderer was gonna say yes? But I was sure gonna follow up on this.

"I hope you'll excuse me, Faye. I don't think I can go on with our plans."

"That's copacetic, Jim."

I got up and started toward the door. Jim behind me.

"Nice to meet you, too," Mother said.

"Thanks."

"Please forgive me, Faye. I'm so shocked."

"I don't blame ya. If there's anythin you can think of that might help me, you'll let me know, won't ya?"

"Of course," he said. "Thank you for being so understanding."

I nodded and took my leave. I wanted to get to my phone to call Marty. Maybe he could find out something about one James Duryea, antique dealer and liar.

NINETEEN

*M*arty wasn't at the precinct or at home, and I didn't feel like going uptown to his usual gin mill. So I gave Smitty's a jingle and got the night bartender, Coburn.

"Is Marty Mitchum there?"

"Who wants to know?" He had a voice like a meat grinder.

I knew Coburn was protecting Marty from his wife. Or maybe his girlfriend.

"Tell him it's Faye Quick."

"I'm not sure he's here."

"Could ya see?"

"Yeah, sure."

He put the phone on the bar while he pretended to look. Coburn knew Marty was there, but he had to nail it down that I was okay first. A minute later Marty was on the horn.

"Hey, Faye. What's goin on?"

"I need ya to check somebody out, Marty. It's important or I wouldn't call ya there."

"That's jake. Who's the party?"

"Name's James Duryea or Jim Duryea."

"It might take a while. Skeleton shift is on."

"That's okay."

"Ya home?"

"Yeah. But I'm goin out for a bit."

"Don't worry. I'll catch ya later."

We hung up.

I grabbed a jacket and my pocketbook and left the apartment. Outside I headed toward Blondell's, which was an eatery I could afford. I was damn hungry and in seventh heaven I didn't have to eat a rabbit.

But that was the only thing I was glad about. This case was under my skin and getting more wacky all the time.

I turned right on Grove and left on Barrow toward West Fourth. Right near Jones Street I happened to look at a window of a first-floor apartment. I stopped. Hanging in it was a small rectangular flag with a red border and a gold star in the middle on a field of white. I didn't see them often in the Village, but when I did my stomach did a yo-yo.

I wondered how old he'd been and if he was their only child. I wondered if he'd ever passed me by or smiled at me, tipped his hat. I wondered how he'd died and hoped it wasn't too painful.

Then I thought of Woody. How would I feel if he was killed in action? This wasn't the first time I'd thought about that. Any war death led me there. In his letters he was always being Woody, cutting up, saying everything was fine except the lousy food. Last letter he said if he ate one more piece of SPAM, his skin was gonna turn pink. Whenever I had the time, I tried to bake and send him cookies, and though he was always grateful, I knew they weren't very good. Still, I guess they were better than SPAM. All he could think about, he wrote, was a juicy porterhouse, and a big baked potato. When he came home, I planned to take him to the Blue Mill Tavern, where steaks were the specialty.

I pulled myself together and went on. I didn't look up at any more windows just in case.

When I got to Blondell's, it was empty. This wasn't a place where dining started at nine o'clock. I said hello to Skip Ireland, one of the owners.

Skip said, "Sit anywhere ya like, Scrumptious Susan, the place is yours." He laughed like *haw-haw,* and his big face got redder than a stoplight.

"Thanks," I said, and took a booth.

"What can I do ya?"

Skip knew I didn't need a menu.

"A bowl of vegetable soup and a cup a joe."

"Comin right up, my Prairie Princess."

He always called me something different, and I asked him why one time, and he said he liked the metaphors. I knew he meant alliteration.

I lit a cig and waited for my meal. Why did Jim Duryea lie about Claudette West? It was no coincidence that we were both involved with her, and he just found that out. It was coincidence enough that we lived in the same building. He had to know I was on the case and that was why he'd invited me to dinner. It had nothing to do with his mother.

And what was Dragon Lady all about? Had Jim prepped her to bring up Claudette? Or wasn't that part of the plan?

"Here you are, Delicious Doll. One bowl of homemade vegetable soup, a roll with margarine, and one cup a joe. Ya look kinda tired tonight, my Little Ladybug."

It was doubly funny that Skip used these terms because he was such a big palooka. He stood about six feet and must've weighed over two hundred pounds. He wore his raven black hair in a military cut, and his eyes were black, too, iris and pupil the same. His nose was long and crooked from being broken in too many fights, and a deep scar ran the length of his left cheek. I'd always wanted to know what that was from but had an inkling I shouldn't ask.

"I guess I am tired, Skip. Rough week."

"Yeah, me too. Me, too. But we got it lucky and shouldn't be cryin the blues. Think if we were over there with them Krauts. My brother's in the thick of it, ya know."

I did know. Skip told me every time I came in. But I nodded cause I knew he was proud of Fred, and it made him feel better that one of his family could be fighting for our country. Skip's club foot had kept him home.

"Yeah, he's on the front lines, makin us all proud of him. But you and me, my Candied Cassandra, we're here and eatin bowls a good soup an havin lemon meringue pie for dessert." He flashed me a toothy grin.

"Yer kiddin," I said.

"Nope. Joanne made it herself."

Lemon meringue was my favorite, and I hadn't had it since eggs had been rationed.

"It's only for special customers. I have it under the counter. I'll bring ya a nice big piece when ya finish yer soup. Eat up, my Tiny Tomato."

This news made me want to pour the soup down my throat, but I didn't. I at least had to eat like a lady.

I stubbed out my butt in the ashtray and started on the soup.

I couldn't get Jim Duryea outta my mind. The truth is, when I first laid eyes on him I thought he might be a pansy, not that I cared, but that's why I was so bowled over when he invited me to dinner. Then I thought it was to impress his mother, make her think he liked girls. But now, finding out he wanted to date Claudette, I was all balled up.

Why did he want me to know that he knew her? And he did. If Dragon Lady hadn't brought her up, I was sure Jim would've. But he knew his mother would warn me not to hurt her son, mention his last love, that was part of their dance. He could count on her.

And did he really not know Claudette was dead? I decided he *did* know, but that still didn't tell me why he wanted to let me in on their acquaintance.

"Ya finished, Dora Doom? Ya look like death took a stroll over yer face."

"That obvious, huh?"

"Let's put it this way: ya ain't Happy Hannah tonight."

"I got a confusin case, Skip."

"That's what ya say every time."

"I do?"

"Sure ya do, Banana Betty. Ya never know how yer gonna solve them, but ya always do."

"This is a murder case. I never had one a those before."

"No kiddin? A murder case. Wow. A regular Sherlock Holmes, huh?"

"I wish. He always solved his cases."

"You will, too. So who got murdered? Hey, it ain't that gal you stumbled over in January, is it?"

Everybody knew I'd found Claudette cause my name had made the papers. For a while I couldn't go anywhere without somebody mentioning it. The picture they used of me was lousy, more Marjorie Main than Scrumptious Susan. Still, people often recognized me.

"Yeah, matter of fact, it is that case. But I can't tell ya anythin about it, Skip."

"Sure, I know that, my Cupcake Cutie. Ready for yer pie?"

"You bet."

He took away my empty soup bowl, the margarine, and my half-eaten roll. In a flash he was back with the luscious lemon meringue, a piece as big as the Waldorf, and fresh joe for my cup.

"I can't believe it," I said, looking at the pie. "Ya know how long it's been since my last slice?"

"Prolly not since '41."

"Yup. That's about right." I was almost afraid to eat it, put my fork through, scared it might topple.

"Go on, try it."

I did. And omigod, it was the best thing I'd ever tasted. It was a holy experience, like being blessed by Mahatma Gandhi or some-body.

"Who'd ya say made this?"

"Fred's wife, Joanne."

"It's the best of the best, Skip. You tell her for me, okay?"

"I will."

I ate in a trance, savoring every morsel, and when I was done I wanted to lick the plate but controlled myself.

I paid my check, and after reminding Skip to toss a bouquet to Joanne, I went out into the night.

The streets were quiet as I walked home. Nightlife was at a minimum these days. And most windows had blackout shades, so the streets were pretty dark.

When I turned the corner of Fourth and Jones, I could hear footsteps behind me. I knew by the sound it was a man, and I didn't think much of it until I turned the next corner and he was still with me.

I sped up, and so did he. I didn't wanna turn around, but it was either that or taking a chance a being decked or worse. I stopped. So did he. I swiveled around. There was nobody there that I could see. But it was pitch on the street.

"Who's there?" I didn't really expect an answer. If you're shadowing somebody ya aren't about to tell them. But I wanted to let whoever it was know I was onto him. Now what? I couldn't stand there all night. I wasn't far from home, so maybe I could run for it. I knew he'd run, too, but what could he do once I got to my building?

I turned on a dime and hit the grit as fast as I could. So did he. Right in the middle of my block I got it on the back of my head.

Slices of lemon meringue spun around me, and I kept trying to grab one, but I couldn't get a grip on anything. It was like being on the merry-go-round, reaching for the brass ring and missing every time.

Then I came to. I saw a lotta faces looking down at me. Beyond that I saw my ceiling. I could tell cause of the carved cherub in the corner of the molding, and I realized I was in my living room on one of my sofas.

"How do you feel?" A woman. "Oy vey. Some night."

No mistaking that voice. It was Dolores, my next door neighbor. What was she doing in my apartment? What were all these people doing? And who were they?

I tried to sit up, but the pounding in my head made me dizzy and I lay down again.

"Like death warmed over," Dolores said.

"I think we should get an ambulance." A man. "She could have a concussion for all we know."

That was Jerome Byington. I'd know his baritone anywhere. He lived on the fourth floor.

"No ambulance," I said.

"I don't think she needs stitches." Bruce Jory. Across the street.

"Are you a doctor, may I ask?" Dolores.

"I think we should all calm down." Ethel Kilbride. Across the hall from Byington.

I refused to ask what happened like I was in some detective pulp. I kept hoping somebody would say.

"A drink of water," I said.

"Get it."

"You get it."

"I'll get it."

"Are you in a lot of pain, dearie?" asked Ethel.

"It hurts some."

"Who would bang a nice girl like Faye on the head, is what I want to know?"

There it was. And then it came back to me. The footsteps, the running, the . . . nothing. I guessed that was when I got it.

"Well, we all know what line of work she's in," Jory said.

"So? Who says a detective has to get a bang on the noggin?" Dolores.

"Tell us what happened, my dear." Byington.

"I really don't know how it happened," I said.

"You were lying like a lox in the middle of the block."

"Well, it wasn't a burglary," Jory said.

"Robbery." Ethel.

"What?"

"Robbery. A burglary is stealing from a place. Not from a person."

"Burgle gurgle, who cares? The thing is our Faye got clobbered by some gangster."

"I doubt it was a gangster, Dolores."

"What's all the nitpicking? The important thing here is to see if she needs a doctor."

Someone handed me a glass of water. I took it and sat up slightly to drink it.

The pounding was terrible, but the thirst was worse. When I was done, I held it out and a hand took it.

"No doctor," I said.

"Why no doctor?"

"I can tell I don't need one." I'd be taken to St. Vincent's, which I had nothing against, but I didn't want to get stuck in the emergency room all night. I remembered I was waiting to hear from Marty.

"Did the phone ring?" I said.

"I didn't hear anything."

"No ringing."

"You hearing bells in your head, Faye?"

"I don't mean now. However long we've been here. Did the phone ring?"

"No."

"No ringing."

"I didn't hear nothing."

"Nope."

"You was some lucky girl, Faye."

"I know. I guess I coulda been killed."

"That, too. But I mean being found like that."

"Who found me?"

"I did," Jim Duryea said.

TWENTY

You found me?"

"Yes. I'd taken a walk, and on my way back there you were, right in the middle of the block. I tried to carry you here, but I couldn't manage, so I knocked on Jory's door. Fortunately he's on the first floor. He came running, and we carried you home," Duryea said.

I wanted to say, Isn't it more likely you hit me over the head? but I didn't. "Thank you."

"Who wants coffee?" Dolores said.

There were a couple a takers.

"I'll be right back."

At least she was gonna make it in her own apartment. It seemed like we were having a party.

The phone rang and I tried to get up, but Ethel Kilbride gently pushed me back.

"Would somebody answer that?" I said.

Jerome picked it up on the third ring.

"Miss Quick's residence, may I help you?"

When I groaned, they all thought my head was getting worse.

"Well, who are *you,* sir?"

"Is it Marty Mitchum?" I said.

Jerome asked the caller. "Right you are, Faye."

"Tell him to get over here pronto." I wasn't about to be left with Duryea playing nursie, and it could easily go that way.

Byington hung up. "He said he'll be right over. Rather a rude fellow, isn't he?"

"He can be abrupt," I said.

Dolores came back with a tray full of cups and a coffeepot. "There's milk—from powdered, naturally—but no sugar. I ran out of stamps."

"Let me help you with that," Duryea said.

"I want Faye to get some of this down, it'll be good for her."

Easing up to a sitting position set off the tom-toms in my head, but they weren't as loud as they'd been.

"Careful."

"Easy."

"Don't be too much in a hurry."

Dolores said, "You shouldn't sit up, you might exasperate it."

When I finally got myself up, I looked around. I didn't think I'd ever had this many people in my place at one time.

"Milk?" Dolores asked.

"Black."

She poured my coffee, a slight shake in her hand rattling the cup and saucer as she held them out. "Family tremor," she said.

I nodded but didn't have the vaguest what she was talking about.

"Drink slow, Faye."

"I will."

Jory said, "You think coffee is going to cure the bump on her head?"

"*Alevei,*" Dolores said with a wave of her hand.

From talking with her I knew this Yiddish expression meant something like "it should only happen to her."

"She should have a doctor."

"She doesn't want a doctor."

"Who cares what she wants. She doesn't know what's good for her."

"I say . . ."

It went on that way for what seemed like hours, and then the doorbell rang and I knew I was saved. Jim Duryea, that jack-of-all-trades, played doorman, letting Marty in.

I don't think I'd ever been so happy to see a man in my life. I *knew* I'd never been happier to see Marty.

"What the hell is goin on here?" he said, seeming to accuse them all as he looked from one person to the next.

I said, "It's okay, Marty."

He came over to the sofa. "What happened, Faye?"

I started to explain, but the help from the chorus only got Marty confused.

"Hey, hold it. One person at a time. Who found Faye?"

Duryea said he had.

Marty asked him to give details, and he blabbed the same spiel he'd told before, word for word. I was glad Marty was getting a load of Jim so he'd know who I was talking about later.

"Ya want some coffee, Mr. Marty?" Dolores asked.

"No, thanks. You've all been swell to Faye here, but she needs some quiet now."

Oh, thank you, Marty.

"And will you be staying?" Byington asked.

"Yeah. Me and Faye got some business to discuss."

Jory said, "Why should we leave her with you? For all we know, you're the one who bashed her on the head."

"No," I said. "Marty's a cop and a friend."

"You're with the police force?" Ethel asked.

"Yes, ma'am. I'm a detective with the New York Police Department."

"That must be very exciting."

"Okay, Ethel, Marty ain't here to entertain us. Let's go." Dolores was like a sheepdog herding them all toward the door.

"Your coffeepot and cups, Dolores."

"I'll get em tomorrow."

When they were gone, Marty said, "Lemme see that bump, kid."

"It's nothin."

"Lemme decide that."

He sat next to me on the sofa, and I bent my head so he could get a good look.

"Size of an egg," he said. "A big one." He touched it. "That hurt?"

"A little."

"It didn't break the skin."

"Feels like it did."

"Nah. Ya don't need stitches or nothin, but ya could have a concussion."

"Ya think so, Dr. Mitchum?"

"Hey, anybody would know that."

"I'm just razzin ya, Marty."

"Yeah, okay. But ya know what ya have to do if ya have a concussion, don'tcha?"

"What?"

"Ya gotta rest."

"Rest how?"

"Rest, ya know, rest."

"In bed?" I was scared he'd say yes.

"Maybe not, but at least here on the sofa."

"Why?"

"Cause this was no tap, Faye, is why. It could be dangerous ya go runnin around."

"What if I don't run?"

"C'mon, Faye, ya know what I'm sayin."

"Marty, I'm working a case . . . you know that . . . I can't take time off."

"Ya have to take a day at least. Ya don't wanna make things worse. Can't ya do some work from here?"

Enough of playing the patient. "Ya know the guy who told ya what happened to me?"

"What about him?"

"He's Duryea. Did ya have a chance to check him out?"

"Matter a fact, I did. He's got a yellow sheet long as my arm. But only two arrests stuck."

"Yer kiddin. What for?" Now I was sure Duryea had been the one to knock the daylights outta me before coming to my rescue.

"Mostly fraud."

"What kind?"

"Antiques."

"That's what he does now. He says he has an antique store."

"He does. Nothin to stop the guy. He's done his time."

"He's been in the slammer?" That knocked me back on my heels.

"Twice. Once when he was in his twenties and once about ten years ago. First time he tried to pass off a copy of a royal wheelchair as the real deal, some Louis or other. Next time it was somethin called a highboy belongin to the 'father of our country,' accordin to Mr. Duryea. Even had a piece a Georgie's writin in a drawer. Nice touch, don't ya think? Only problem was, another drawer had the name of a New Jersey furniture factory stamped on its underside."

"I tell ya, there's one born every thirty seconds."

"Ya can say that again. And he got a load a money both times before anyone caught on. But there musta been plenty who didn't.

"The wheelchair got him six months, the other, three. And the jail time was only cause the piker wouldn't pay a fine."

"Listen, Marty, he knew Claudette West. He says she was a customer. His mother says he was in love with her. I'm beginnin to think maybe he killed her."

"Why would he?"

"Maybe he was tryin to pull his scam again with Claudette, and she found out and threatened him. Maybe she led him on, then dropped him. Maybe she sweet-talked him, but he saw her with other guys."

"Ya think maybe he beaned ya?"

"It's lookin more like that with each passin minute."

"Don't ya think it's, well, queer that this character lives in your buildin?"

Cops believed in coincidence less than I did. "Yeah, I do. But ya know, somethin just occurred to me. He only moved in about a month ago. I wasn't on the case then, but as ya know it was in all the rags that I found Claudette."

"Yer thinkin maybe he tracked ya down and there just happened to be an empty apartment in this buildin?"

"Why not? And that apartment was vacant for months."

"Okay. Let's say that's true. Why is he interested in *you*? Especially since ya wasn't on the case yet?"

"I'm not sure."

"Ya know what, Faye? I think we should ask him."

"When?"

"Now."

"His mother's with him."

"So we'll have the jerk come down here. What number is his crib?"

I told him. "Ya sure this is a good idea, Marty?"

"Why not? If nothin else, we get him rattled. And I don't think he'll come after you no more."

I had a sec when I didn't want to be left alone, but I blew it away as having the heebie-jeebies for no real reason. Nobody was gonna bust into my place while Marty was upstairs. Besides, the most likely one to do that was the same guy Marty was going after.

"You'll be okay?"

"Sure. Go."

When he was gone, I was sorry I hadn't told him to lock up and take my keys. But then he woulda known I was a scaredy cat, and that wouldna been good for me and him working together.

I'd never been attacked before, and it sorta had me rattled. I didn't remember Woody warning me about that. He said a lotta stuff before he left, told me to watch my back, be careful, but not that I might get clobbered. Least I didn't think he did.

I slowly inched forward on the sofa and reached my pack of butts, shook one loose, and lit up. The thing was, whoever kayo'd me wasn't out to kill me, so what was the point? Was it a high sign for me to take a powder from the case? The only person who'd care one way or another would be the killer. So he knew where I lived and had followed me home from Blondell's. And I knew it was a man cause of those footsteps I heard.

Would the next time be more than a warning? Would he kill me as well? But even if he knocked me off, wouldn't the Wests hire somebody else? Well, nobody ever said murderers were smart.

The door opened, and I held my breath until I saw Marty. Jim Duryea was right behind him.

"Mr. Duryea has agreed to honor us with his company."

Jim smiled weakly.

"Take a load off, Mr. Duryea." Marty pointed to my reading chair.

As he sat he said, "Please call me Jim."

"Okay. Would ya like a drink or anything, Jimbo?"

"Nothing, thank you."

"You okay, Faye?"

"Solid."

Marty sat on the other sofa, putting Jim between us.

"Jimbo, we got a few questions, like I told ya upstairs."

I wondered how Marty had gotten him to come down.

"I certainly hope we didn't wake my mother."

Ah. "Were ya yellin?" I asked.

"Our pal here got a little riled up at one point, didn't ya, Jimbo?"

"Do you have to call me 'Jimbo'? I'd prefer Jim."

"Right."

"What did ya get riled up about, Jim?" I asked.

"Well, I . . . it's hard to explain."

"I think he doesn't wanna talk about Claudette."

"No. I don't."

"Have ya told Jim about what we know, Marty?"

"Not yet."

"Know? What do you know?"

Marty took a pad outta his pocket, flipped it open, and pretended to study what was there.

"Let's see now. We know about the wheelchair con for one."

"Wheelchair con?"

"Yeah, the first one that landed ya behind bars."

Jim looked like he'd eaten a bad piece of rabbit. And then he put his head in his hands. Marty and I looked at each other. We knew he'd spill the beans now.

Duryea mumbled something.

"Speak up, Jimbo. We can't hear ya."

He lifted his head. "My mother doesn't know about any of this. She thinks I was out of the country for those six months. I had a friend forward my mail from India."

"And the three months?" I asked.

"Africa."

"Let's talk about tonight," Marty said.

"What about it?"

"Did you knock out Faye?"

"God, no. I like Faye."

I said, "How come you moved into this building? And don't tell me it was cause ya liked the apartment."

"I *did* like the apartment. But that wasn't the only reason."

"Faye was the other reason, wasn't she?"

"Yes."

"Cause of Claudette?" I asked.

"Yes."

"I wasn't even on the case yet, Jim."

"But I knew about you. You found her."

"You kill Claudette, Jimbo?"

I couldn't believe Marty was asking him that.

"Kill her? I loved her."

"Let me run this by ya, Jimbo. Claudette found out some con you was cookin up and ya had to get her outta the way."

"No. I told you, I loved her. And I've gone straight. No more cons."

"So why did ya want to be here . . . in this buildin . . . cause of me?"

"It's stupid. You'll laugh at me."

"Nobody's laughin," Marty said.

"I picked up the paper and there was Claudette, front page, and the headline SOCIALITE MURDERED."

"You told me ya didn't know she was dead."

"I lied. I didn't want my mother to know I read the papers. All she knew about Claudette was that she hadn't come back to the shop, that's all."

"Ya always tell yer mother when yer interested in a broad?" Marty asked.

"I know how it sounds, but I do."

"It sounds like what it is," I said.

"Yeah? What is it, Faye?" Marty asked.

"Givin Mama scraps."

"Something like that," Jim said. "She's the most intrusive person I've ever met, and I can't not tell her something because she'll go out and mess around in my life until she finds out what it is she wants to know. So I gave her just enough."

"Which was what?"

"Claudette's name, and that I found her appealing. I told her about the lunch and then later that she hadn't come into the shop again. I invited you to dinner, Faye, hoping it would come out that Claudette was dead. Then my mother would stop taunting me with her disappearance from my life."

"Ya know, Jimbo, this still doesn't explain why ya moved in here to be close to Faye."

"It doesn't, does it?"

We stared at him, waiting.

"I wanted to be close to Faye because she was one of the last people to see Claudette."

"But she was dead when I found her."

"I know. It didn't make any difference. Being near you, even if it was as an upstairs neighbor, made me feel closer to Claudette. It was a kind of tie to her, and that was better than nothing. It made me feel I'd hung on to some small piece of her."

"Well," Marty said, "that's what makes horse races."

TWENTY-ONE

*L*ike they say, I was back to square one. Not entirely cause I still had Cotten, ex-boyfriend; Brian Wayne, English professor; Leon Johnson, aka Rockefeller; and Jim Duryea in my sights. And if I wanted to, I could've added *Mrs.* Duryea to my list, but I didn't want to.

She had motive, maybe opportunity if I ran it down, and probably means, but it didn't sit right with me. I couldn't picture Dragon Lady out in the snow on Bleecker Street at ten o'clock in the P.M., whacking Claudette West, no matter how jealous she was of her. It just didn't gel.

Jim Duryea and the rest of the group were pretty flimsy suspects, but they were all I had so far.

My notes were in my office, and I was taking the day like I'd been told to. It made me mad that I hadn't outfoxed my attacker. If Woody knew about it, he'd probably have me close down the office. I'd called Birdie to tell her, but it was strictly on the q.t. Not that she was gonna tell Woody, she'd never even met him, but it made me feel better to keep it hush-hush. Who was I kidding? The whole neighborhood knew. The mouth of Dolores alone could get it in the *Daily News*, should they be short of stories.

I had a slight headache, and every so often my vision was blurred up. Lying around never appealed to me, and my eyes kept me from reading. So I put on the radio for company and sorta listened to Don McNeil's *Breakfast Club.*

While I was lying there, I decided I had to work backward. What was Claudette doing on Bleecker that night? Was she *going* to meet someone or *coming* from seeing someone?

As for the father of Claudette's unborn child, there was no one I could rule out. Not even Johnson/Rockefeller, cause no matter what he said about no sex, it didn't have to be true. I hadn't asked Cotten about their sex life cause, I had to admit, it hadn't entered my noggin. How could I've been such a dumb bunny? Well, I was learning on the job, after all.

But maybe that wasn't it, me being a knucklehead. Asking about people sleeping together was always a tricky question. And at the time I saw Cotten I didn't know Claudette was three months pregnant when she died.

Course this brought me back to Brian Wayne. I'd have to check on sex between Cotten and Claudette, but if that didn't pan out, Brian Wayne was the obvious next choice. Maybe he was the first choice. Even so, I had to ask Cotten first.

I started feeling excited, like I wasn't at a dead end after all. But I was sidelined, on the bench, having to rest.

I sat up and slowly swung my drumsticks over the edge of the sofa so I was sitting straight up, feet on the floor. I felt a little dizzy, but that passed. Pushing off with a hand on the sofa arm, I stood, real gingerly. The dizziness happened again, but like the first time, after a few secs, it did a Judge Crater. The trick was to take a few steps. I did. I felt fine, well, maybe a little wobbly, but I knew that would fade. I took a few more steps, then another few, and before I knew it I was in my bathroom. I wanted to take a bath, but I was afraid I might fall, so I washed up as best as I could and then went into my bedroom. I picked out a nice polka-dot dress and red pumps to match. No creep in the night was gonna keep me down.

When I was ready, I sat at my telephone table and dialed. Cotten answered on the second ring. I told him who I was.

"I thought you were through with me."

"Did I say that?"

"No."

"Okay, then. I have to ask ya a question, Richard. It may be embarrassin, but I need to know."

"What?"

I could feel myself blushing. I wasn't sure how to put it. And I didn't even know if he knew she was pregnant. Then I realized I should do it that way.

"Well, this may or may not come as a bolt outta the blue, I don't know."

"Would you please just ask. I have a class I have to get to, and I'm going to be late as it is."

Okay, smarty pants. "Did you know Claudette was pregnant when she died?"

There was a long silence on the other end, but I could hear him breathing.

"Richard?"

"Yes. I'm here."

"Did ya know?"

"No. I didn't."

"Was it yours? The baby?"

"No."

"You sound pretty sure of that."

"I am."

I knew the answer, but I had to ask anyway. "How come yer so sure?"

"You're right. This is embarrassing. I'm sure because I never slept with Claudette. She wouldn't."

"Never?"

"Never."

"Got any idea who the father might be?"

Silence and breathing again.

"Richard? Ya got any idea?"

"Do you know how pregnant she was? I mean, how many months?"

"Three months. Why?"

"Oh."

"Oh?"

"Well, six months before she died we stopped seeing each other for a short time."

"What's a short time?"

"Two weeks."

"She seein somebody else then?"

"I don't know. She said she wasn't, but if she'd been six months pregnant then it would've been during that time."

"Did you believe her, Richard? That she hadn't stepped out on ya?"

"We'd broken up. She wouldn't have been *stepping out* on me."

Touchy. "Yer right. It wouldn't a been that. But did ya believe her that she hadn't dated anyone durin that time?"

"I didn't say she hadn't dated anyone. You asked if she had been *seeing* anyone. The implication is—"

"Yeah, yeah, yer right." I wanted to give this joker a kick in the keister. "So who was she datin?"

"She told me she had one date."

"Who with?" No wonder Claudette dumped this guy.

"I think his name was Garfield."

"First name or last?"

"Last. I can't think of his first name."

"Ya gotta try, Richard."

"What difference does it make? It's the wrong time period, and Claudette would never have slept with a man she went out with one time."

I didn't think it would be helpful to suggest that the lack of sex he'd had with Claudette might have been his own fault.

"Do ya think she might've seen him again later?"

"You mean when we were back together?" He sounded like this would be impossible.

"Well, yeah."

"Claudette would never have cheated on me."

Why should I clue in this also-ran that she probably had a lotta boyfriends while she was supposed to be with him? "Can ya think of Garfield's first name, Richard?"

"I can't."

"Could ya work on it today?"

"I'll try."

"Okay. I'll give ya my office number and ya can leave it with my secretary cause I'll probably be out."

I gave him the number and hung up. Everything was getting real interesting again.

I dialed Birdie at the office.

"Bird," I said. "Anythin goin on?"

"If ya think me and Pete fightin is somethin goin on, yeah."

"It's not."

"How're ya feelin, Faye?"

"I'm fine. Reason I'm callin is a guy named Richard Cotten—"

"The boyfriend."

"Right. He might call today with a name for me."

"And?"

"I want ya to be sure to take it."

"Ya know, Faye. That's insultin. What else would I do with a name somebody gave me?"

"Yer right. I'm sorry."

"And why can't he call you at home?"

"Well, I—"

"Yer goin out, ain'tcha?"

I didn't want a lecture, but what could I do but tell the truth. "Yeah, I am. And don't say anythin about it, Bird."

"Lips zipped."

"Keep tryin to get me once ya get that name, cause I'll be in and out, okay?"

"Right."

"And I'll try you off and on durin the day."

"Right."

"Ya mad at me?"

"Lips zipped."

"Oh, come on, Birdie."

"Ya don't wanna hear what I have to say."

She was right, but I couldn't leave things like this between us. "Okay, tell me what yer thinkin."

"I'm thinkin yer a dumb cluck, is what I'm thinkin. Ya were told to rest and what're ya doin? Yer gonna be out and about doin God knows what. What're ya gonna be doin out there? What's so important yer hell bent to go out there?"

"Ya done?"

"Maybe."

"There's somebody I need to interview."

"Ya can't wait till tomorrow?"

"No."

"I give up."

"Don't be mad, Bird."

"Yeah."

"Tell me what you and Pete are fightin about."

"What's the dif?"

"I wanna know."

"Same old thing."

"He wants to get married?"

"You got it."

Most girls would've jumped at the chance to get married and have the security, but not Birdie Ritter. She liked her independence. Also Pete was not exactly dream husband material.

"Says he wants to make me respectable. I told him I thought I was respectable already."

"And ya are."

"Yeah, well he doesn't think so. Says if we don't get married soon, he's not gonna see me anymore."

"Would that be so bad?"

"It's not like there's a lotta fish in the sea right now in case ya hadn't noticed, Faye."

"Ya know what, Bird. We need to go to a USO dance together."

"And what? Meet a lotta soldiers and sailors who're probably gonna be killed soon?"

"We should do it for them."

"That's different. But what's that gotta do with Pete?"

"Nothin. I just thought it would be a change for ya."

"Meanwhile, I gotta get Pete outta this rut. He's drivin me nutty."

"Tell him you'll marry him after the war."

"I'd be lyin."

"So?"

"I got my own regulations, Faye."

"Well, I don't know what ya should do. You'll figure somethin out."

"Yeah, I guess. Ya goin out now?"

"Yeah."

"Take it easy, will ya, Faye?"

"I promise. Now could ya look up somethin for me?"

She said she would and gave me an address. The bulb clicked on over my head while I was getting dressed that I should try to interview Brian Wayne's wife. I wasn't sure how I was gonna get her to talk to me, but I had to give it a shot.

TWENTY-TWO

*M*rs. Wayne lived on West Ninth Street between Sixth and Fifth. It was a small white building, set back from the street. A nicely trimmed hedge bordered a little plot of grass. The door was painted red. There were three names on the bell roster. Wayne lived on the third floor. I knew I was taking a chance not calling ahead, but I pushed the bell. In about a minute I heard somebody coming down the stairs.

When the door opened, I saw a pretty woman about my height and weight. She wore a blue and white dress with a jabot and puffed sleeves. On her feet were blue and white pumps.

"Yes?" she said.

"Mrs. Wayne?"

"Yes."

"My name is Faye Quick and—"

"Faye Quick? What kind of name is that? Quick? Did you make that up?"

"No. Why would I do that?"

She stared at me.

"I'd like to talk to you for a little bit."

"Talk to me? Are you selling something?"

"No." I was afraid to mention her husband before I got in. "I'm not sellin anythin. I'd like some information."

"Oh, you must be interested in the apartment next door."

I thought about pretending that I was, but when she found out I wasn't she might not trust me. "No. I wonder, could I come in? This is a confidential matter."

She squeezed her dark brows together so they looked like one.

"Are you one of *his*?"

"His?"

"Brian's. You're one of his sluts, aren't you?" She started to close the door, but I put my hand up against it and held it there.

"I'm not one of anybody's sluts," I said.

"Then what the hell do you want?"

I had no choice. "I wanna talk to ya about yer husband."

"I knew it. I have nothing to say to you. Brian no longer lives here and—"

"Mrs. Wayne, I'm not a girlfriend of his. I'm a private investigator."

"A what?"

"I'm a detective."

"You certainly are not."

I dug around in my purse and found my license, which I handed to her.

"How do I know you didn't have one of those people on Forty-second Street make this for you?"

I could tell this dame had been hit before. "Ya *don't* know, but why would I come here wantin to talk to ya? What would I gain?"

"What do you girls ever gain?"

"I'm not one of those girls. Mrs. Wayne, your husband is involved in a murder investigation." It wasn't a total lie. *I* was investigating him.

"I thought that was all over. It was months ago, wasn't it?"

"True. But it's not over. I've been hired to look into it again."

"Who hired you?"

"I can't tell ya that."

She stared again.

"And you don't have to cooperate with me, but I wish ya would."

"I don't see why I should, but come in." She opened the door wider, and I stepped into the vestibule. The stairs were covered by a red runner.

"I'm on the top floor," she said.

Mrs. Wayne led the way. When we got to the third floor, she opened the door to a large room with a skylight letting the sun stream in. The furniture was big and floppy and a far cry from most of the stuff I'd seen on this case. Ya just wanted to sink down in one of the chairs and read or take a nap. The floors were wood, no rugs. In one corner there was a box with toys piled neatly inside. And a big black hairy cat was stretched along the back of the sofa.

"What's the cat's name?"

"Rathbone. Do you like cats?"

"I do."

"Have any?"

"No."

"Then you don't really like them."

"I do. I shoulda said I don't have any right now." I thought about that white ball of fur, and my heart filled with sadness. "Mine died about a year ago. His name was Cedric."

"Oh. I'm sorry."

"He had a good life. But I miss him a lot."

"Aren't you going to get another?"

"One of these days."

"Would you like some tea or coffee, Miss Quick?"

"Coffee if it's made. And call me Faye."

"It's made, Faye. Please call me Maureen."

Funny thing about cat lovers, we stick together cause more people like dogs. Cats are kinda second-class citizens in some eyes.

I sat on the rose-flowered sofa, putting Rathbone's purr near my ear. It was a surprisingly small sound for such a big cat, but still comforting to me.

Maureen came back with coffee for us both.

"I hope you don't mind it black. I can't stand that powdered stuff."

"I wouldn't know cause I always take it black."

Maureen sat down in a comfy-looking chair across from me.

"So what can I do for you?" she asked.

"As you know, Mr. Wayne was questioned in the Claudette West case."

She nodded.

"The case still hasn't been solved."

"And that's why you were hired? By the parents, I'd guess?"

I didn't say anything.

"Sorry."

"You seem quite angry at your husband."

"Wouldn't you be? He's been involved with one girl after another."

"Claudette West bein one of em?"

"I don't see why not."

That was less than I'd hoped. "How long have ya been married?"

"Ten years."

"And how long has he been up to his . . . shenanigans?"

"An interesting way to put it. Brian, as far as I know now, has been cheating on me since the second month of our marriage."

That was quick off the mark. A real track star, Brian. "And when did ya find out?"

"I'm ashamed to tell you." She lit a cigarette and made a big deal outta blowing out the match.

I wasn't sure she was gonna tell me, and I didn't think I had the right words to encourage the confidence. All I could think of was, "I'm sure I've heard worse things, Maureen."

"I'm sure you have, but this is the worst thing I've ever done. What I mean is, to stay with a man for five years after you find out he's making a fool of you."

Whew. "So ya found out five years ago?"

"Six. I finally kicked him out a year ago."

"Are ya divorcin him?"

"I'm a Catholic, Faye. I don't believe in divorce."

"Under the circumstances wouldn't ya get some special dispensation or somethin?"

"I could have it annulled, but I don't believe in that either."

"Yeah. I can understand that. So when ya found out six years ago, what did ya do?"

"I foolishly kept it to myself for another year. I didn't want to have to ask him to leave at that time. I had two very small children. But then one of his floozies showed up here, and I had to confront him. He denied everything the way they all do."

"All?"

"Men."

I knew a lotta guys cheated, but Wayne seemed like he was a major leaguer. "And ya believed him."

"No. I didn't. But he confessed and promised he'd be a good boy from then on."

"And ya believed that?"

She sighed. "I'm afraid I did. It was more hope than anything else."

"And these other gals, were they mostly his students?"

"I think so. The ones that came to me were."

"More of them came to you?"

"It's hard to believe, isn't it? But, yes, they did, some begging me to give him a divorce when Brian had told them I was the only reason he wouldn't marry them. Ridiculous. He no more wanted to marry any of them than pigs can fly."

"What did ya tell the girls?"

"The truth. That's what I told them. By the way, Brian had never asked me for a divorce. In fact, he still hasn't. And he's not a Catholic. I think being married is convenient for him, gives him an out if his sordid little affairs get out of hand. It was the last one who came here that made me kick him out."

"What was different about her?"

"She was pregnant . . . and it wasn't a ploy. I could see that she was. Of course there was no way to prove it was Brian's baby, but I knew she was telling the truth."

"How long ago was this?"

"As I said, a year ago."

I'd forgotten, and I'd gotten my hopes up. "What did ya do?"

"I told her I'd never give him a divorce. That I was sorry he'd gotten her in that condition, but that there was nothing I could do for her. She said if I didn't help her, she was going to have an abortion." Maureen's expression turned into one of disgust. "Imagine threatening me with *that*."

"Pretty brazen, I guess."

"You guess? She knew how I'd react to it."

"And how did ya?"

"First I told her to have her child and then I ordered her out of here."

"Didn't any of these girls go to the dean about Brian?"

"It's amazing, isn't it? I think they were too ashamed. But it wouldn't have done them any good anyway. Brian and Dean O'Hara are best friends."

It was time to tell her about Claudette. "You probably don't know this cause it isn't common knowledge, but Claudette West was three months pregnant when she was murdered."

Her hand flew to her chest as though to keep her heart in place. "No . . . but you don't know if it was Brian's, do you?"

"Not for sure. But it's beginnin to sound more likely with every word ya say."

"Wait a minute. You don't think Brian killed her because she was pregnant, do you?"

I shrugged.

"Listen, Miss Quick, Brian's a terrible man. An adulterer, a liar, a predator. But he's not a murderer."

"How can ya be so sure?"

"He's my husband."

I kept myself from smiling. "I don't mean to be cruel, Mrs. Wayne, but ya didn't know for years that he was cheatin on ya."

"That's different."

"How? How is it different?"

"There are certain things you know about a man when you live with him all those years. And I *know* he's not a murderer. It's different because although he hurt me and the children, not to mention those girls he had affairs with, he wouldn't steal a life."

"Did Brian ever hit ya, Mrs. Wayne?"

"Absolutely not. I would never have put up with anything like that."

Her words hung in the air like the hollow things they were.

"Would ya say then that Brian's not a violent man?"

"I would. He wouldn't hurt a fly."

If I had a nickel for all the times I'd heard that one. "And ya don't know if he was havin an affair with Claudette or not?"

"I haven't known anything about Brian for about a year."

"Claudette West never came to you, did she?"

She stood up. "I think it's time for you to leave, Miss Quick."

"Why's that?"

"Because I don't like your inferences. Now you're questioning *my* veracity."

"I'm just doin my job. I have to ask these questions."

"No, you don't. I told you I knew nothing about this Claudette, and you continued to ask me this and that about her."

"But ya can't be sure that she wasn't one of Brian's girls, can ya?"

"Of course not. But I'd swear on a stack of Bibles that he had nothing to do with her death. Now I'd like you to leave."

I got my cigs, put them in my pocketbook, stood up, gathered my coat and hat, and made my way to the door. Maureen Wayne was right behind me like a shadow. She reached in front of me to open the door.

"I have one last thing to say to you, Miss Quick."

I had a flash of hope. Maybe she'd give me a crumb to go on.

"What's that?"

"I think what you do for a living is disgusting. I don't know what kind of woman would do something so sordid."

"Now ya do."

"What?"

"Now ya know what kind a woman. Me."

I took my time going down the stairs. Out on the sidewalk I lit up even though I knew *nice* women didn't smoke on the street, or so my aunt Dolly said. Truth was, I hardly ever did, but my little skirmish with the perfect Maureen Wayne made me want to rebel.

It must be swell to be so sure of things. But I couldn't take Maureen Wayne's word for gospel. I didn't know her Brian the way she did, but I *did* know that even though he wouldn't hurt a fly, that didn't mean he couldn't kill a girl.

TWENTY-THREE

I needed to find a phone booth to call Birdie and see if she'd heard from Richard Cotten about Mr. Garfield.

On Sixth Avenue I looked up at the Jefferson Market Courthouse. I loved that building with its big four-sided clock in the tower. I wished I'd been around to catch the Harry Thaw trial there, but, as they say, I wasn't a gleam in my parents' eyes yet. In fact, they hadn't even known each other.

To the left of the courthouse I could hear, as always, the women yelling from the House of Detention. Sometimes they shouted pretty off-color things.

I walked down Sixth Avenue to Eighth Street. Walgreen's was on the corner and across from it a phone booth. I went in, shut the door behind me, and sat on the wooden seat. I was feeling weak and woozy, and I needed to rest. Maybe I shouldn't have gone out after all.

A knock on the glass made me jump. A tall man in a Superman costume stood outside. He was a fixture around the Village.

I opened the door. "Hey, you don't need this booth, yer already changed."

We both laughed. He said, "I don't want it for myself, it's just that you looked like you needed help."

"That's real nice of ya, Superman. But I'm fine."

"Are you sure?"

"I am. Thanks."

"All right," he said. "But if you feel bad, give a shout, I'll hear you."

"Swell."

We smiled at each other, and he walked away. I shut the door again. Probably anywhere else on the island of Manhattan Superman would be locked up. But in the Village we saw strange people all the time. Superman was the least of them.

I stood and scrabbled around in my pocket to come up with some change. I found a coin and dialed my office.

"A Detective Agency," Birdie said.

She told me there'd been no call from Cotten, but Barry Shields, one of my clients, had checked in. Shields had a cheating wife, and once a week I followed her to the Plaza, where she met up with a man named Arthur Fitzgerald. A regular tryst, you might say. I'd passed this on to Shields, so I wasn't sure what more he wanted me to do. If it was pictures, I'd already told him I didn't do that. Fact was, I hated this kinda work. But when I'd started the case, it had been a slow month.

"How ya feelin, Faye?" Birdie asked.

"I'm fine."

"Yeah, well, ya don't sound fine."

"I bet ya say that to all yer bosses."

"Very funny. I'm serious. Ya get yerself in a mess today you'll be out of commission more days than you'll like."

"I'm just gonna do one more interview and then I'll go home."

"I'll be callin ya at home."

And I knew she meant it. She would call me to check up. But what could I do? I was so close to NYU. I left the booth and made my way across Eighth.

I wondered if Richard Cotten was ever gonna give me the first name of the Garfield guy. It had occurred to me that maybe there wasn't any Garfield and Richard was shining me on. But why? The only reason would be cause he was guilty, and the more I talked to him, the more I didn't think he was.

It was time to have a chinfest with Dean O'Hara, even though Maureen claimed he and Brian were in cahoots. I might get something from him, maybe a different bead on Wayne.

I turned at MacDougal, and when I hit the park I took a left toward the university.

While I waited in the dean's outer office for him to become available, I flipped through a *Life* magazine. It had a Montgomery beret on the cover and, among other things, a photographic essay about the kaiser's empire inside, but I couldn't concentrate enough to look at it. My head was giving me a good spin, and I hoped O'Hara would be free soon. But not right now. I didn't want to pass out at his feet. I leaned back and shut my eyes. Worse. I opened them again and stared at his secretary, who seemed to have the phone permanently attached to her ear. I focused on her nose, which was of the Jimmy Durante variety, and I started to feel steadier. I wasn't sure why this worked, but I didn't question it except to wonder if my cure for dizziness belonged in *Ripley's.*

A few minutes later the Nose told me I could see Dr. O'Hara. I got up real slow and took my time getting to his office. I knocked, and he told me to come in.

O'Hara was standing behind his desk, a man of medium height with a long face and white hair. His eyes were sharp and smart, and I knew I had to be a straight shooter with this one.

"Please sit down, Miss Quick." He gestured to the maroon leather chair on my side of the desk. Where else was I gonna sit?

"Thank you."

He sat when I did. "I must say you look too young to have a child at the university, so it must be a sibling you're inquiring about." He smiled easily. Too easily, I thought.

"I don't have anyone here, Dr. O'Hara."

He looked down at the paper in front of him. "But it says here that you—"

"I lied."

"Young lady, I don't find this a bit amusing. I'm a very busy man."

"Yes, I know. But I do have someone I want to talk to ya about. I didn't think you'd see me if I told the truth."

"The truth is always best, Miss Quick."

"I agree. But in some cases, well . . ." I started over. "I'm inquiring about Brian Wayne."

A big storm cloud covered his puss.

"I don't discuss my staff with outsiders. Who are you, and what do you have to do with Dr. Wayne?"

"I'm a private investigator, and I'm lookin into the death of a student from this university. Claudette West."

"Ah, yes. That was unfortunate."

Unfortunate? "She was murdered ya know."

"Yes, I do know. Was that case solved?"

"It wasn't." I couldn't believe he didn't know.

"And what does this have to do with Dr. Wayne?"

"Claudette was one of his students. And there's reason to believe that Wayne had an illicit relationship with her."

"That's absurd." His cheeks seemed to puff up along with his chest.

"Why is that?"

"Because Bri . . . Dr. Wayne would never have relations with a student."

Was this guy serious? "From what I've heard he's had affairs with lots of students."

"Then you've heard wrong."

"I don't think so. You and Dr. Wayne are good friends, aren't ya?"

"What are you implying?"

"It's just a question, Dean. You friends or not?"

"Yes, we're friends. I'm friends with many people on my staff."

"I'm sure ya are. And it's yer job to protect them, isn't it? All yer staff, I mean."

"I look after them, of course. Keep their interests in mind. What are you getting at?"

"As dean, would it be part of yer job to cover up for members of yer staff?"

"Cover up? I don't like the sound of that."

"I understand why you'd want to do that. But we're talkin murder here."

It looked to me like beads of sweat were forming on the dean's brow.

"You think I'd cover it up if I knew about such a murder?"

"Ya might not realize that murder was involved. Ya might just know about the affair. So let's try this again. Did ya know that Brian Wayne was havin an affair with Claudette West?"

"I did not."

"How about other girls? Did ya know he had affairs with other students?"

He took a deep breath. "I heard . . . there were rumors."

"And ya never asked yer good friend Brian about these rumors?"

"That would have been an insult to him. I'm not in the habit of questioning my staff about every tale that gets told around here, every bit of scuttlebutt, much of it malicious."

"I see."

"I'm not sure you do. A university is like a small town, Miss"—a speedy glance down—"Quick. Rumors, whispers, gossip. It's part of the territory. If I took all the things I hear seriously, I'd have no time for anything else. If they were all true, professors would have no time to teach. Student–teacher dalliances are a staple."

"You've heard this about other professors?"

"Of course . . . with great regularity."

"And you've never looked into any of them?"

"Only if a student came directly to me. Or a parent."

"And no one ever approached ya about Wayne?"

"Never."

"They weren't shy about talkin to Mrs. Wayne, ya know."

He batted her name away like an unruly Ping-Pong ball.

"Maureen Wayne is an unstable girl."

"Is that so?"

"Have you met her?" he asked.

"I have."

"Then you must have recognized that she's a neurotic."

"Nope."

He sniggered. "That doesn't say much for your detecting skills."

"Maybe not. Did ya know that a lotta girls went to Mrs. Wayne, beggin her to give Brian a divorce?"

"Mrs. Wayne supplied this information, of course."

"She did."

"Then it's not to be taken seriously. As I've said, she's most unreliable. She's being treated by a psychiatrist."

I managed not to fall off my chair hearing this info. A lot of people thought this was an indictment, roughly equal to being locked up in Bellevue Hospital. But not me. Although I couldn't see me ever going to a psychiatrist, I have a cousin who sees one, and I know a man who gets the same treatment. I don't think either of them is crazy.

"So she sees a psychiatrist, what does that prove?"

"Simply what I've been saying about her. She's very fragile and tends to make up things."

"Ya mean like Brian Wayne seein other women?"

"Exactly. Now, if there's nothing else I can do for you . . ." He stood.

"Just one more question."

"Yes?"

"Is it possible that Brian Wayne could've been havin an affair with Claudette West and you didn't know about it?"

He cocked his head to one side to show me he was thinking.

"Of course that's possible."

"Thanks for yer time, Dean."

Once again I waited outside of Brian Wayne's office. I could tell no one was inside, but I hoped he'd show up soon. Think of the devil. There he was, turning the corner toward me, and then he stopped.

"You again?"

"Yeah. The bad penny."

"What now?"

"Same thing."

"I told you everything I know."

"Yeah, but that was before I talked to your wife."

He took a step backward. "You saw Maureen?"

"I did."

His face squirreled into a mask of hate. "You had no right to do that."

"I didn't?"

"Who told you you could talk to her?"

"For the record, nobody. Nobody had to, Brian. Why are you in such a lather?"

"My wife has serious problems."

"Far as I could tell, her most serious problem is you."

"Let's not stand out here." He walked past me and unlocked his door.

Inside the small room it looked like trouble lived there. Books and papers were everywhere. If he coulda managed it, I was sure he'd have had them on the ceiling. A chaise longue and a desk took up most of the space. I wondered how many professors kept a chaise in their offices.

It smelled of smoke and the unmistakable odor of perfume. Many perfumes. The chaise was covered in a fabric of green diamond shapes and little yellow and pink flowers, on a field of white. I wondered if Maureen had done that for him. It was an oddball choice for a man, I thought. But girls would like it and probably think it was his homey side or something corny like that.

I picked up some papers from the straight-back chair on my side of the desk and held them in my lap. He put out his hands, and I reached across the desk to give them to him.

"Sorry about the mess," he said. "I get so involved I don't get around to tidying up."

Involved with what? I wanted to ask, but thought I wouldn't get a straight answer so I deep-sixed it.

"Before we go any further, where were ya last night?"

"I was playing poker with friends."

"Can ya prove that?"

"Of course."

"Good." I didn't really think Brian had attacked me, but I had to rule him out.

"Just what did Maureen tell you?"

"That you're a ladies' man. But then I knew that."

"You can't believe anything she says."

"But I do. Even so, she didn't seem to know about Claudette West."

"I told you there was nothing to know." He shot his cuffs, and a ray from his lamp threw a glint in the air. Cuff links.

"Nice links," I said.

He looked at one of them as though he was surprised it was there. "Thanks."

"Who gave them to ya?"

He pursed his lips together and didn't answer.

"Ya hear me, Brian?"

"Yes."

"So who gave ya the cuff links?"

"I bought them myself."

"No ya didn't."

"Prove it."

"I can't."

"Then let's move on," he said.

"Claudette give them to ya?"

"As a matter of fact, she didn't."

"Who did?"

"Another girl. Look, what does this have to do with anything? My cuff links."

"What girl?"

"I'm not about to tell you that."

"I think you'd better. I happen to know Claudette bought some cuff links for a man."

"Not for me."

"Then who gave them to ya?"

"What kind of cad do you think I am? I'll never tell you her name."

"Very honorable, Doctor. Don't make me laugh. Those cuff links could put ya right in the hot seat." They couldn't, but he didn't know that.

He looked like he'd just swallowed a dose of cod liver oil. "Her name is Joan DeHaven."

What a true blue guy!

"Do you have to talk to her? Ask her about the cuff links?"

"Of course I do." I wasn't so sure about that.

"Oh, God." He slumped in his seat.

"Did ya think about what I told ya last time we spoke?"

"You mean about Claudette being pregnant?"

"Yeah."

"What about it?"

"How come she didn't tell ya, do ya think?"

"That's not something a nice girl would tell her professor."

"Can it, Brian. We both know you were sleepin with her."

"I told you—"

"Yeah. You told me. Now I know different. The daddy couldn't be Cotten cause they never did it, and Leon—"

"Who?"

"Doesn't matter. Anyway you're the only one left."

"All right. I did have an affair with Claudette, but it was over a year ago. I had nothing to do with either her pregnancy or her death."

I was set back on my heels that he admitted the affair. And if he was telling the truth, then he couldn't have been the father.

"Any way ya can prove when ya broke it off with Claudette?"

"Of course not. But I'll tell you this." He sat up straighter. "Claudette still considered me a friend. And even though she didn't confide that she was pregnant, she did tell me she was in love. She couldn't say who it was."

"She ever mention the name Alec Rockefeller?"

"Yes, she did. But that wasn't who she was in love with. She said she was seeing Alec to keep her parents happy."

"Why would she tell you about this secret love?"

"Because she knew I cared about her. And I did."

"You always step out on the girls you love, Mr. Professor?"

He looked away. "I can't help it. And I don't even enjoy it. I swear every time that it won't happen again, but it always does."

"Maybe you're the one should be seein a psychiatrist, not your wife."

"I don't believe in that mumbo jumbo."

"Let's get back to the point. Yer tellin me that Claudette was seein someone she didn't want anyone to know about?"

"Yes. And she wasn't happy about it."

"Oh?"

"She said it could never work out."

"Because he was married?"

"She didn't say that."

"What *did* she say?"

"She called it 'a stinking mess.' That was the way she put it."

"Did you ask her if the guy was married?"

"I didn't."

"Why not?"

"Because . . . well, because I didn't want to remind her of us."

"She gave ya no clue as to who he might've been?"

"Nothing, except that her parents would have hit the ceiling because this was a worse choice than Richard Cotten."

TWENTY-FOUR

J lay on my sofa, Harry James in the background playing "I Had the Craziest Dream." The canary was Helen Forrest. It fit my mood to a T. Everything I'd been hearing seemed like a crazy dream.

I didn't seem to be moving forward on this case . . . more like I was running in place or going round in circles. Didn't I start the day right where I was now?

I knew there was a missing man in Claudette's life, and I couldn't find out who it was. Was it this Garfield character whose first name I didn't even know? And all Anne could say was that some man was violently trying to make Claudette do something she didn't want to do. That wasn't much help. The war scenes I could forget. I'd left the sweater with Anne in case she wanted to take another stab at it, but I wasn't counting on it.

Then there was me getting clobbered. I had no more idea who did that than I'd had the night before. It still didn't make sense to me. I guess I had to face that it was a warning to lay off.

The phone rang and I got up slowly, walked across the room, and picked up. It was Birdie.

"Just let me sit down a sec, okay?"

"Sure. Ya feel that bad, Faye?"

"Nah. A little dizzy is all."

"Ya think ya should see a sawbones?"

"Nah. I'll be all right."

"Ya shouldn't a been out and about all mornin."

"Birdie, if I'd a wanted a mother I'd a hired one."

"I'm bein a friend, not a mother. There's a difference."

"So don't be a friend right now. Be my secretary. What's cookin there?"

"The boyfriend called with the first name of Garfield."

"Give."

"Warner."

"Warner?"

"Whatcha want from me? That's the monkey's name."

"Don't tell me . . . he lives on Park Avenue, right?"

"Wrong. Hell's Kitchen."

This Claudette had across-the-board taste. Hell's Kitchen was bad enough, but the next thing I'd hear she had a boyfriend on the Bowery.

"Did Cotten tell ya where he lived?"

"No. I looked him up. I know it'll come as a shock, but there ain't a whole lotta Warner Garfields in the phone book."

"Gimme the address."

"Nine ninety-one West Forty-third. Are ya goin there now, Faye?"

"Gimme his phone number."

She did. "Answer me. Ya goin to Forty-third?"

"I'm not sure what I'm gonna do right now."

"Ya'll be the death a me, Faye."

"Now ya really sound like a mother. Or an aunt."

"It ain't safe there, Faye."

"Yer thinkin in the past, Bird. You and Pete still fightin?"

"Yeah."

"Okay, tomorrow night we're goin to the USO. Whaddaya say?"

"Yer gonna go dancin with a bum head?"

"I dance with my feet, not my head."

"That's side-splittin, Faye."

"Ya wanna or not?"

"Sure. Then I can pick ya up when ya fall down."

"Right. Now don't go makin plans with Pete if he wants to make up."

"I hate girls who do that. Don't worry."

"Okay. See ya tomorrow."

"If yer still with us."

"I'll be the one with the rose in my teeth. Bye."

I cut the connection before she could say anything else.

I looked down at the paper where I wrote Garfield's name, address, and phone number. Claudette dating somebody from Hell's Kitchen still surprised me. Not that everybody who lived there was a crook or a rough-and-tumble kinda guy. The place had cleaned up a lot since the Ninth Avenue El came down, and I'd heard a lotta actors lived over there cause it was cheap.

Maybe Garfield was an actor. Warner Garfield. It had an actor's ring to it. That was probably it. And it fit. An actor wouldn't be Porter West's cup a tea. For him an actor probably *would* be worse than Richard Cotten, student.

And maybe the baby Claudette was carrying belonged to Garfield. Let's say she succumbed to Garfield's charms, instead of resisting like she did with Richard. The time period he'd given me wouldn't have left her three months pregnant when she died. But she coulda picked up with Garfield again without Richard knowing or catching on. Maybe three months after her first breakup with him. Maybe keeping both guys on the string while dating Alec Rockefeller, too, even though that one was for show.

I dialed Garfield's number, but there was no answer. I knew sitting around my apartment would drive me batty while there were still threads to follow. Or even territory I could go over again. A second look can pay off sometimes, Woody had taught me.

Maybe Leon knew something about this Garfield guy. I felt a little woozy standing up, but I steadied myself and checked my pocketbook. My trusty little pad was inside with Leon's number in it. But there was no answer when I tried it. On about the fifth ring the face of Gladys Wright swam into my think box. Maybe that's where he was. The lovebirds in their nest.

Gladys answered, and when I ID'd myself, her groan practically took my ear off.

"Is Leon there?"

"Why?"

"I need to talk to him."

"Well, he's in the bath."

"Get him out."

"No."

"Ya want me to come over and do it myself?"

"Not particularly."

"Then get him out of his bath and on the phone."

"Oh, all right."

She slammed the phone down, assaulting my ear again, and I could hear her steps moving away, her heels tapping the floor. For a sec it made me think of my mother.

Before the morphine sank its hooks in her, pinning her to her bed, she used to dress every day, and the sound of her heels and the swish of her stockings made me feel safe somehow. I'd never really felt safe, that way, since then.

"Hello?"

"Leon?"

"Yes, Miss Quick."

"Call me Faye."

Silence from his end.

"I got a question for ya, Leon."

"What's that?"

"Does the name Warner Garfield mean anythin to ya?"

More silence.

"Are ya there?"

"I'm thinking."

"Either it does or it doesn't. It's not like I'm askin ya about Joe Jones."

"Who?"

"Never mind." Was Leon playing me? "Warner Garfield. Ya know the name?"

"She mentioned it. Claudette."

"What did she say that he wanted?"

"She said he was after her for a date."

"How'd she know him?"

"I don't know."

"Ya didn't ask? She was supposed to be yer girlfriend."

"But she wasn't."

"Ya woulda asked if she'd really been your girl?"

"I guess so."

"So why didn't ya tell me about Garfield before?"

"I forgot about it."

Too busy making whoopee with Gladys. "What else did Claudette say about him?"

"That he was a queer duck and he gave her the heebie-jeebies."

"And?"

"And that was it."

"Ya let it go at that?"

"Well, what in the Sam Hill do you want me to say?"

"I guess I was hopin for a little more curiosity, Leon."

"Look, our whole thing was a phony deal . . . what would you expect me to do?"

"Ya tellin me that ya didn't give two figs about a girl who found this Garfield guy creepy? Ya didn't think she might be in danger?"

"It didn't sound dangerous to me. Claudette was very dramatic, you know."

"No. I didn't know. How?"

"She was always in a squeeze about something. If it wasn't her father, then it was her ex. Or it could be she didn't have the right dress for some deb ball. She could make anything seem like life and death."

"And one of those times it was," I said.

"Yeah, well . . ."

"So anythin else about Garfield?"

"Not that I can remember."

"She did go out with him, ya know. At least once, maybe more."

"I had no idea. It didn't sound like that when she mentioned him. She gave me the impression that he *wanted* a date but there was no way in hell he was going to get one."

"Did Claudette ever give ya a pair of cuff links?"

"No. She never gave me anything."

"Okay. Yer sure that's all ya know about Garfield?"

"I swear."

"Forgive me, Leon, but you swearin to somethin doesn't exactly pack a punch for me."

"Well, that's too bad. I can't prove it, but if I knew anything more I'd tell you. I sw—"

"Okay, if ya think of anythin, call me."

"I will."

"Do ya swear?"

"I . . . goodbye."

I was smiling when I hung up but not for long. There was a possibility that Warner Garfield was a danger to her, at least in Claudette's eyes. How could I know what was what until I got hold of him?

I tried his number again, and he answered. Or some man did. I hung up. I knew I was taking a risk that he wouldn't be home when I got there, but I didn't think he was the kinda guy I should give a heads-up to.

I didn't like carrying a gun, but it didn't seem like such a bad idea, considering where I was going and who I was planning to drop in on.

Woody had given it to me right before he left.

"Take some lessons, Faye. Havin a gat doesn't do much good if ya don't know how to use it," he'd said.

"I don't even want to touch it, Woody."

"Ahh, Faye, ya gonna be a gumshoe or what?"

"Can't I be one without that thing?"

"No. Most of the time ya won't need it, but that one time will come along you'll be glad ya got it."

Maybe this was the one time.

I had taken some lessons. Marty couldn't sneak me onto the official police shooting range so he took me out to an empty lot in the Bronx and taught me. I turned out to be pretty good. A natural he said. But I never liked it. Not the feel or the sound. Nothing about it appealed to me. Still, I knew it was dumb not to take the thing with me just in case.

I kept it on a high shelf in my bedroom closet. I hauled a chair over and stepped up, grabbing the frame of the door cause I wasn't that steady on my pins. I don't know why I had to hide the heater in the hardest place to reach. It wasn't like there was anyone else who'd find it. I guess I was hiding it from myself.

I moved some hat boxes and reached for the Van Dyck cigar box I kept it in. I'd found this on the street one night, just sitting there, like it was waiting for me and my bean shooter.

I almost slipped climbing down off the chair, but I got back to terra firma in one piece. When the cigar box was on my bed, I opened it with the same joy I'd have for poking in a hornet's nest.

One of the things I liked about this particular box was that printed on the inside cover was QUICK ON THE DRAW. Made for me, ya might say. Whoever put together the boxes for this brand had some vision.

I could see the outline of my gun through the piece of old white sheet I'd wrapped it in. It wasn't loaded, so I took one end and pulled until the thing rolled onto my bed.

Ugly. That's how it looked. Woody'd told me it was a Colt .38 pistol. I picked it up by the trigger guard and dropped it into my pocketbook. And then I heard his voice just like he was in the room.

"So what good is an unloaded rod gonna do for ya, Faye?"

I knew he was right. If I was gonna take this thing with me, it better be loaded. I opened the top left drawer of my dresser and reached all the way in the back under my panties. Stashed there were what Woody called the magazines. I don't know why the name, I didn't ask and I didn't particularly care.

I got the gun outta my pocketbook, opened it up, dropped in a magazine, then slid it closed. I didn't take the extra with me cause if I used up the one in my gun I'd probably be dead.

I thought I'd better empty my handbag before I dropped the pistol back in. A mountain of stuff spilled onto the bed. There was:

A compact (that wouldn't close)
Two lipsticks
A wallet and change purse
One fresh handkerchief
Two crumpled handkerchiefs
The laundry bill
Three tickets from the dry cleaner
One address book
One pack of opened cigarettes
Three packs of matches
Lots of ration books (including expired ones)
Two scraps of paper with telephone numbers and no names
One hairnet
One bottle of vitamins
One fountain pen
Two pencils
One parcel of V-mail letters from Woody covering several months, held
*   by a rubber band*
And an old nylon stocking with ladders up and down it that I
*   couldn't face chucking*

I left most of the stuff on my bed and carefully laid the gun inside my pocketbook like it was a corpse in a casket. In the living room I grabbed my coat and left the apartment, toting a gat.

TWENTY-FIVE

J took the subway and got off at Forty-second and Seventh and walked west. Hubert's dime museum was one of my favorite places in Times Square. I never passed without going in, but today I didn't have time. Still, I knew what it felt like to be inside.

You paid your dime at a booth in the back then went down some rickety stairs and sat waiting with the other customers, a lot of sailors and soldiers lately, and tourists. Sooner or later, the worn curtain would open and there, one after the other, appeared the freaks. My favorite was Albert-Alberta, half man, half woman. He/she was a hideous-looking person with long hair on one side and short on the other. The rest of the body was done the same way: stocking on one leg, trouser on the other. Then, if you were of a mind to pay twenty-five cents more, Albert-Alberta was willing to show ya his/her privates.

I knew it was all a fake even while Albert-Alberta told us about his/her life in a croaky voice that was supposed to be a cross between the two sexes. And I did wonder how he/she pulled off the most amazing part of the act, but I still wasn't ready to find out for myself.

The museum's main attraction was Professor Leroy Heckler, who proudly presented his flea circus. The fleas made a carousel go round and round, raced chariots, juggled teeny, tiny balls, and did other amazing tricks. The problem was I could never actually see the fleas, just the objects moving around. I believed in the flea circus anyway. I hated missing it today, but I had other fish to fry.

I passed the many movie theaters, crossed Eighth Avenue, turned uptown to Forty-third, where I hung a left and started into the heart of Hell's Kitchen.

By and large it was a pretty poor neighborhood, a place with a long history and a big bad reputation. The grisly stuff was mostly in the past, although the area still had some active gangs. But I knew it wouldn't be smart to walk along these streets at night, even with an escort.

I found Garfield's tenement, but there were no names listed by the door, no bells. Beyond the front door was a small vestibule with mailboxes along one wall. Garfield's was near the left end. But it didn't tell me what floor he was on or what number his apartment was.

The inside door was unlocked, and I knew I had two choices. Either knock on every door or find the super, if there was one. The looks of the hallway made me suspect the job was going begging. So I started knocking. First apartment no one answered, second someone did.

"Yeah?"

He was big. Big head, big shoulders, big chest. He wore a not-too-clean undershirt and brown trousers. His head of black hair was big, too. He had a face like a Model T Ford.

"I'm lookin for someone," I said.

"Yeah?"

"Would ya know if a Warner Garfield lives here?"

"Why?"

"I need to talk to him."

"What about?"

"That's private."

He started to shut the door.

"No. Don't. This is important."

"You his old lady?"

"No. I'm a private investigator."

He laughed, but I was used to this.

"Whatcha want with Garfield?"

"I have to ask him some questions about a case I'm on."

"Yeah? What case is that? A case a beer?"

A real wit. This time he roared with laughter, like they say.

"Can ya tell me what apartment he lives in?"

"Why should I?"

"It's not a matter of *should.*"

"What's it a matter of?"

"A murdered girl."

His eyes narrowed. "And Garfield did it?"

"I didn't say that."

"What did ya say?"

"I just want to talk to him."

"About this murdered girl?"

"Yeah."

"How much is it worth to ya?"

Boy, was I thick. Usually I knew when they were trying to hit me up for some moola, but I hadn't caught on.

"How much do ya think?"

"How about a sawbuck?" he said.

"How about a fin?"

He nodded.

I opened my purse and took a bill from my wallet. I handed him the five.

"He's on the fourth. Number 402." He slammed the door shut.

"Thanks," I said.

I climbed the stairs, kicking papers, a crust of bread, and other garbage I couldn't identify, out of my way. The smells coming from the different apartments were not appetizing. Whatever they were, mixed together they almost made me gag.

When I reached 402 I gave it only a fifty-fifty chance Warner Garfield was still at home. I knocked.

Nothing.

I put my ear to the door and thought I could hear running water in the distance, like it might be coming from a faucet at the other end of the place. There was no other sound.

I knocked again.

Still nothing. I did that four or five times, then like Woody had taught me to do in these situations, I turned the door handle. The place was unlocked.

This never ceased to surprise me. And if I was being honest it spooked me, too. I opened the door just a crack and again I heard Woody's voice in my mind.

Take out the gun, Faye.

I knew it was the right thing to do even though it made me more scared than I already was. I opened my purse and carefully lifted out the gun and, like Marty showed me, held it out in front of me at arm's length.

I wanted to laugh. If my pop could see this, he'd bust a gut, then make book on it.

Real quiet, I pushed open the door, hoping that it wouldn't squeak. It didn't. The sound of running water was louder. It was coming from the other end of the place. This was a railroad apartment, with all the rooms lined up one after another off a hall. The whole joint was dark except for a little light at the far end of the long hallway.

I had to make another call. I could keep sneaking down the hall, peering into rooms until I found someone or didn't, or I could announce myself with a holler. Of course, finding me with a pointed gun might not make the tenant too happy. Even so, I chose the yell.

"Hello. Anyone home?"

Nothing. Just the running water.

I tried again, but nobody answered. So I inched in, step by step, until I came to a door on my right that was open.

Gun in front of me, I looked in. A bedroom with a mussed-up bed, a dresser, and a wooden chair, a pair of trousers and a shirt hanging over the back, an undershirt on the floor. But nobody was in there.

I inhaled, only then realizing I'd been holding my breath. My underarms were clammy, and I could feel the droplets of sweat on my forehead turning to trickles starting down my face.

I had to keep going. So I took some more baby steps, the gun sorta wavering in my wet grip like a divining rod.

"Anybody home?" My voice didn't sound too good. It was more like a warble than a shout.

Nobody answered. I don't know what I woulda done at that point if somebody had.

Next I came to the kitchen. It had a range, sink, ice box, and a small table with two chairs. But no one sitting there.

As I moved down the hall the sound of running water got louder and louder until I was outside the door where it was coming from. The top half of the door had pebbled glass, and through it I could see the glow of a light inside.

The water sounded like it was turned on full force in a sink. Bath water would've made a different sound. I stood to one side of the door. Although I couldn't see through the glass, if anyone moved inside the room I knew I'd see a shadow.

No dice. And the water kept running. I coulda walked back down the hall and out the door and nobody woulda been the wiser. I thought of the boys at Stork's and what a laugh that would give them if they knew, which they wouldn't. But *I'd* know, and that made me dig in my heels and tighten my grip on the gun. It was a job I had to see through to the end, no matter what.

After a couple a deep breaths I slowly turned the door's porcelain knob until I heard the click that told me the door was ready to open. I inched it inward little by little.

The water was pounding against the sink like I'd thought, and the ceiling light was on. The bathtub curtain, streaked with mildew, was pulled closed, but not for long. I knew I had to look behind it. This was worse than going to the dentist.

With the gun in my right hand, I reached out with my left and grabbed the edge of the curtain in my fingers, then yanked them back like I'd burned myself. I felt like a horse's ass. What was so tough about tugging a stupid bath curtain? Everything. I had the terrible feeling I'd find something I didn't wanna find in that tub. Something I didn't wanna see.

Okay, Quick, I told myself, you can do it. Think of Woody. I did. There he was probably in some miserable foxhole, tired and dirty, and here I was in an apartment bathroom, able-bodied, clean, water spraying on me from the sink, afraid to open a moldy old curtain. I wished I'd joined the Wacs.

Enough. Do it. I reached out again and this time I held on and pulled back the curtain, exposing the tub. And what was in it. I couldn't stop myself. I gasped.

He was dead. That was clear. He was in his drawers. His trousers, shirt, and undershirt were missing. He was stuffed into the tub so that his legs bent at the knees. One side of his head, the side I could see, was smashed in and covered with blood. I couldn't get a look at his face, but it didn't matter. I was sure I didn't know this stiff, although I had to assume he was Warner Garfield cause he was lying in Garfield's tub. But it coulda been someone else. A guest. A neighbor. A salesman who hawked at the wrong door. No telling.

When I looked more carefully, I saw two bullet holes in his chest.

I had to call the cops. I left the bathroom and walked still farther down the hall to the living room. On a table next to a broken-down sofa was a phone. I picked up the receiver and dialed zero.

"Operator."

"I wanna report a murder."

"Where are you located?"

"Nine ninety-one Forty-third Street. Apartment 402."

"I'll connect you with the precinct in that area."

The desk sergeant took the details and told me to sit tight, the cops were on their way.

I needed a break from Garfield's digs, so I stood outside in the hall, lit up, and took a big drag filling my lungs, my nose, my mouth with the smell and taste of tobacco. I knew the guy in the tub hadn't been there long cause the smell woulda driven me out sooner.

You don't bleed after yer dead. Woody had told me that. So I figured Tub Man was kaput from the head injury by the time the killer pumped lead into him.

I hadn't looked around the place cause I didn't want to disturb anything or spread my fingerprints around. I knew they were on every door I touched, but that was about it.

I heard them coming like a herd of buffalo. It sounded like the whole police force as they ran up the stairs. But it was only four cops with drawn guns.

And they were all pointed at me.

"Hey," I said, holding my hands up in front of my face like they could shield me.

"Who are you?"

"I called this in."

"Yeah? Where's the victim?"

"In the bathroom down the hall. In the tub."

"Drownin?"

"No."

He eyed me suspiciously. "Webb, you stay with her for now."

The other two followed him.

"Name?" Webb asked.

"Faye Quick."

"Ya know the victim?"

"No."

"How'd ya happen to be in his bathroom?"

I knew this was just the first of many times I'd have to answer this and the first of many times I'd get the look or the laugh.

"I'm a private detective."

Webb laughed.

TWENTY-SIX

*D*etective Lake didn't laugh.

He was tall and thin and wore his trilby toward the back of his head. He had a long face with deep-set brown blinkers and a nice nose and mouth. I liked the way he looked.

I figured he was about thirty. He wore a gray suit, and a short chain dipped into the small pocket of his vest where he kept his watch. His hands were in his trouser pockets as he paced back and forth on the worn rug in Garfield's apartment.

"So you didn't know Garfield at all, is that right, Miss Quick?"

"That's right."

"Tell me again why you came here?"

"A case I'm workin on. I wanted to question him."

We were interrupted then by a cop bringing in the guy from downstairs who'd told me which crib was Garfield's.

"What the hell, you do this?" He pointed at me.

Lake said, "Shuddup, bud. What's your name?"

"Jack Gorcey. Why?"

"You know Warner Garfield?"

"I seen him around. Why? What's goin on?"

"Then you know what he looks like, right?"

"Sure. Why?"

"Take him," Lake said to the cop holding Gorcey's arm. To me he said, "Excuse me, Miss Quick. I'll be right back."

I nodded and smiled like some schoolgirl. But that's what I felt like. Sort of all fluttery inside.

I was alone in the crummy living room. Detective Lake was taking Gorcey to identify the body in the tub. I was almost sure it was Garfield cause of the trousers and shirt hanging in the bedroom and the missing ones from the body. And I was sure Lake was, too. He just wanted a formal ID.

Suddenly I heard a noise from down the hall. It was definitely someone throwing up, and I didn't think it was Detective Lake or the cop.

When they came back to the living room, Gorcey looked like he'd aged about twenty-five years. He was pale and shaky, the tough-guy pose gone.

"Sit down," the cop said.

Gorcey fell into a stained and shabby chair.

"When's the last time you saw Garfield?" Lake asked.

"Yesterday. Why?"

"Can the why, Gorcey."

"Why?"

"What did I just say?"

"Yeah. Sorry."

"How did Garfield look when you saw him?"

He shrugged. "I don't know. Regular."

"What's regular?"

"He looked like he always looked. Wh—"

"Which was what?"

"Like Garfield."

"Look, Gorcey, right now you're the last person who saw Garfield alive, so you better stop cracking wise."

"I ain't crackin wise. I dunno what else to say. And I ain't the last person to see him alive."

"Yeah? How do you know?"

"Because I didn't whack him."

"Who did?"

"How should *I* know?"

Gorcey looked like a squashed can. I almost felt sorry for him.

"You ever see Garfield with anyone?"

"Sure."

"Who?"

"I dunno. I mean, I didn't know him or his friends."

"You see him with men or girls?"

"I seen him wit boat."

"Was he with anyone when you saw him yesterday?"

"Nah."

"Where'd you see him?"

"By the mailboxes."

Lake nodded to one of the cops, and he left the room.

"Did you talk to him?"

"We said hello, that's all."

"Was he coming in or going out?"

"Goin out. After he got his mail he left and turned right. That's it. That's the last I saw of the mug."

"Excuse me," I said.

Lake turned to me, a surprised look on his face. I guess he wasn't used to being interrupted when he was grilling someone.

"I'm sorry to butt in, but I'd like to show Mr. Gorcey a picture."

He took a beat, then agreed.

I got Claudette's photo out of my purse and passed it to Gorcey.

"Do you know who that is? Ever seen her?" I asked.

"I seen her somewhere, but I ain't sure it was with Garfield."

Everyone had seen her at the time of the murder. This snap had been in all the papers, and that made it heavy sledding for me.

"Think," Lake said.

I coulda clicked my heels that he was helping me out.

"I'm thinkin. Yeah. I coulda seen her with him. But not in a long time."

"What's a long time?" I asked.

"Maybe six months."

"What was she doin with him?"

"How should *I* know?"

Lake said, "You can stop saying that along with 'why.' "

"But I *don't* know what the broad was doin with Garfield. What am I, a mind reader?"

This made me think of Anne. I needed something that belonged to Garfield. But there was no way I could explain this to Detective Lake.

The cop came back with something in his hand. Papers. No, mail.

He handed the letters to Lake, who shuffled them like a deck of cards before handing them back to the cop.

I said, "Mr. Gorcey, did he seem chummy with this girl?"

"She was holdin his arm when they went down the street, that's what ya mean."

"That's just what I mean." I looked at Lake. "Just one more question." Back to Gorcey. "Do ya think she coulda been his girl?"

Gorcey dropped his head into his hands.

Lake said, "He doesn't know."

"Okay. Thanks, Detective."

"My pleasure, Miss Quick." He smiled, and he looked adorable.

"Okay. Did you see anyone you didn't know come in here between yesterday and today?"

"Only her." He pointed at me. "And I wouldna seen *her* she hadn't knocked on my door."

"You live in a front apartment, don't you, Gorcey?"

"What about it?"

Right then my hand slipped between the sofa cushions and landed on something. Something that wasn't the sofa.

"Your windows face the street?"

"Window. Yeah."

"You never look out?"

"What's ta see? I lived on these streets all my life, I don't need ta look out ta know what's goin on."

"So you only saw Garfield when you were at the mailboxes at the same time?"

"Or in the hall."

"How about the other tenants in the building? You know any of them?"

"I keep myself ta myself."

"Right. Okay, Mr. Gorcey, go back to your palace and don't take any sudden trips."

I carefully pulled what was lodged between the cushions until I saw it was white crumpled cotton. Whatever it was was probably Garfield's. I slipped it into my pocketbook while nobody was looking.

Detective Lake handed out assignments. "You two question the other tenants. After the coroner and the fingerprint guys get done, you two toss this place. I'll be back soon."

Then he turned to me.

"Miss Quick, may I escort you out?"

How could a girl refuse? "Sure."

As we walked down the hall, I realized my palms were sweating. The three flights seemed like twenty before we got down to the ground floor, through the door, and out to the street.

"Well," I said, "thank you, Detective." I hoped my voice wasn't shaking like my insides were.

"Would you like to have a cup of coffee?" he asked.

Trying to sound easygoing, I said, "Why not?"

We walked in silence toward Eighth. When we reached the corner, he pointed across the avenue.

"That's not a bad coffee shop over there."

The sign spelled out KELLAWAY'S. I nodded.

As we crossed I kept bumping him cause I was walking like I had a few too many. I hoped he didn't notice. When we got to the place, he opened the door for me and we went in.

It was your regular coffee and eggs joint, and we took a booth near the middle. The crowd was light this time of day. I lit a cig right away, and so did he.

A waitress with a rag of brown hair came to our table.

"So?"

"What would you like?" he asked.

"Just a cup of j . . . coffee."

"Same," he said.

"We got a nice blueberry pie," she said.

I love blueberry pie and usually I woulda snapped up the offer, but I didn't think I could eat in front of him. Besides, it would turn my teeth blue.

"No thanks," I said.

He shook his head.

She looked at us like we were the scum of the earth for turning down the pie, then went to get our coffee.

Detective Lake smiled that smile. "I don't think she likes us."

"Not too much," I said.

"So, Miss Quick, tell me how you happened to become a private investigator?"

"It's sort of a long story."

"I have time."

The waitress put our coffee in front of us. I wondered if I'd be able to pick it up without my hand shaking. It was too hot to try, so I started my tale of how I became a gumshoe.

Lake listened without interrupting, which was a first from any man I knew, and halfway through the story I picked up my java and nothing shook cause I was concentrating on my tale.

"That's very interesting," he said when I was done. "Can you discuss the case you're on now? I thought I recognized the girl in the picture you showed Gorcey."

"Then ya know what case it is."

"I suppose I do, but I thought it had reached a dead end."

"Somebody didn't think so."

"I won't ask who hired you."

I knew I woulda told him if he had. After all, he was a cop. A detective, no less.

"Sorry," I said.

"No, no. I understand and respect you for your professionalism."

"Thanks." I was such a phony I embarrassed myself. "What about you? What made ya become a cop . . . a policeman."

He laughed, and the sound was deep, real genuine, and full of fun. "You can call me a cop, Miss Quick. That's what I am."

I smiled. "And you can call me Faye. That's *who* I am."

"I'm John, but most people call me Johnny."

We exchanged a look that lasted a few seconds, and my stomach did a roller coaster.

"I became a cop because my father was a cop and his father was a cop. Not an interesting story like you have."

"But ya like it, don't ya?"

"I do. Especially since I made Homicide. I don't usually mention that to girls, but I know you understand."

Girls. Plural. I wondered how many there were. "Yeah, I do. It's a lot more excitin than catchin burglars or breakin up car rings, I imagine."

"How about you? Do you find murder cases more . . . interesting?"

"I'll tell ya a secret. This is my first one."

"And Garfield was your first body?"

"No. I'm the one who stumbled over Claudette West lyin on Thompson Street."

A spark lit up his peepers. "Ah, that was you."

"Yeah. Me."

"That must have been quite a shock. Well, both of them must have been shocks."

"I was almost expectin Garfield. At least once I got into the apartment. I could hear the water runnin and nobody was answerin my calls. I knew there was a good chance I'd find a body."

"I can see that. But the West discovery was a true surprise."

"That's fer sure."

He took out his gold pocket watch, and my heart sank a little.

"I should get back," he said.

"Me, too. Not back to Garfield's, but I got plenty a work left to do."

The check was on the table, and he picked it up after laying down some change for a tip.

I waited while he paid, and then we went outside.

"Well, Faye, I've enjoyed meeting you."

I thought I might die right then. He was gonna leave, and that was gonna be that.

"Yeah, me, too. Thanks for the coffee." I held out my hand to shake.

He took it and kept it wrapped in his. "We should exchange phone numbers . . . since our cases overlap, and who knows? One of us might come up with something that might help the other one." He let go of my hand.

Struggling not to come apart at the seams, I said, "Yeah. That's a good idea." I reached into my pocketbook and rattled around in there, bumping against the gun, until I came up with a paper and pen.

He was already writing on a pad. When we were both done we traded our numbers.

"When the boys finish tossing the apartment, they'll probably come up with something for you."

"Thanks."

He put out his hand, and I took it. I wondered if he'd forgotten that we'd already done this.

"It's been really nice, Faye."

"Yeah, it has."

He let go of my hand and touched the brim of his hat. "Goodbye for now."

"Goodbye."

He turned and crossed Eighth and I turned away fast, in case he looked back. I walked down Eighth toward my subway.

Nah.

I floated toward my subway.

TWENTY-SEVEN

*O*n the way home I'd realized that during our yakety-yak Detective Lake and I had never once mentioned Warner Garfield. I didn't know anything more about the clown than when I'd gone to his door, except he was dead and a lousy housekeeper. If he'd had a girl around, she wasn't a practitioner of the domestic arts either. Which made me think of what I'd stuffed in my pocketbook.

Back on my sofa, the last thing I wanted to do was get up. Birdie'd been right. I'd done too much. But hell, how could I have known I'd be walking into a murder? Besides, if I hadn't gone looking for Garfield, I would never have met Detective John Lake.

But so what that I'd met him? I'd probably never see the guy again. On the other hand, I had to remember that he'd said, "Goodbye *for now.*" He didn't just say goodbye. *For now* were two very important words. Ah, the hell with it. Who was I kidding? For all I knew the monkey was married. I had to make myself stop thinking about him and concentrate on my case.

When I walked across the room to where I'd left my pocketbook, I wasn't dizzy anymore.

Inside my purse, crumpled in a corner and underneath the grip of my gun, was what I'd lifted from Warner Garfield's sofa. I scooped it up and shook it out. An undershirt.

With dried blood on it.

It could've been Garfield's, but why would the killer stuff it in between the cushions like that? Also I'd seen an undershirt lying on the floor in Garfield's bedroom. Maybe this one belonged to the killer. And the *blood* on it was Garfield's. That made more sense. But stuffed in the sofa? That made no sense. Whoever it belonged to, I knew I should've turned it over to the police. To Johnny. I could give him a call to say I had it. But what would he think of me holding out like that? I had another idea.

I went to the phone and dialed Anne. I filled her in and we agreed to meet the next day. Then I called the West house.

A man answered and I asked for Porter. When he asked who was calling and I'd told him, he said, "Oh, hello, Miss Quick. Cornell Walker here."

Myrna West's half brother. We made some chitchat and then he got Porter. After our initial hellos, I said, "Did Claudette ever give ya a set of cuff links, Mr. West?"

"Of course."

"Why, 'of course'?" I asked.

"Daughters often give their fathers cuff links for a birthday or Christmas."

"I thought they gave them ties." I was thinking about my last gift to Pop. A yellow tie with bluebirds on it. I thought it was the most beautiful thing I'd ever seen. Now it made me shudder.

"I suppose in some families they do."

It didn't take much to know whose family he meant. I wanted to slap his face.

"So about these cuff links. When did she give them to ya?"

"Claudette has given me many sets over the years."

"How about in the last year?"

"No. Not since she was in high school."

"Yer sure?"

"Of course I'm sure. Is there anything else?"

"Yeah."

"I'm waiting."

"Another name's come up. Did Claudette ever mention Warner Garfield?"

"Never."

"Is Mrs. West there?"

"Yes."

"Could ya ask her if she knows the name?"

"If I don't, she doesn't."

He had Myrna West on some tight leash. "Could ya ask her anyway?"

"There's no point."

"How about your brother-in-law? Could ya ask him?"

"What does Cornell have to do with this?"

"Maybe Claudette mentioned the name to him in passin.'"

"Who is this person? What did he have to do with my daughter?"

"I'm not sure yet. That's why I'd like you to ask Mrs. West or Captain Walker."

"Is Garfield a suspect?"

"Like I've said, Mr. West, everybody's a suspect until I rule them out."

"What about Garfield?"

Talking to Porter was like being conked from behind over and over. It took a lot out of a girl.

"For the moment I haven't ruled him out." I didn't want to tell West yet that Garfield was dead. "So could ya ask Walker if ya don't wanna ask yer wife?"

"It's not that I don't *want* to ask her. I already *know* her answer. Hold on."

Softly, I started singing "That Old Black Magic" and almost got to the end before West came back on the line.

"Cornell has never heard that name. Now tell me what this is about."

"No sources, Mr. West, is that understood?" I wasn't about to tell him I got Garfield's name from Cotten.

"I know that's what you've told me, but I can't say I understand it since I'm paying the bills."

"That's just the way it's always been."

"Never mind. Tell me who Garfield is."

"Was," I said.

"Was? You mean he's dead?"

"Yes."

"Then what could he have to do with Claudette?"

"He's only been dead about twelve hours."

"Oh."

"He was murdered."

"Who murdered him?"

"We don't know."

"We?"

"The police and I." I felt myself blushing.

"Are you working for the police now?"

"Mr. West, I found the body and called the police."

"Again? You found a body again?"

I ignored him. There was nothing else to do. "I know that Claudette knew him, but I don't know how she met him or what their relationship was. That's what I'm tryin to find out."

"Do you think he may have had something to do with Claudette's death?"

"It's possible."

"This has gotten very complicated, hasn't it?"

Like it was my fault. He didn't even know about me getting hit on the head. "Murder is always complicated, Mr. West. Even if it's open and shut." At least that's what it said in the books.

"What's your next move?"

Telling him that I was going to turn Anne loose on a bloody undershirt didn't seem like the right answer to give Porter.

"Pinnin down Garfield's particulars and his connection to Claudette." All true.

"Yes, of course."

"So you'll keep your ears open for anythin about him?" Me and Porter. A real team.

"Certainly."

As always he told me to call him the next night, and we hung up.

After I put the receiver back in the cradle I sat at the telephone table, unmoving. I found myself staring into the room. I *did* need to find out what the connection was between Garfield and Claudette, but I had no idea where to start. No respectable PI would ever admit this to anyone, but it was something Woody had warned me might happen. You're working on a case, moving along, and suddenly a wall comes up in front of ya and there's no way over around or under it. When that happens, he'd told me to take a break. Go to a movie. Drop into your favorite restaurant. Knock back a few drinks. I wasn't going to do any of these things by myself. Not tonight. I dialed my office, and when Birdie answered, I asked, "What are ya doin tonight, Bird?"

"Nothin."

"How about we go to a USO dance instead of tomorrow?"

"Faye, I don't think ya should be jumpin around after what happened to ya last night."

"Is that how you dance, Birdie? Ya jump around?"

"Don't get smart with me. You know what I mean."

"I feel fine, and I need some distraction from this case. It'll free up my mind. Woody told me so."

"Ya heard from Woody?"

"No. He told me before he left. He said, 'Quick, when the case isn't jellin, ya gotta do somethin real different. Ya gotta forget all about it for a few hours.' "

"Yeah?"

"Yeah. So whaddaya say, Bird? We meet up for a couple a cocktails at the Hotel Astor, then have a sandwich at Lindy's followed by a piece of cheesecake, then ankle over to the USO."

"You buyin?"

"Who else?"

"What time ya wanna meet?"

While we walked to the USO from Lindy's, Birdie said, "So, these soldiers and sailors, do they expect anything from ya, Faye?"

"Like what?"

"Ya know. After. Later."

"I suppose some might, but that depends on how ya act with them. Tell ya the truth, mostly these guys wanna talk. They're away from home in Idaho or Tennessee or some hick place for the first time in their lives, and they're homesick. They wanna talk to ya about their girlfriends or their hometown folks. Stuff like that."

"Ya mean they ain't New Yorkers?"

I stopped dead in my tracks. "Bird, don't ya get the point of this place? If they were New Yorkers, they'd be with their families. These guys just wanna go home."

"To Idaho? Who'd wanna go there?"

"Listen to me. Ya gotta be interested in these guys. They're real nice, and they're real lonely. They want the companionship of us girls but mostly to talk to. They want somebody to tell their problems to. They've been over there fightin for us, Bird. Now we do our part."

"I get it."

"Good."

When we got there, some of the boys had spilled out onto the sidewalk.

"Hiya, fellas," I said. "How ya doin?"

They all said something, and Bird and me nodded and smiled and went inside.

There was a girl at a table right inside the door who took our names and what we were volunteering for. Some girls played Ping-Pong, cards, were hostesses, or handed out doughnuts and coffee. And then there were others, like us, who wanted to dance.

We went into the large main room where the girl spinning the platters had on Bing Crosby singing "All or Nothing at All." Lots of couples were on the floor, but there were still plenty of boys standing around, waiting for the right girl or, as I'd discovered before, just too shy to ask.

"What now?" Birdie asked.

"Ya pick out a guy and ask him to dance."

"*I* gotta ask *him*?"

"Yeah. It works that way sometimes. C'mon, I'll show ya." I spotted a couple a guys standing near the table with doughnuts on it, and I grabbed Birdie's hand and pulled her over with me.

"Hiya, soldier," I said to a red-haired, freckle-faced kid. "I'm Faye and this is Birdie. Wanna cut a rug?"

His eyes lit up like I was a Kewpie doll he'd just won.

"Sure. I'm Lon. This is Rory Tracy."

"Hiya, soldier," Birdie said, following my lead.

Rory said, "I'm a Marine."

"But yer all soldiers, aren't ya?" she asked.

"No, Bird, not exactly. I'll explain later."

"I'll explain now," Rory said, and asked Birdie to dance.

Bing was winding up as we moved away from the sidelines. The next number started right away, and it was a jitterbug.

"Can ya do it?" Lon asked.

"You bet," I said.

And we were off. That soldier knew his stuff. He swung me around, slid me through his outstretched legs and up again, spun me behind him, pulled me back, and generally wore me out.

When it was over, I told him I needed a break, and we sat down listening to Glenn Miller's band playing "Chattanooga Choo Choo."

Private Lon Calhoun was from Iowa and told me all about himself for the next half hour. I didn't have to pretend I was interested cause I was. I'd always liked to hear about other people's lives.

Later we danced again, many times, until I had to tell Birdie that we had to go. The boys offered to see us home, but we said we'd grab a checker instead.

"They were nice boys," Birdie said. "But they wore me out. Jeez, Louise, I can't get Pete to do a fox-trot. He woulda busted a gut had he seen me with that Marine."

I realized nobody woulda cared about me dancing with Lon all night, and that made me a little sad. But it wasn't what was bothering me. Maybe my strange feeling had to do with Detective Lake. But right away I knew that wasn't it.

I'd distracted myself, forgotten the case for a few hours, and where was I now? Feeling like something was just out of reach, something important that would help me with the case.

Birdie chatted on.

I heard her words, but my mental picture of that soldier and Marine, our dancing partners, nagged.

And nagged.

TWENTY-EIGHT

Sitting at my desk the next morning everything seemed easy. I guessed my night on the town had done the trick. That made me think of Lon and Rory and the nagging feeling came back for a flash then disappeared.

The first thing I did was to call Claudette's friend June Landis. After the niceties were out of the way, I asked her if she'd ever heard Claudette mention Warner Garfield. She clammed up like I'd asked her for the combination to the family vault.

"June?"

"Yes. I'm thinking."

I knew if she was thinking about it, it was whether to tell me or not.

"She did talk about him, didn't she?" I said.

"Yes. I think so."

"You know so, June."

"All right. What about him?"

"Was she datin him?"

"Hardly." June couldn't help herself. She sniggered.

"Not her type?"

"She couldn't stand him. But he wouldn't give up on pestering her for a date."

Leon had said the same thing.

"Do ya know how she met Garfield?"

"I think she said she'd met him through this acting group she was involved with. God, don't tell her parents she hung around with actors."

"Do ya think that'd make a lotta difference to them now, June?"

"Guess not." She sounded sad.

"When ya say she was involved with this group, do ya mean she was actin?"

"Oh, no. She just liked being with them."

"What's the name of the actin group?"

"I don't think I ever knew that. I know they were in Greenwich Village though."

Big help. "There are tons of actin groups in the Village. Can ya tell me anythin that might help me find them?"

"Gee, I don't think so. Wait, I remember a play they put on last year that she went to. It had an *M* in the title . . . two *M*'s maybe . . ."

June was trying so I kept quiet.

"*Moons and Mulberries.* That's what it was called."

The title alone probably made it a big hit. "This was for the payin public . . . tickets and all?"

"I think it was just for invited guests."

"So it wasn't reviewed."

"I doubt it."

"Yeah, me, too. Well, thanks." I hung up. Maybe Peggy Ann Lanchester, who'd helped me once, could do it again. I'd kept her number, and I dialed it. A maid told me she wasn't home. I left my name and number and said to tell Peggy Ann it was urgent that she call me back.

I had to find that acting group. Maybe there was something in Garfield's papers that would help.

I opened my pocketbook. The paper Detective Lake had given me was in a small pocket in the lining. I stared at it. He'd put his precinct in the upper-right-hand corner and his work phone number below his name, *Johnny Lake*. I dialed.

The desk sergeant took the call and put me through. I could feel myself blushing all over when I heard his voice.

"Miss Quick, good to hear from you."

"Faye, remember."

"Right. Faye."

I loved the way he said my name. "I need some help."

"What can I do for you?"

"I imagine when ya tossed Garfield's apartment ya came away with a lot of paper, right?"

"Yes."

"I was wonderin if any of those papers named an actin company?"

"I don't know but I can find out."

"It's very important."

"Hold on a minute."

"Sure." My hands were sweaty, and my heart was thumping like a bass drum. I felt ridiculous, but I couldn't stop either thing. I tried to remember if I'd ever felt like this and all I could come up with was Spencer Nelson. Fourth grade. Pretty pathetic.

"Faye?"

"Yeah, I'm here."

"My guy tells me there are three cartons full of papers. So far they haven't come across anything about an acting company. I have to go through a lot of it myself once it's winnowed down. I told them to be on the lookout for it, though."

"Thanks."

We dummied up for a few seconds.

"Anything else I can do for you?" he asked.

A few things came to mind, but I wasn't about to say them. "No. That's all I need. At least it's all I know I need. Maybe they'll come across somethin I'm not privy to right now." I sounded like a moron.

"When we've finished, I think I can arrange for you to have access."

I knew this could take forever.

"That's nice of you, John."

"Johnny."

"Johnny. Maybe ya could mention to your guys to also be on the lookout for anything that links Garfield to Claudette West."

"I've already told them that."

I smiled. "Thanks." I didn't want to hang up, but I was clean outta Garfield questions.

"Now that I have you, I was wondering if you'd like to have dinner sometime. We can discuss the case."

"Well, yeah, sure. That'd be nice."

"Great. I'll call you."

"Swell."

We said goodbye. I felt depressed. How come he didn't ask me right then for dinner? I knew I shouldn't be complaining. He brought up the subject of a date. At least I thought it was a date. But maybe not. He did say we'd discuss the case. Course that could be an excuse. Maybe he was too shy to ask me outright? I wished girls could ask men out. If I was a man and saw a girl I liked, I'd just ask. Oh, the hell with it.

Maybe if I went to some of the established theater companies and asked, someone might be able to point me . . . and then I thought of it. Claudette's things. I was sure the Wests hadn't thrown anything away. Claudette might've kept a playbill.

I decided not to let the Wests know I was coming. I went into the outer office.

"How long ya goin out for, Faye?"

"I'm not sure. What's with you?"

"Meanin?"

"Ya look like ya swallowed a robin."

"Canary."

"I know. So what's up?"

"My Marine called me."

"No kiddin?"

"No kiddin."

"Ya gonna see him again?"

"Tonight."

"Well, that's swell, Birdie."

"Yeah. Pete can eat worms."

For now, I thought. What happens when her Marine goes overseas? But I didn't want to put the kibosh on it. "Good riddance."

"Yeah. Sergeant Rory Tracy is my kinda guy."

"Don't get too carried away, Bird."

"Nah. Don't worry. We're not gonna run away and get hitched or anything like that."

That never entered my mind. "Good thing. I need ya here. I gotta go now."

"Call in once in a while, will ya?"

"Right."

Captain Cornell Walker was the only member of the West household at home. When we were settled in the living room and he'd gotten the maid to bring us coffee and biscuits, he finally asked the reason for my visit.

"I don't think you'll be able to help me, Captain. That's what I was sayin at the door." Before ya steamrolled me in here, I wanted to add.

"Well, try me, Miss Quick."

"I need to know what plays Claudette saw in the last, let's say, six months of her life."

"I can name some of them."

"How's that?"

He smiled, but his blue eyes didn't have a twinkle in them.

"I took her to a few."

"Was one of them *Moonbeams and Mulberries*?"

"No. That sounds dreadful."

"Yeah, it does." I figured that wasn't the only play this group ever did. "So what were the titles of the plays you took her to see?"

"Let's see. We saw *Blithe Spirit* and *The Eve of Saint Mark* and—"

"No offense, Captain, but those are Broadway shows, aren't they?"

"Yes, of course."

"I was thinkin more along the lines of small theater companies, produced downtown, maybe."

He looked like he was smelling a dead mouse. "No, that wouldn't interest me, and I'd never take my niece to something like that."

He acted like I was talking about burlesque. "What if I told ya she hung around with actors and actresses from one of those groups?"

"I'd wonder where you got such information."

I ignored this. "I was hopin maybe I could look through some of Claudette's papers, keepsakes, a scrapbook if she had one, that might turn up a lead to the group I'm tryin to find."

He stood up. "I certainly can't allow that, Miss Quick."

"Yeah. I guess not." But I made no move to get up or leave. "When will Mrs. West be home?"

"I don't know." He sat down again. "Why repeat rumors to Myrna about Claudette associating with theater people? You'd only distress her."

"What've you got against theater people?"

"Nothing. We just have different . . . our worlds are poles apart, Miss Quick."

"Ya don't get murdered too often either, I bet."

"I beg your pardon?"

"Nothin. You mind if I wait for Mrs. West?"

"I was on my way out."

"That's okay. I don't need to be entertained."

"It's not that. Well, I can hardly leave you here alone, can I?"

"Ah, don't think a thing of it. I'll be fine right here. I'll read my book. See?" I held up my copy of *Valley of Decision*. "I never go anywhere without a book just in case somethin like this happens."

"You're being difficult, Miss Quick." He started talking to me like he was my father.

"I don't mean to be difficult, it's just that your brother-in-law is payin me to work on this case and that's what I'm tryin to do."

"I simply can't leave you in the house alone."

"Yer afraid I'll go snoopin, aren't ya?" I tried to make my eyes sparkle, but I wasn't any good at it.

"I thought no such thing."

This bozo was turning out to be a stiff. Then I remembered what Gladys had said about him. Boring.

"Still, Miss Quick, I—"

We heard the door open, then footsteps. "Cornell? Are you home?"

"In here, Myrna." To me he said, "I guess that solves the problem."

"Yeah, guess it does."

She came in with a twirl although her suit skirt didn't budge. "How do you like it?"

Cornell looked embarrassed. So did Myrna when she realized I was there.

"Oh, Miss Quick. I didn't know . . . I wasn't expecting . . ."

"I like it, Mrs. West."

"Excuse me?"

"Your suit. I like it." It was royal blue, the jacket boxy with its padded shoulders.

"Thank you." She'd pulled herself together. "Well, I don't want to interrupt your little chat."

"We were finished, Mrs. West. The captain helped as much as he could, but it's you I need now."

She exchanged a look with Walker that I couldn't pin down. "What can I do for you?"

I told her I needed to look through her daughter's mementoes. And her face fell.

"I'm not sure I can bear to do that."

"If you just lead me to them, I can do it myself."

Walker said, "That would be out of the question." When Porter wasn't around, he had no trouble taking the lead. He went to his half sister and put a protective arm around her.

"It's all right, Cornell. Perhaps you could go in the room with her."

I didn't like that idea at all. I had a feeling Walker would interfere somehow.

"Before we look at anything let me ask you somethin, Mrs. West."

"Yes?"

"You ever hear of a play called *Moonbeams and Mulberries?*"

"Awful title. But it seems familiar. Yes, I think Claudette went to see that play. She said she knew someone in it. Not well, of course. A cousin of a cousin of a friend or something like that."

I didn't want to get too excited. "A small actin company put it on, I think."

"Yes. They were down in Greenwich Village. Near her school. Oh, I begged her not to go to that place. I knew it meant mingling with those ragtag people all the time. Why couldn't she go to Bennington or Radcliffe? None of this would have ever happened if she hadn't insisted. She never would have met that horrible boy."

She dropped into a chair, exhausted. It was more than I'd heard her say in all the times I'd seen her.

She waved a hand in front of her face. "I'm sorry."

"Perfectly okay, Mrs. West."

"What was it you wanted to know?"

"The name of the actin group that put on that play, if you remember."

"How could I forget? HeartsinArts. All one word."

TWENTY-NINE

When I left the West apartment, I made my way over to Seventh Avenue, where I knew I'd find a phone booth with a directory. I didn't have high hopes that the acting company would be listed, but it was worth a try.

I stood in the booth and opened the phone directory to the *H*'s, ran my finger down the pages but there was nothing. The best thing for me to do was to get back downtown and start asking questions.

I hopped a subway. I laughed to myself at the way Myrna West viewed the Village. *Ragtag people,* she'd said. Did she think I lived in my office? Course not. She didn't think about where I lived at all. I didn't register with her as a person who had a life of my own. I was a worker performing a job. One who might solve the murder of her daughter. That's all she saw. And that was on the beam.

I was in my own backyard in ten minutes and knew exactly where to start, and probably finish, now that I had the name of the group. At the intersection of Seventh, Christopher, and West Fourth there was a triangle of a store named Village Cigars. It was sorta like Stork's but smaller cause of its odd shape. And there was no poker game going on in a back room that I was wise to. I knew Nick Jaffe, the owner, cause that's where I bought my cigs downtown.

He had one customer who left as I went in. Jaffe was behind the counter.

"Pack a Camels coming right up, little lady."

"Thanks, Nick." I didn't need a pack but I would tomorrow so why not buy one today? Grease the wheels, like they say. We made our transaction, and I slipped the pack into my handbag.

Nick was about sixty, and he wore a cap with a narrow brim. Most people thought it was cause he was Jewish, but I knew it was cause he was going bald. I wasn't a detective for nothing.

Jaffe had had a cig in his mouth since Hector was a pup, leaving one brown eye always closed, the smoke going up and past it.

"How you doing today?"

"Just fine."

"You got a fella yet?"

My mind went directly to Lake and hurried back again. "Not yet, Nick."

"Well, with the war it's a sum of a gun to find somebody kosher. Ya know what's going on?" As usual he motioned for me to come closer. Nick always had news, and sometimes it sounded straight and other times crazy. I leaned across the counter so he could reach my ear.

"They're taking the Jews and gassing them. Then burning them up."

"Oh, come on, Nick. Who is?" This was one of the crazy ones.

"Them Nazis . . . all over Europe."

"Who told ya that?"

"I ain't gonna reveal my sources . . . any more than you would. But it's on the level. I know it here." He thumped his heart with his fist, which started him hacking. But the cig never moved.

"If it's true, why isn't anybody puttin a stop to it?"

He shrugged. "Why? Why anything?"

I needed to cut this short, so I moved back and hit him with my question. "Nick, I need to know somethin, and I think yer probably the only one who can give me the skinny on this."

"Yeah?" He didn't light up like I thought he would. He looked sad, thinking about what he'd told me, I guessed. I wished people wouldn't tell him these stories.

"I'm lookin for an actin group, the name of HeartsinArts. Ya know where they meet?"

"Sure I know. Nice kids. Nice but they should get jobs. A few *faygelehs,* but some of the boys has gone in the army, like a lot of my customers." He shook his head in despair. "I'm glad they don't draft girls, Faye."

"Me, too. Where does this group put on their plays, Nick?"

"They're over on Perry Street near Hudson. I don't know the exact address, but that's where they are."

"Thanks. Ya just made my life a lot easier. Take care of yourself, okay."

As I started to leave Nick yelled after me, "Tell people, Faye."

"Tell people what?"

"What I told ya."

"About the gas and the burnin?"

"Yeah. Ya never know, it gets around somebody might do a mitz-vah."

"Okay, Nick. I will." I hated lying to him, but if I told that to anyone they'd think I was loose in the upper story. I gave him a wave and headed west down Christopher.

In five minutes I was where Perry met Hudson. Being it was such a nice day, a few people were sitting on stoops. I picked out a gal, maybe in her forties, who looked friendly.

"Excuse me."

"Yes?"

"I wonder if you'd be so kind as to respond to an inquiry?"

"Why are you talking like that?"

"Like what?"

" 'Be so kind?' 'Inquiry?' "

"What's wrong with that?"

"Everything. How about, *Could I ask you a question?*"

"I was just tryin to be polite." What a pain in the neck.

"Well, don't try so hard. Be natural. Take a deep breath."

"I'm not in the market for breathin lessons."

"In, out. Go on, do it."

"Lady, I don't mean to be rude, but I just wanna ask ya a question."

"I'm trying to get you to relax."

"I'm already relaxed. *Yer* makin me nervous."

"If you were relaxed, nobody could make you nervous. In, out." She demonstrated.

I was about to move on when she said, "So what do you want to ask me?"

"Have you ever heard of an actin group called HeartsinArts?"

She looked at me funny for a sec, then burst out laughing.

"Heard of it? Honey, you're looking at it."

"Excuse me?"

"It's my troupe. I run the group, such as it is." She stuck out her hand. "Dinah Dumont. Who are you?"

I took her hand. "Faye Quick."

"Nice to meet you, Faye Quick. That your stage name?"

"I'm not an actress."

"So what do you want from me?"

"I'm a private investigator, and the group came up in a case I'm workin on."

She burst out laughing again. I waited until she stopped falling all over herself. By that time the other stoop sitters were all staring at us.

"Come on, honey, you rehearsing a role?"

"No. I'm tellin ya the truth. I'm a PI."

"What's the name of the play?"

Forget my relaxation level. It didn't exist, and my frustration was rising. "Okay, ya don't wanna believe me, will ya answer some questions anyway?"

"Why not?" She stuck a cigarette in her mouth and lit up. "Want one?"

"I have my own, thanks." I wasn't about to take anything from this gal.

"Ask away."

"You ever heard of Claudette West?"

"Familiar, but I can't place the name."

"How about Warner Garfield?"

Her face went dark. "That one."

"What about him?"

"I kicked his behind right out of my class and my troupe."

"Why?"

"I don't wanna talk about it." Smoke trickled from her nostrils.

"You said you'd answer my questions."

"Did I know you'd be asking about that dirty dog?"

I got that excited feeling I always got when I knew I was close to something. "Why was he a dirty dog?"

"Look, honey, you don't want to know about this stuff. Trust me."

"Whether I want to or not, I need to know it."

Dinah Dumont stood up. "I have to teach a class now."

"Can I watch?"

"No." She turned to go up the steps.

"Wait."

"Why?"

"Warner Garfield's been murdered."

She turned back to me. "You're kidding me."

I shook my head.

"Well, good riddance to bad rubbish."

I couldn't help being a little shocked by that reaction. "You don't care that he was murdered?"

"After all the ones *he* murdered?"

I felt a thump in my gut. "Whaddaya mean?"

"I mean Warner Garfield was a murderer, plain and simple. I have to go."

As she started to turn away I grabbed her arm. "Please. Explain that to me. What're ya talkin about?"

"Garfield does abortions. Or did. Believe me, I didn't know that when he joined the troupe or he never would have gotten through the door."

"An actor doin abortions as a sideline?"

"And second rate at both. I eventually found out that he'd been kicked out of medical school a few years before he turned up here."

"But how did ya know he was doin abortions?"

"One of the girls told me . . . that's when I gave him the boot."

"How long ago was that?"

I watched her do a mental count.

"About four months ago. You really *are* a private eye, aren't you?"

"Yeah. I am."

"You trying to solve Garfield's murder?"

"No. I'm tryin to find out how Garfield was connected to Claudette West."

"She have an abortion?"

"No." But she probably was going to, I thought.

"Claudette West. I think I know who you mean. She was a friend of one of my actresses, Audrey Todd."

"Could I talk to her?"

"Now?"

"Yeah."

"She has a class with me in a few minutes. I'll send her out."

"Thanks. You've been very helpful."

"Anything that hurts Garfield is a good day's work, far as I'm concerned." She disappeared inside the building.

I didn't think it was a smart idea to remind her that Garfield couldn't be hurt anymore.

An abortionist. I wondered if I'd been standing in his operating room at any point. Had he killed a girl accidentally and then somebody paid him back? This abortionist news made me think his murder had nothing to do with Claudette. On the other hand, maybe she'd been planning to have an abortion and Garfield was the one who was gonna do it.

"Excuse me."

I looked up into the face of a dewy-eyed girl with blonde hair that turned up in a roll at the bottom.

"I'm Audrey Todd," she said.

I introduced myself.

"Miss Dumont said you wanted to talk to me."

"Yeah. Thanks. Does the name Claudette West mean anything to ya?"

Audrey looked stricken. "Yes."

"She was a friend of yours?"

"Yes."

"How did ya know her?"

"We were in a history class together at NYU."

"And you brought Claudette here?"

"I told her about HeartsinArts. She sat in on some rehearsals and came to some plays. But she knew her parents would kill her if . . ." She slapped a hand over her mouth.

"It's okay. Go on."

"Well, she wanted to act, but she knew her parents would have a fit if she did. So she just watched."

"And what about Warner Garfield?"

"He had a crush on Claudette. But she didn't like him. Actually, nobody did."

"Why not?"

"There was this creepiness about him. Then we found out what he did to make a living."

"Abortions?"

She looked down at her shoes. "Yes."

"Did Claudette know he did that?"

"Yes. We all did once Miss Dumont kicked him out."

"Do ya know if Claudette ever had any direct contact with Garfield after he got the shove?"

"No. Why would she?"

"I guess she wouldn't." Claudette obviously hadn't confided in Audrey that she was pregnant. "Thanks a lot, Audrey. You've been a big help."

"I hope so. Did Warner kill Claudette?"

"I don't know. Maybe."

I expected Audrey to say goodbye, but instead she said, "Somebody should pay for her murder." She sounded like she wouldn't mind doing it herself.

"I'll do my best," I said. "Thanks again."

She nodded and ran back up the steps.

Walking away from the HeartsinArts building toward my street, I thought again that maybe Garfield did kill her. Motive: Passion? Rejection? But if he did, who killed him and why? Maybe the two murders, like I'd thought, *weren't* connected. Claudette may have set up an abortion with Garfield, but somebody killed her before he could do it. Probably the father of her unborn child.

Did Garfield know who the father was? Or the murderer? I didn't think it would be beneath Garfield to blackmail someone. That someone probably killed him. And knocked me over the head as a warning. Whoever clocked me would have no problem putting my lights out permanently. Not a comfy thought.

THIRTY

I hotfooted it home. The phone was ringing as I walked into my place. It was Birdie.

"Where ya been?"

"Workin."

"I got a whole lotta calls for ya."

"Name em."

She did, and I jotted down two from other clients. Then she said, "And three from Detective Lake. He said it was real important."

My heart thwacked against my chest.

"He's not at his precinct, so here's the number ya can reach him at."

I hung up in a hurry, but then I felt nervous about making the call to Lake. I knew I was being a dodo about this cause probably all he wanted was to give me some info about the case. I dialed the number.

"Joe's Chili Parlor," a woman's voice said.

I told her the number I wanted, and she said I had it right. "Is Detective Lake there?"

"Yup. Hey, Johnny." The phone banged in my ear as she put it down. It felt like forever until he picked it up.

"Hello."

"It's Faye."

"Faye. Thanks for getting back to me."

"Yeah, sure."

"How are you?"

"I'm fine. You?"

"Fine."

This didn't seem like a business call to me. Neither of us said anything for a few secs, then he said, "I have some information for you."

"Good."

"We found the name of the acting company."

Should I or shouldn't I? I had to. "I got it."

"Oh." He sounded down in the mouth.

"We also found out that Warner Garfield did some nasty stuff on the side."

Now what? Do I tell him I know this? I didn't want to sound too smart for my own good. I decided to play it out. "What kinda stuff?"

"He . . . he helped out ladies in trouble."

Was I supposed to act like I didn't know what that meant? Make him think I was a birdbrain. I couldn't. If that was the kinda girl he wanted then he wasn't the guy for me.

"I heard that," I said.

Silence.

"Sounds like you've been doing all right without my help," he said.

Oh, jeez. I couldn't make out the sound in his voice. Was he upset or proud of me? Hell's bells. I had to be who I was and not worry about him every minute, no matter how the ladies magazines said I should act with a man.

"I had some luck." This was true. "But what I don't know is his connection to Claudette West."

"I have that." His voice sounded sunnier.

"Can ya tell me?"

"Garfield had a little book with pages of dates and initials. The initials C.W. were there in early January, but they'd been crossed out. They appeared again the day after Claudette was murdered. Not crossed out. She probably got cold feet the first time. I know this doesn't prove anything, but I think on circumstantial grounds we can assume that she'd made arrangements to . . . see him. To have him take care of things."

That made me smile. Lake was being so careful not to offend me in any way. I guessed I shoulda appreciated it. But he'd have to know the true me sometime if we were gonna . . . gonna what?

"That's about it," he said.

."Well, that's a lot."

"Most of it you already knew." Down again.

"Not the most important thing . . . the connection between the two."

"That's true." Up.

"Do you have any idea who knocked Garfield off?" I asked.

"Not yet. Could've been any number of people. But we'll find out."

I knew this wasn't necessarily true. "Yeah. I bet ya will. I'm wonderin if the same person who killed Claudette killed Garfield."

"What would be the motive?"

"Another thing I gotta pin down."

"I think . . . ," he said. "I think we should meet and talk this over, compare notes."

"Okay." My pulse was racing.

"How about tonight? Dinner?"

"Let me check my calendar." Now that was just plain stupid. As if I wouldn't know what I was doing that night. Those magazines, which I read only at the beauty parlor, had infected my brain. I was never gonna read them again.

"Johnny? Tonight would be fine."

"Good."

"What time?"

"How's seven for you?"

"Fine. Where?"

"Where do you live, Faye?"

Did he want to pick me up at my place? For some reason that made me very nervous. You'd think I was a slob or something when I was really very neat.

I told him where I lived.

"Okay. I'll pick you up at quarter to seven. You think about where you'd like to go. See you later."

"Bye." But he'd already hung up.

The thought of him coming here gave me the jimjams. I looked around my living room. There was the empty space waiting for my piano. How could I explain that unless I told him the truth? So, I'd tell him the truth. All he could do is laugh. But right away I didn't think Johnny Lake would laugh at me cause I wanted to play and sing. It wasn't like I thought I was gonna perform in clubs and become a star. Lots of regular people had pianos.

So why was I so nervy? It'd been a long time since I'd had a real date, and I wanted this guy to like me. But if he didn't like me already, why'd he ask me out to dinner? He coulda talked about the case on the phone or asked to meet me for a cup of coffee. Dinner was different. Dinner was the real thing. Enough.

I sat on my sofa with a yellow pad and a fountain pen. I needed to figure out who knew both Claudette and Garfield and also who knew she was gonna have an abortion.

Claudette met Garfield at HeartsinArts. That was probably during the first time she broke up with Richard. When she split with him again she went back to the acting group and Garfield was still there. Then Dinah Dumont chucked him out. And that woulda been a plus for Claudette to learn what else he did besides act badly, cause by then she knew she was gonna need him. Maybe one of the actors was the baby's father and he set up the appointment with Garfield. That way, Garfield woulda known who the father was, known he probably killed Claudette, and he coulda been blackmailing him. But why would the father need to kill her if Claudette was gonna get rid of the baby?

It didn't add up. How about the other way around? The father hired Garfield to knock off Claudette cause he didn't know she was planning an abortion and Garfield wasn't about to tell him. But was Garfield a killer? Performing abortions wasn't the same as killing an adult human being in cold blood. At least, I didn't think so.

If that theory was gonna fill the bill, the father would have to have some loot. I didn't know any actors with extra greenbacks to throw around. And paying somebody to rub out your pregnant girlfriend wouldna come on the cheap. The idea of an actor being the dad was starting to look flimsy.

Why did Claudette say Garfield was trying to date her? Even if he was, she made him sound like a lounge lizard trying to wear her down. According to Cotten and June she thought of him as a pest. If he was gonna perform an abortion on her, why mention him at all? When she'd told Cotten she'd dated him, she didn't know she'd be needing his services down the line. Maybe she was just trying to make Cotten jealous.

The important thing was that Claudette had scheduled an abortion twice and her second appointment was the day after she was killed. Then months after Claudette's murder somebody knocked off Garfield. Once again I tumbled to the fact that there might not be any connection between these two murders. But it seemed a lead-pipe cinch there was.

The father of Claudette's unborn child was the number-one suspect. And come to think of it, Anne's vision of a man forcing Claudette to do something against her will coulda been having the abortion. Maybe she'd decided against it a second time . . . three months was risky enough, and papa settled on wiping out everything the night before. Two for one.

It felt like I was on to something. The father had set up a meeting in the Village then crowned her on Bleecker Street because she refused to go through with the abortion.

Why the Village? Because he lived there. The three I knew about who were connected to Claudette even slightly were Gregory Flynn, Marlene Hayworth's paramour; Jim Duryea, my upstairs neighbor; and Brian Wayne, her professor. Flynn had an opportunity when he went out for cigs, but why would he have gotten Claudette down to the Village when he knew he was gonna be with Marlene Hayworth? More than that, I really didn't think he'd been involved with Claudette.

Brian Wayne was another story, and he still wasn't off my list. Neither was Jim Duryea. I didn't think Duryea could've been the father, but he might've murdered her for rejecting him. Nah. Besides, why would he kill Garfield? But I couldn't know for sure so he stayed on my list.

Brian Wayne was my first choice as father and killer. I had to find out if he knew Garfield. How? I needed to check his alibi for the time of Garfield's murder. Before I did that I needed to meet with Anne to give her the undershirt I'd taken from Garfield's apartment.

When Anne opened her door she said, "Who's Johnny Lake?"

"Ah, no. Is it written on my forehead?"

"In green."

I thought back to her explanation of colors' meanings. "So it's sexual then?"

"Probably. So who's Johnny Lake?"

"Can I come in?"

"Sorry."

Today Anne was wearing a qipao, a mandarin dress made of blue silk with a brocade of flowers. She'd gotten it before the war when she'd been in China. Anne had done a lot of traveling. I hoped I could do that some day.

"Tea?"

"No. Nothin, thanks." Whenever I could avoid that green tea, I did.

We sat down in the living room.

"Johnny Lake?"

"Just a cop on a case."

"But you like him, don't you?"

"I'm havin dinner with him tonight."

"Are you sure?"

"What's that mean?"

"I don't know. I feel something blocking the date."

"Is he married?"

"No."

"Then why—"

"I'm not telling you anything else about your date. That would ruin all the fun."

"But you don't even think I'll be havin the date. That's not fair."

"What's fair have to do with it? So you have something for me?" she asked.

I reached in my pocketbook and pulled out the rolled-up bloody undershirt and handed it to her.

She shook it open. "Oh, nice. Is this what I think it is?"

"Far as I know."

"You want me to tell you what type of person this belongs to or if there's a trauma connected with it?"

"Both would be nice."

"Well you know I can't do one from column A, one from column B."

"Why ask then?"

"My pitiful attempt at a joke."

"Stick to bein psychic."

She ran her hands over the shirt and soon she closed her eyes.

"It belongs to a violent man. He has blood on his hands."

And his shirt, I thought. This could be Garfield, but I didn't think so.

"I see an *M*."

"Any other letter?"

"No. Books. Lots of books. And a gun."

I knew there weren't any books in Garfield's place. I'd have to ask Johnny if he'd found a gun.

"The *M* is very strong. Flashing red."

"What else?"

"Oh, no," she said. "The damn battle scenes." Her eyes opened. "I'm sorry, Faye. I think I'm going to have to give up this part of my gift. These war scenes are ruining everything."

"Maybe when the war is over it'll stop." I tried not to show my disappointment.

"I hope so . . . although these were a little different."

"How different?"

"I'm not sure I can explain, except to say these felt connected."

"Connected?"

"To the shirt."

"In what way?"

"That I don't know."

"You mean other times when this happens to ya, there's no link, no hook?"

"Yes. The pictures of war are separate. Let's just say it felt different this time. But that may not mean anything."

I wasn't so sure, even though I couldn't put it together.

"Tell me whose shirt this is?" Anne asked.

"I don't know. I found it in a guy's apartment tucked in between some sofa cushions."

She gave me a look.

"No. Nothin like that. There was a dead guy in the bathroom. I don't know if it's his shirt or somebody else's."

"I'm sorry I couldn't help, Faye."

"But ya did. At least now I have an initial."

"That *M* could stand for anything."

"But maybe it's the initial of the killer."

"Could be. There's something else it could stand for though."

"What's that?"

"Murderer," she said.

THIRTY-ONE

I went from Anne's to Blondell's to have a cup of joe, but when I got there the place was closed up like a clam. And then I saw the sign on the door: CLOSED DUE TO A DEATH IN THE FAMILY.

My stomach flip-flopped. I think I knew right away, but I couldn't let myself take it in. I just kept staring at the words like they were gonna change if I eyeballed them long enough. But they didn't. They stayed the same in big black letters.

I don't know how long I stood there like that before a tap on my shoulder made me jump.

"Sorry," he said. "Didn't mean to scare you."

It was Mickey, who owned the stationery store down the block.

"That's okay." He'd know who'd died, but I couldn't ask.

"You okay, Faye? Ya look pretty pale."

"I'm all right."

"Ya didn't know, huh?"

I shook my head. I was waiting for his words to fall on me like bricks.

"Yeah. They heard yesterday."

Heard. So it had to be Fred. I couldn't say his name out loud. It was like I'd keep him alive as long as my lips stayed buttoned.

"Why don'tcha come on down to my store for a minute?"

Like a robot I matched my steps with his, ordering my feet to move. The door was open, but the place was empty. From behind the counter Mickey brought out a folding chair and set it up for me. I sat.

"Skip took it pretty hard."

"Why wouldn't he?"

"Yeah, why wouldn't he?" Mickey said. "He loved that kid like he was his son . . . more than a brother."

"How's Joanne holdin up?"

"I ain't seen her, but I guess she's pretty broken up."

"Yeah. Why wouldn't she be?"

"Yeah."

"No mistake, huh? No missin in action or anythin like that?"

"No."

"It's an ordinary name, maybe . . ."

"Faye. It was him."

"Yeah."

I stood up. "Guess I'd better be goin."

"You sure?"

"Yeah."

"Thanks, Mickey."

"It's okay."

"See ya."

"Yeah."

I left the store and started walking east. I had no idea where I was going, I just knew I needed to walk. Until I hit Washington Square Park, and then I knew I had to sit and landed on a bench facing the fountain. But I coulda still been staring at the shelves in Mickey's store for all I saw. Neither one of us, I realized, had said Fred's name. But that wasn't gonna bring him back to life.

"Fred." I kept my voice down. Saying his name was the least he deserved. I felt like a louse for waiting so long.

I wondered how Skip was, and if he'd ever be the same. Joanne, too. I'd lost my brother, but I was only a baby. And Don McCallister, the guy I'd been writing to and barely knew, had been killed. Claudette was the first dead person I'd ever seen. Firsthand, I knew beans about death. And I didn't know diddly-squat about losing someone ya loved.

What if something happened to Woody? I guessed he was the only person I loved besides Anne. Maybe my pop. But Woody was different. I chose him, not in a romantic way, but I loved him like I mighta loved my brother. And if Woody got killed over there? Just having the thought made me feel like bawling. If I hung on to it, I'd start.

I speedily switched over to the A agency he'd left in my hands. And the case I'd put on the front burner.

What was that letter *M* Anne saw? She said it was flashing, so it must've been important. I was convinced it was an initial, but the only *M* people connected with the case, who I could think of, were Marlene and Myrna. I couldn't see either one of them killing Claudette. Marlene had no motive, and Myrna was her mother.

Not that mothers never killed their kids. It was rare, but it happened. Still, Myrna West was not a killer. Especially of her daughter. But maybe Myrna knew something she wasn't telling. Maybe she didn't even know she knew it.

Porter tried to keep her under lock and key, and even though I'd seen her show a bit of spunk, I wasn't sure how often that would happen. I was sure Porter didn't fill her in on everything that I told him. Maybe I could jar something loose if I gave her a complete report. But how was I gonna get to her?

The West apartment was out. If Porter wasn't there, her brother might be. Or the maid might let something slip later. I had to get Myrna out of the house. But would she meet me somewhere or would she be too afraid?

Gladys Wright! Myrna's stepsister. True, these two didn't seem to have much use for each other, but maybe in this case the relationship could be useful.

I got up and started walking toward the phone booth on Thompson, flipping through the pages of my notebook until I found the number. Gladys answered.

"He's not here," she said after I gave my name.

"I'm not interested in talkin to Leon. I wanna talk to you."

"About?"

"Myrna."

"Yuck."

"Gladys, I need to talk to her, and I need to talk to her alone. I figured if you called her and asked her to meet ya, she would."

"Then you think wrong. Myrna doesn't want anything to do with me."

"If ya told her it had somethin to do with Claudette, she'd see ya."

"Hey, what is this?"

"A trick."

"You want me to trick my stepsister into seeing you?"

"Right. Will ya do it?"

"It's sort of amusing. All right, sure."

"Tell her to meet you in the park by the Garibaldi statue in an hour and not to tell anybody where she's goin. I'm in a phone booth, so ya can call me back here."

I gave her the number, pushed down the button on the cradle, but held on to the receiver and made like I was still talking so nobody would try to get the booth. About five minutes later Gladys called me back.

"She'll be there. You could've knocked me over with a feather. She was even nice to me. But when you turn up, I guess she'll hate me again."

"I'll try to smooth things over."

"Ah, who cares?"

She did, I thought.

"Thanks, Gladys. I won't forget this."

"And that means?"

"It means if you're ever in trouble, let me know."

"Oh, goody." She hung up.

When I stepped out of the booth, I remembered I hadn't eaten and was hungry. Since I was near MacDougal Street, I thought I'd go to the Reggio. I had a little less than an hour for a cap and a bite and to get back to the park in time to ambush Myrna.

The place was pretty empty. Maria wasn't on cause she worked nights. None of the regulars were there at this hour either. Along with my cap I ordered a plate of fruit and cheese.

I had a hard time swallowing cause I couldn't stop thinking about Fred. He was only nineteen. And his wife, Joanne, about to have a baby. Nineteen years old. Sure he wanted to serve his country. They all did. But why did he have to die?

I drained my cup but left most of my food. After paying the tab I still had twenty minutes left till I met Myrna. I went back to the park and sat in a place where she wouldn't see me, but I'd spot her standing by the statue.

Behind me and across the street was the building where Brian Wayne taught and had his trysts with young girls. A terrible realization hit me. I *wanted* Wayne to be the killer. It didn't matter that he had an alibi. They can always be gotten around. No question . . . I hated this Casanova. But I couldn't let that cloud my thinking. Stick with the facts, Quick, with the evidence, not by the outcome you think would be hunky-dory.

About five minutes to the hour Myrna West appeared at the right side of Garibaldi. Still not sure how I was gonna handle this, I got up and walked toward her. When I was almost there, she turned and saw me.

"Miss Quick?"

"Hello, Mrs. West."

"I'm meeting my sister. I'm surprised to see you. . . ."

She got it then. Her expression was less angry than sad.

"I see," she said. "I'm *not* meeting my sister."

"No. Yer meetin me."

"Why this subterfuge? It's very annoying."

"I'm sorry. Let me ask ya this: If I'd called and asked ya to meet me, would ya have done it?"

She looked down and fiddled with her brown handbag. "Porter has told me I'm not to talk to you alone."

"That's why the sham, Mrs. West."

"You're not married. You don't understand."

"I'm not married, but I *do* understand. I don't think I could have a marriage that handcuffed me that way, but I accept your marriage is different from what I'd want."

"Then why aren't you respecting it?"

"I can't. I'm on this case for ya, and what I might do in normal so-cial circumstances just doesn't apply. Ya see what I mean?"

She pouted like a little girl but finally nodded.

"Will ya talk to me?"

"I might as well. I'm here now. But I'll get my head handed to me if Porter ever finds out."

"There's no way he's gonna find out unless you tell him."

She looked around like she was a hooligan on the lam. "I guess we shouldn't stay here . . . out in the open. But I don't know this area. You decide on some place discreet. Is that possible down here?"

I took her back to the Reggio, where she ordered an espresso and I had my usual.

"This seems pleasant enough," she said. "It reminds me of cafés in Italy. Have you ever been abroad, Miss Quick?"

"No, I haven't. Please call me Faye."

"Well, now is no time to go, of course. Perhaps when the war is over. What did you want to talk about?"

She'd blindsided me, and I didn't know what to say for a few secs. Then I hit the ground running.

"I'd like to tell ya everythin I know so far about the case, Claudette, everythin. And then I'd like to see if anythin new rings a bell. Do ya understand?"

"Yes, I suppose."

"So as I'm tellin ya this stuff, I want ya to interrupt me at any time yer reminded or hear of somethin we haven't talked about before."

"All right." Her little finger stuck straight out as she lifted her espresso.

I started to talk like I was telling a story, everything in order. She said nothing. But I kept going. And then she interrupted me.

"Warner Garfield?"

"Ya've heard his name?"

"You might as well know, Miss Quick, I always knew that Alec Rockefeller was a fraud."

"How?"

"Claudette told her uncle, and he told me."

"You mean Captain Walker?"

"Yes."

"What exactly did he tell ya?"

"Cornell told me 'Alec' was a fabrication, gave me the boy's real name, and said Claudette pretended to date him when she was seeing her real boyfriend, Warner Garfield."

My head was reeling. "And did he tell ya why Claudette was doin that?"

"He said Warner Garfield was an actor and she knew we wouldn't approve of him."

"And was Captain Walker right?"

"An actor wouldn't have been my first choice for my daughter."

"What did Mr. West say about this?"

"Porter didn't know. Cornell and I decided it would be best if we didn't tell him. We agreed she'd probably get over this fellow, but if Porter knew he'd make a terrible fuss and perhaps force Claudette's hand."

"Meaning what?"

"She was so rebellious." A slight smile snuck onto her face. "When Porter carried on about Richard, I think it made Claudette stay with him longer than she would have, and Cornell and I thought the same thing could happen with this Garfield boy if Porter knew about him."

I recalled that Captain Walker had denied knowing anything about Warner Garfield. Under the circumstances, what else could he do?

"I can see yer reasonin. So ya didn't tell Claudette ya knew either."

"No."

"And your brother didn't tell her he'd told you?"

"No, of course not. He wanted to remain her confidant."

"Yeah, sure."

"Was Mr. Garfield the father of Claudette's child?" Myrna asked.

"I don't know. But I doubt it. You see, Warner Garfield was—"

"Well, well, look who we have here," said a voice.

And when I looked up I saw that it was Captain Cornell Walker.

ornell. What are you doing here?" Myrna asked.

"I might ask you the same."

"But yer not gonna, right?" I said.

He pulled out a chair. "May I join you?"

I wanted to say no, but I thought that was Myrna's place. It was a stretch to think this was an accidental run-in.

"As you can see," Myrna said, "I'm having coffee with Miss Quick."

He sat. "Yes, I can see that."

"Are you following me, Cornell?"

"Don't be foolish. I was walking by, and I saw you inside."

"But what are you doing down *here*?"

For these people, as I'd heard over and over, being in the Village was as likely as being on the moon.

"I often come to Greenwich Village, Myrna. I enjoy the atmosphere."

Myrna turned to me. "Cornell plans to be a painter when the war is over."

"Is that so?" I said.

"I dabble."

"That's not true. He's very good."

He shrugged, trying to take the shine off her words.

A waitress came and took Cornell's order.

"So why'd ya follow her, Captain?"

"I just said I didn't."

"Yeah, I know what ya said."

"Miss Quick, if my brother says—"

"Mrs. West, I'm a detective, and it's my job to detect. That's what I'm doin."

"It's all right, Myrna. Actually, the detective is right. I did follow you."

"Why?" She looked shocked by his giving away the show like that.

"Because I promised Porter I would. He's worried about you."

"Worried? I can't imagine why."

Walker reached out a hand to cover Myrna's. He patted it gently.

"He knows, dear, as I do, how frail you are."

What the deuce was up? "I thought you didn't like how Mr. West treated his wife. And she looks fit as a fiddle to me."

"I'm referring to her soul, Miss Quick."

He may as well have shouted I was a moron when it came to understanding people's sensitivities.

"So you're frail inside, Mrs. West?"

"I don't know what he's talking about. If you mean do I mourn my daughter's death? Then yes, that's true. This isn't something you can understand, Cornell. You don't have children."

"But I *do* understand," he said.

"Then why are you and Porter treating me like I'm a mental case? The next thing I know you'll be wanting me to see a psychiatrist."

"Hardly. You know what Porter thinks of them. But I must say I find it odd that you'd meet with Miss Quick by yourself. Shouldn't Porter be consulted when the case is involved?"

I said, "Sometimes a one-on-one works better. But since you're here, maybe ya can help us."

The waitress put an espresso in front of the captain.

"How can I help?" He took a sip of his coffee.

"Ya can tell us exactly what Claudette told ya about Warner Garfield."

He gave Myrna a swift, angry glance.

"Don't worry, I'm not gonna drop a dime on ya to Mr. West."

"I don't have much to tell. Claudette thought she was in love with Warner Garfield. I decided it was best not to tell Porter since the fellow was an actor. I knew Myrna wouldn't prevent Claudette from seeing him."

"Did ya ever meet Garfield?"

"No."

"Why not?"

"Claudette didn't want me to for some reason. I assumed she thought I'd find him wanting and never pushed her for an introduction. I never thought it would go so far."

"So far. Whaddaya mean?"

"Claudette was pregnant, so obviously it must've been Mr. Garfield's child, wouldn't you think?"

"Did you know she was pregnant before she died?"

He hesitated a moment. "Claudette told me everything."

"And you didn't tell me, Cornell?"

"I'm sorry, Myrna. I couldn't. I knew it would destroy you."

"Oh, don't be so dramatic. Destroy me."

"Well, what would you have done if you'd known?"

Without a moment's thought she said, "I would've sent her abroad to have the child and then given it up for adoption."

Myrna West was far from frail, it seemed to me.

"You wouldn't have wanted her to have an abortion?" Cornell whispered the last word.

"Of course not."

"Your friends must know someone reliable," he said.

"Certain people do. But I don't happen to believe in that."

"Did Claudette?" I asked him.

"Believe in abortion? I don't know."

"So what was she plannin on doin?"

He lit another cigarette although he still had one burning in the ashtray.

"She didn't know what she was going to do."

"Did she wanna have it?"

"No. I mean, she did, but she didn't know how to tell Myrna and Porter."

"Ya know, Captain, earlier ya said 'obviously it musta been Mr. Garfield's child.' Do ya remember sayin that?"

"Yes."

"Didn't ya know? Didn't Claudette tell ya who the father was?"

"No, she didn't."

"Didn't you ask?" Myrna said.

"I never questioned Claudette. She told me what she wanted me to know."

"And she didn't want ya to know who the father was?"

"Apparently not."

"Didn't ya wonder why?"

"I think she was afraid I might do something."

"Somethin like what?"

"Fly off the handle at her foolishness, perhaps."

"What exactly does that mean? Do somethin violent?" I asked.

"I don't know. Maybe she thought I'd confront the father. Garfield."

"Weren't you curious, Captain?"

"Of course I was. I've already said that. But what could I do? It was obvious that she didn't want me to know. Do you think he did it?"

"Who?"

"Whoever the father was."

"Might be," I said. "Wouldn't be the first time a pregnant mother was murdered by a boyfriend who didn't wanna play proud papa. Think of *An American Tragedy.*"

"That's a novel."

"So what? Novels say a lot a true things."

"Now you're a philosopher, Miss Quick?" Walker said.

"I'm a reader. But let's not get sidetracked here. Ya brought up a good point, Captain. If we could find out who the father was of Claudette's baby, we'd probably find out who killed her."

Myrna said, "Well, Cornell's right. It must be this Garfield man."

"We'll never know."

"Why not?" she asked.

"Because he's dead."

Myrna's gloved hand flew to her mouth.

Walker said, "How do you know?"

"I found the body. But let's not get into that."

"You make it sound like he was murdered, Miss Quick," Myrna said.

"He was."

"Wait a minute." Walker said. "This doesn't make sense. Somebody kills Claudette months ago and now kills the father of the baby?"

"Then Mr. Garfield couldn't have killed Claudette, could he, Miss Quick?"

"He *could* have, Mrs. West. But I don't think he did." I weighed telling them more about Garfield and Claudette's scheduled appointment with him the day after she was murdered. But I had a feeling the less I told, the better it would be. For what, I wasn't sure.

"Who killed Garfield?" Walker asked.

"Don't know yet. It just happened."

"It had to be someone who knew he and Claudette were connected, don't you think? Someone who knew he was the father of her child?"

"Anyone come to mind?"

"I think it takes us right back to Richard Cotten," he said.

"Does it? Ya think Claudette told him she was pregnant by another man when she wouldn't sleep with him?"

"How do you know she wouldn't . . . sleep with him?" Myrna asked.

"He said so. And he was pretty upset about her bein pregnant, which I told him. He didn't know before that."

"And you believe him?"

"Why shouldn't I believe him? He and Claudette split several weeks before she was murdered. It was a mutual agreement."

"That's not what she told me," Walker said.

"No? What did she tell you?"

He waved his hand at the waitress. "Anybody want another?"

We both said yes.

Then he made a circling gesture with his hand ordering our coffees and settled into his chair like he was about to tell us a long story.

"Claudette told me that she'd tried and tried to get Richard out of her life, especially when she'd fallen in love with Warner. But he wouldn't let her go."

"What's that mean, *wouldn't*? How could he stop her?"

"He threatened her. He said if she tried to leave, he'd kill her because he couldn't live without her."

"Wait a minute. How come ya didn't tell the police that at the time of the murder?" I asked.

"For one thing I wasn't here. I was in South Carolina. Parris Island."

"But you came home for the funeral, Cornell."

"That's true."

"So why didn't ya tell the cops then?"

"I did."

"But you never told us," Myrna said. Her voice had gone up a register.

"I didn't want you to know then how much I knew. I thought the police would handle it. It's not my fault they could never get anything on that boy."

I made a mental note to check with Marty as to how much Walker told the cops.

Myrna turned to me. "Does anyone know why Mr. Garfield would've been murdered?"

"The investigation's just beginnin, Mrs. West."

"It has to be Richard," she said.

"The cops'll shake him down for an alibi on Garfield's murder."

"Oh, he'll have one. He's very smooth," Walker said. "So you found the body. Again. In a movie you'd be the first suspect." He smiled, making his perfect looks more so.

"Yeah. I would be. But this isn't a movie. And anyway, I've got no motive."

"Technicality," Walker said, laughing at his half-baked joke.

"How about you, Captain? Ya have an alibi for Garfield's murder?"

He stared at me.

"Let's see. I remember the first time I met ya, you said ya loved your niece. And you've just told us how she confided in you. It wouldn't be outta left field to think you'd wanna avenge yer niece's murder."

"Loving someone doesn't mean you'd kill for them, Miss Quick."

"Sometimes it does."

"Well, not this time."

"Can't take a joke, Captain?"

"I don't think this is a laughing matter."

"Really? *You* just joked about it . . . sayin I might be a suspect in a movie. What's good for the goose is good for the gander, like they say."

He gave me a glorious smile. "You're right. You have me there."

"By the way, Captain, did Claudette ever give ya a set of cuff links?"

"Cuff links?"

"Cornell, she did. This past Christmas."

"Oh, that's right. She said they were for me when the war was over. Beautiful things, too."

"They were," Myrna said. "Jade."

After finishing his second espresso, Cornell said, "Well, Myrna, I think it's time to go."

She looked at him like he was loony. "I didn't come with you, Cornell."

"I know, dear. But you're going to leave with me. It's for the best."

It was pure and simple blackmail. "Go ahead, Mrs. West, I think we're finished here. Thank you for seein me."

Myrna gave a slight nod and stood up.

"Goodbye, Miss Quick," Walker said.

As they got to the door Myrna turned her head and gave me such a down-in-the-dumps look I almost went after her and hauled her back. But I knew there'd be no point. Then they were gone.

I sat sipping my cap and smoking a cig. So Walker believes Garfield was the father of Claudette's baby. Not cause she told him but cause he thinks he's put the puzzle together. And that Richard's the killer. Even though Richard had no idea Claudette was sleeping with someone until after she died.

And I felt about Richard as I always had . . . no passion.

Why would Claudette tell her uncle that she was in love with Warner Garfield? He was an actor, and no one, including Walker, would approve of him. But she told others, like Richard and June, that she thought Garfield was a creep who wouldn't leave her alone. And why use Alec/Leon to cover seeing Garfield when she was probably using Garfield to cover her real lover?

So who was her sweetheart? Immediately I was back at Brian Wayne. He'd told me his affair with Claudette ended a year before she died. That didn't make it true. He could've been seeing her right up to the end. Or maybe he cut her off when she told him she was pregnant. But how did he hook up to Warner Garfield?

Wayne could've been afraid that Claudette might expose him so he'd arranged for an abortion. Either he knew of Garfield from an unknown source or Claudette told Wayne herself. So what'd that prove?

But if Wayne never laid eyes on Garfield why would he kill him? Maybe he was afraid Claudette had given Garfield his name and he wanted to clear the slate. That was possible.

Did he have an alibi for Garfield's murder? I'd meant to find this out earlier, and now I really needed to have another talk with Dr. Wayne. The sooner the better.

THIRTY-THREE

*B*rian Wayne and I sat in a booth at Pete's Tavern on Eighteenth Street. It was a neighborhood Italian restaurant that was cheap but had pretty good food. The story went that O. Henry wrote "The Gift of the Magi" there. Who knew if it was true or not? We each had a glass of Pete's famous Original Ale in front of us. It was the middle of the day, and I wasn't about to order a manhattan.

Wayne looked like hell. He had deep bags under his eyes, and the crags in his face were like cracks in a dried-up field.

"Ya look like ya haven't been sleepin much, Brian."

When he glanced at me, I saw that his eyes were small and red-rimmed. I thought of a rat.

"I've been under a lot of pressure."

"Yeah? What kind?"

"Work."

"How about yer girlfriend?"

"What girlfriend?"

"Whoever's the current one."

Our food arrived. Eggplant parm for me, and he had spaghetti with meatballs.

"I don't have a current girlfriend. I'm trying to stop all that. I know it's going to get me in more trouble. I've already lost my wife and children."

"But not your job."

"No."

"Why is that, Brian?"

"No one has gone to the dean, I suppose."

"And if they had, Dean O'Hara would sweep it under the rug, wouldn't he?"

He took a slug of his ale. "I don't know what you mean."

"Never mind." I had a bite of my eggplant. The mozzarella was hot. I remembered my aunt Dolly saying, Always be careful cause there's nothing hotter than hot cheese. I had often questioned this wisdom, but it had finally proved true. I'd burned the tip of my tongue. I put my forkful back on the plate and took a swig of ale instead.

"What's wrong with you?" Wayne asked. "You have tears in your eyes."

I waved a hand in front of my mouth. "Hot."

"Oh."

Oh? Thanks a lot, Mr. Sympathy.

"Why did you want to see me again?"

"New developments."

"What kind?"

"Another murder."

"Who?"

I forked a new bit of eggplant, touched it with the tip of my finger, then popped it into my mouth. Delicious. Eggplant was a favorite of mine.

"Don't interrupt savoring your ambrosia, but when you have time could you tell me who was killed?"

I bet dollars to doughnuts he'd think I didn't know what ambrosia was. "The food of the gods, thought to confer immortality."

"What are you talking about?"

"Ambrosia."

"Miss Quick, who was murdered?"

I told him about Warner Garfield.

"What's that got to do with me?"

"That's why I'm here, Brian. I'd like to know if it has anythin to do with you."

"I never heard of Warner Garfield."

"You admitted to havin an affair with Claudette."

"Over a year ago."

"Yeah, that's what ya said. But now I'm wonderin if maybe ya picked up where ya left off, ya know what I mean?"

"I do, and I didn't."

"Ya said Claudette confided in you."

"Yes."

"She tell ya she was gonna have an abortion?"

"I told you before I had no idea that Claudette was pregnant. So how would I know she was going to have an abortion?"

"I know exactly what ya told me before, but this is now. I'm givin ya a chance to set the record straight."

He mashed out his cigarette. "I knew Claudette, I had an affair with her more than a year ago, I didn't know she was pregnant or that she was going to have an abortion, and I've never heard the name Warner Garfield until today. That's the straight record."

"Where were ya night before last?"

"I was with my wife, begging her to take me back." His humiliation and sense of shame showed.

"And is she gonna?"

"No."

Good for her. No wonder he looked the way he did. "I can easily find out if that's true or not."

"Help yourself."

"You were there the whole night?"

"No. I left our . . . her house about ten o'clock and went to the San Remo to get drunk."

"Did ya?"

"Get drunk? Yes."

"Ya remember what ya did when ya got drunk?"

"I didn't black out, Miss Quick."

"Okay, so ya went to the San Remo. Did ya meet anybody there?"

"I went there so I *wouldn't* meet anybody. San Remo is a working-class bar."

"Did any of the smelly workin class speak to ya?"

"No. And I'm not implying that—"

"Can it. Would anyone remember that you were there?"

"I don't know. The bartender might."

"What was his name?"

"Vic, I think. Or maybe Vinnie."

I jotted this down in my notebook.

"I wouldn't advise you to go in there, Miss Quick."

"Why not?"

"It's a little . . . well . . . rough around the edges. Not a place for a girl."

"Thanks for the tip. So after gettin plastered at the San Remo, where did ya go?"

"I went back to my room." He chewed at the inside of his cheek.

"Which is where?"

"Across the street from the San Remo on MacDougal. I rented a little place. Pretty dingy, if you want the truth."

"I always want the truth. Anybody see ya there?" I worked on my eggplant while noticing that Brian had taken only one bite of his spaghetti. "Somethin wrong with your food?"

"I'm not hungry."

It looked pretty good to me. Especially the meatballs.

"You want it?"

"What?"

"My food."

"Brian. What makes ya think such a thing? I haven't finished my own meal."

"It looked like you were coveting it."

"Well, I wasn't." I gave my fork a rest though. "So anyway, did anybody see ya at yer place?"

"No. Of course not. It was about two in the morning."

"So you just went to your crib and went to sleep?"

"My crib?"

"Yer room. Yer apartment."

"Why do you call it a crib?"

"I dunno. That's just what it's called. Ya went home and went to sleep?"

"I passed out. On the floor."

"Nice."

"Believe me, I'm not proud of it."

I figured he was telling the truth. Much as I wanted it to be true, I didn't have too much hope that he'd killed Garfield.

"And ya swear ya never heard the name Warner Garfield from Claudette?"

"Why wouldn't I tell you if I had?"

"Lots of reasons. Ya wanna hear my theory?"

"No."

He wasn't gonna get off that easy.

"You're the father of the now-deceased child Claudette was carryin, and you wanted her to have an abortion by Garfield. She said she would but then she changed her mind, so you whacked her. Then

Garfield, who knew you were the father, started blackmailin you, so ya whacked him, too."

"Can I go now?"

"Yeah, beat it."

You'd think I was a boozehound the way I was going from one bar to another. I met Marty Mitchum at Smitty's around four o'clock. He had a boilermaker, and I had a Coke.

When he started off complaining about his wife, Bridgett, I didn't want to hear it and told him so. He was another one cheating on his wife. I was turning into a cynic, and I didn't like it.

"Ya never minded before, Faye."

"Yeah, well now I mind."

"Why?"

"I dunno." But I did. I knew it was cause I was thinking about a guy for the first time in a long time and I didn't wanna foul it up with a dim view of the opposite sex.

"Tell me about Garfield?" I took out my notebook.

"Yeah. He's got a sheet. Small stuff."

"Abortion?"

"Nah."

"Anything on his whereabouts the night he was croaked?"

"Nobody seen him that night."

"Except for whoever knocked on his door, I guess."

"Yeah."

"How many guys who do abortions just open their doors to any-body, ya think?"

"I'll take a wild guess. None."

"That's what I'm thinkin."

"So ya sayin Garfield knew his killer?"

"Sounds like it to me," I said.

"So who was that?"

"That's what I wanna know. It could be almost anyone, Marty, but I think it was somebody familiar, somebody has a tie with Claudette."

"How'd ya get there?"

"She knew Garfield at HeartsinArts, an actin company, and she was scheduled for an abortion the day after she died. And ya know how much I like coincidences."

"Bout as much as I do. But if the man did abortions for a lotta girls, they all had boyfriends, probably fathers, and maybe brothers."

I doodled on my pad. "Yeah, I know. And there are a lotta guys connected to Claudette. But not a one of them knew she was pregnant, accordin to them. Except her uncle, and he didn't know who the father was."

"So somebody's lyin is yer thinkin?"

"That's it. I mean, this wasn't an Immaculate Conception."

"That ain't what the Immaculate Conception is. Everybody gets that one wrong. You think it has to do with Jesus, right? And Mary had him without . . . ya know."

This seemed like the wrong time for catechism. But once Marty got hold of something you'd do best to hear it through. Otherwise, he'd sulk and keep bringing it up anyway. "What is it then?"

"It has to do with Mary bein born without original sin. That's the Immaculate Conception."

"No kiddin?"

"That's it."

"Fascinatin, Marty." And it was, for another day. "But I gotta focus on the case."

"Yeah. Sorry."

"The point is, Claudette had to sleep with somebody to get pregnant."

"I'd say that's a good bet."

"So I'm thinkin that the father of the baby went to Garfield's with Claudette to set up her appointment and that's how Garfield knew him."

"And then what . . . so he went with her . . . so?"

"I think Garfield was blackmailin him cause he knew the guy knocked off Claudette."

"Why would the guy kill Claudette if she was havin an abortion?"

"That's where I get caught in a goat's nest."

"What are ya doodlin there?" Marty reached for my pad.

I tried to stop him, but I wasn't fast enough.

"Who's Johnny?"

"Nobody."

"Ya can't fool me, Faye. C'mon, who's Johnny? Hey, what's wrong? Ya look like ya seen a ghost."

I was staring across at the pad. I'd been scribbling Lake's name, but I'd also been doodling *M*'s, the initial Anne saw when she touched the undershirt.

"Excuse me, Marty, I gotta make a call."

"Ya leavin?"

"I'll be back. I gotta get to that phone booth down the street." I raced out like I was being chased by a bear and made it to the booth.

I found a dime in my pocket, dropped it in, and dialed.

Anne answered on the second ring.

She said, "I'm so glad you called, Faye. I have something to tell you."

"What?"

"I tried an item of clothing from someone else and there were no battle scenes."

"Great but—"

"No, listen. Then I gave another go at the undershirt you left with me."

"Yeah?"

"Battle scenes."

"So?"

"I think they mean something. I don't believe they're random after all."

"From two tests?"

"You know me better than that. I collected a bunch of items on the street—bottle tops, an old sock, an envelope, things like that."

"And?"

"No battle scenes. But when I went back to the undershirt, there they were again."

It probably did mean something, but all I could think of was my question. "Okay, Anne, I hear ya. But I gotta ask you a question."

"Go ahead."

"You remember the *M* ya saw flashin?"

"When I did the undershirt? Sure."

"Did it happen again?"

"Yes, it did. Something like that doesn't change."

"Well, here's my question, Anne. Could that *M* have been a *W*?"

She was silent for a second.

"Well, sure. Why not?"

"That's all I wanted to know. I'll call ya later."

I hung up and stood on the corner for a minute. When I'd looked across the table at my pad the *M*'s I'd doodled looked like *W*'s. If *W* was an initial, this case had a lotta those. Starting with West.

THIRTY-FOUR

I went back to Smitty's, picked up my pack of Camels, said good-bye to Marty, and went to my office.

"So," Birdie said, "the protocol daughter returns."

"Any news?"

"Not a whiff."

"Calls?"

"Lots. I put em on your desk."

"Thanks." I hurried into my office. There were a dozen pink memo slips waiting for me. I shuffled through them and put them all to the side cause not a one was important. There were none from Johnny, but that made sense. Why would he call me if we were gonna see each other that night? Only to cancel, so I was glad there was nothing from him.

I got out my yellow pad, picked up my fountain pen, and started making my *W* list.

Porter West
Myrna West
Brian Wayne
Cornell Walker
Gladys Wright

It was a leap . . . let's face it, a long jump . . . to believe Porter West woulda killed his own daughter. It's not unheard of, but the police woulda ruled him out first thing. And his motive? He didn't know Claudette was pregnant until the autopsy, and he didn't know Warner Garfield existed. And why hire me when the case was so cold?

Myrna West. I'd nixed her myself.

Brian Wayne. The most likely. But I still hadda check his alibi for the Garfield murder. This meant going to the San Remo bar and seeing his wife again.

His wife! Maureen Wayne. I'd forgotten to list her. If only Brian had been seeing Claudette this year instead of last, Maureen woulda had a great motive to kill her. Brian said his wife didn't know who the girls were, but that was just his thinking. Maybe Maureen knew Claudette was pregnant and thought, wrongly or rightly, that the baby was Brian's. What kind of alibi did she have? What did she know about Warner Garfield? And did she have a motive to kill him? I wanted her alibi for his rub out, too.

Cornell Walker. He had an alibi for Claudette's murder. But what about Garfield's? Claims he didn't know she was gonna have an abortion, but I only had his word for that. He might've been convinced that Garfield was the father of Claudette's child and thought Garfield killed her. A revenge murder. Where was he the night of Garfield's murder? When I'd asked him, we'd gone into our pitiful comedy routine and he never did answer me. Even if he did kill Garfield, that left Claudette's murder unsolved.

Gladys Wright. Although she was a cold, calculating con, she never had a motive for killing her niece. The plan to get Claudette's money was ruined before her murder. And what about Garfield? Did Gladys even know the bum was alive . . . when he was? Claudette could have told her favorite aunt his name but with which story? Garfield as creepy pest who wouldn't lay off or wonderful Warner her latest conquest?

Either way, would Gladys have done anything about it? And why? Still, I needed to know where she was the night Garfield got it. Leon was her alibi for Claudette's murder. Convenient that they could alibi each other. And they'd probably do the same for Garfield's murder.

So there it was, laid out on my yellow pad, my thoughts on each one. My first two choices were one or the other of the Waynes. If I could knock a hole in Brian's alibi or find out Maureen didn't have one, I might solve this thing.

I looked at my watch. Holy moley. It was quarter after five. I jumped up. Johnny was picking me up in an hour and a half. That didn't give me a whole lotta time to make it home, take a bath, get dolled up, and be ready when he arrived.

When I glanced back at the pad, all at once it struck me. I'd been so fixed on the murders being connected that I also thought they had to be done by the same person. But they didn't.

For instance: Maybe Brian Wayne did one murder and Maureen did the other. Why? Right now I didn't know, and if they were in it together, that didn't make sense. I hadda get their alibis before I could work this out.

But what if the murders had nothing to do with each other? Just because Garfield was gonna perform Claudette's abortion didn't hafta hook up their murders. I'd been looking at this all wrong. I didn't have to connect the murders. I needed to concentrate on one or the other. I'd been hired to find out who killed Claudette West, so that's what I was gonna do. I sat down, and keeping my number-one job in mind, I examined everybody on the pad I'd listed. I went over and over it, and it still turned out that I needed to see Brian and Maureen Wayne first.

There was one rap on my door before Birdie looked in, wearing her hat and coat.

"Ya leavin early, Bird?"

"Early? It's six o'clock. I stayed late to finish some work, ya ungrateful wretch."

"Omigod." I'd lost track of time again.

"What?"

"I got a date tonight."

"Yeah? Yer soldier boy from the other night? Maybe we should double."

"No. It's not him."

"Oh, yeah?" She raised her eyebrows twice like Groucho Marx. "Who ya got on the string?"

"Probably nobody now. I'll never make it home in time. I gotta try to call him. Bird, do me a favor?"

"What?"

"Try to find the home number of John Lake."

"Oh, the cop."

"Detective."

"Forgive me for livin."

"Do it. Please."

She sighed and left my office. I dialed his precinct. He wasn't there, and nobody would tell me where he was. I dialed the chili parlor, where he'd been earlier. Nothing. I was outta numbers. Then Birdie came back.

"So here's his number," she said, throwing a piece a paper on my desk. "Good night."

"Bird, don't. I'm sorry, okay?"

She turned and looked at me, her brown eyes showing hurt. "I'm not yer slave, ya know."

"Jeez, Birdie, I don't think of ya like that. Never. Don't say such a thing."

"I don't like to be talked to that way. I say cop and you say detective. What's the diff?"

"Yer right. There's no diff. I'm sorry. I'm a little overwhelmed here. Forgiven?"

"Okay." She grinned. "So the detective asked ya out?"

"Yeah. For dinner. Tonight."

"Ya like him?"

"I don't know him, but I think he's pretty nice."

"Bout time ya found somebody ya like. Uh-oh, I'm keepin ya from callin."

"That's okay."

"Nah. Call him. I'm gonna skedaddle."

Before I could say anything more she was gone.

I dialed John at home. I felt funny about calling there, but I didn't know what else to do. He answered.

"Hello, Johnny. It's Faye."

"Faye? Everything all right?"

"Not exactly." I had trouble getting out the words. "Listen, Johnny, something's come up. I gotta cancel our date for tonight."

"Oh? I'm sorry to hear that."

"Me, too. It's work."

"Anything to do with Garfield?"

"No. It's the West murder . . . the case I've been workin on."

"I understand, Faye. I've been in the same fix myself plenty of times."

"I hope . . . I hope we can do it some other time."

"Sure."

Why didn't I believe him? I wanted to reschedule right there and
then, but if we did and I had to cancel again . . . well, that wouldn't
be too keen.

"How's the Garfield case goin?"

"We're looking into different angles, different people."

It was clear he wasn't gonna tell me anything.

"Are you getting near the end on your case?" he asked.

"I think so."

"Well, that's swell. I'll call you in a couple of days, all right?"

"Yeah, that'll be fine."

"Good luck, Faye. Bye."

When I said goodbye, I felt like I'd never hear from him again.
And then what would I do? Just the way Birdie said, he was the first
man I'd liked in a long time. Oh, hells bells. I couldn't think about
John Lake now. I had to hold on to my concentration. First stop,
Maureen Wayne.

By the time I got downtown it was dark. Daylight savings time
hadn't begun yet. I walked over to Ninth Street, where Maureen
Wayne lived.

Our last meeting hadn't gone too well, and that was putting it
mildly. She'd kicked me out. And if she was guilty of the murder,
then why in the hell would she let me in?

I had to try. I rang the bell and soon heard her coming down the
stairs. She opened the door, then started to close it as soon as she saw
me. But I got my foot in fast.

"What do you want?"

"I have to talk to you about Brian."

"We've already done that."

"There's been another murder."

Her face showed shock. It looked genuine.

"Who was it?"

"A man named Warner Garfield."

"Who's that?"

"Please let me in."

"I don't know why I should, but all right."

She opened the door and I followed her up, same as last time. We
sat in the living room. She didn't offer me anything to drink.

"So who was this Garfield person?" She lit a cigarette.

"He was an actor and an abortionist."

"Nice combination. What does he have to do with Brian?"

"When did ya see him last?"

"Two nights ago."

"Where?"

"Here."

"Why?"

"He wanted me to take him back. That's what he said anyway."

"What time did he leave here?"

"About ten."

All of it jibed with what Brian had told me. "How did he seem to you?"

"Well, what do you think? He wanted his family back, and he wasn't getting his way. That's what Brian always wants . . . *his* way."

"And when he doesn't have things go his way, what does he do?"

"Well he doesn't kill people, if that's what you're getting at."

I was, but I didn't expect her to tell me that. "Course not."

"But you think he did, don't you?"

"Did what?"

"Killed that man."

"I don't know what to think. What did you do after he left?"

"Why?"

"Did ya go out?"

"I don't leave my children alone, Miss Quick."

I believed her. "So you were here. Did Brian call ya?"

"We'd just seen each other. Why would he call me?"

"Did he?"

"I don't know. I can't be sure."

"Meanin?"

"The phone rang about midnight, but no one spoke on the other end. I heard a lot of noise in the background but nothing from the caller."

"Ya get many calls like that?"

"No. Never."

"What did the background noise sound like?"

"It was just noise." Her impatience was showing.

"Was it car sounds, like the caller was on the street in a booth?"

"No. It was more like people talking."

"Bar noise?"

"I don't know. I don't get a lot of calls from bars. None, in fact."

I was sure it was bar noise and that the caller was Brian. So far his alibi was checking out. At least until midnight.

"I'm gonna ask ya somethin that'll make ya mad."

"As if you haven't already. What?"

"You remember me askin about Claudette West?"

"Yes. You thought Brian might have killed her. I believe she was one of his paramours."

"Yeah. You ever meet her?"

"I told you I hadn't last time. No."

"Can ya tell me where you were on January twentieth?"

"You were right. You're making me mad."

"I have to ask."

"I have no idea what I was doing that night."

"Ya keep a date book or anythin?"

She stared at me. It wasn't peachy. But I didn't look away. "Do ya?"

"Yes."

"Could ya look up that date?"

"You have no real right to ask me these questions, do you?"

"Nope."

"I don't have to get my date book, do I?"

"Nope."

"At least you're honest." She got up and crossed to a mahogany secretary and opened it. There were a couple a rows of pigeon holes. She reached into one and pulled out a burgundy-colored book.

"Here," she said, dropping it in my lap, "find the date yourself."

"Thanks." I opened it at the front.

There it was, January 20: 7:00 dinner with Mother and Dad. 8:30 *Something for the Boys* (Ethel Merman).

"Well? What was I up to?"

I read it aloud.

"Would you like my parents' address in Pennsylvania?"

"No thanks. But tell me, what were ya gonna do if the date had been empty?"

"I wasn't going to do anything. Except to ask you to leave once again. And in fact I'm going to do that anyway."

"I'm sorry. I had to know. I had to rule ya out."

"Please don't ever come here again."

"I don't think I will." I was convinced Maureen Wayne had nothing to do with the murders.

"Good."

I went to the door but turned back when I got there. "One more thing."

"What?"

"How was Miss Merman?"

"Superb. Goodbye."

"Goodbye."

THIRTY-FIVE

J hit the bricks and made my way home. At least part of Brian Wayne's alibi checked out. I didn't think Maureen would lie for him. And odds on, the phone call she got at midnight was from him. Either he'd been too stewed to remember it or didn't want to be knocked from his high horse by telling me he'd made a call like that. I believed he was at the San Remo until he staggered home around two. So for my money neither of the Waynes had anything to do with Garfield's murder.

Maureen was in the clear on Claudette's murder, and Brian didn't look as good as I'd once thought. Most likely he and Claudette had the affair when he'd said they did. And I doubted that Brian Wayne ever looked back. A *new* conquest was the important thing for him.

By the time I got to my building, though, I was not a Little Mary Sunshine cause I was nowhere. It was only eight o'clock, and I wanted to be out having dinner with Johnny Lake. Instead I was gonna eat a bowl of oatmeal by myself. I thought of Anne and how she'd said I wouldn't have a date tonight. Maybe I should ask her if I was *ever* gonna have one with him. Nah, she didn't do stuff like that. She wasn't a fortune-teller, after all.

I opened the big front door, and Dolores was, as usual, sweeping the hall outside her place.

"Pretty late for that, isn't it?"

"Good thing I was out here, *bubee.*"

"How come?"

"Well, I wouldna seen yer boyfriend, would I?"

"Dolores, what're ya talkin about? What boyfriend?"

"And what a cutie he is."

Johnny would never have shown up here after I broke the date. Would he? "I don't have a boyfriend."

"Don't kid a kidder, Faye."

It was useless to keep denying that I had a guy, so I took another tact. "Okay, what did he say to ya?"

"When I came out, he was fumbling with his keys in front of yer door."

Now I knew it wasn't Johnny, and I felt a little panicky. "Dolores, nobody has a key to my apartment but me."

"Oh, c'mon. I won't tell the rest of those *shmendriks* who live here nothin."

"Listen, Dolores. I'm serious. How do ya know this guy ya saw wasn't tryin to break in?"

"Ya think I'm a nitwit? I asked him who he was lookin for and he told me, Faye Quick. That's you, ain't it?" She cackled crazily.

"Did he say why he wanted me?"

"Course not and I didn't ask. He looked like a mensch but a little embarrassed."

"He looked like a crook is my guess."

"No *bubele,* ya got him all wrong. He knew who you was, so right away I know he's not a gonif. And he has a key."

I started to repeat myself about the keys. Also useless, so I cut it short. "Tell me what he looked like."

"Oh, a beauty. Nice dark hair and eyes like an angel."

"What was he wearin?"

She shrugged. "Wearing? A suit. A shirt. A tie. What else would a nice boy be wearing?"

"This key he had, did he use it to go inside?"

"He didn't need to once we'd met and I said I'd be glad to give a note to you."

I counted to ten. "Where is it?"

"In my pocket." She felt around in her right sweater pocket. "No."

Then in her left. "Nope." She unbuttoned her sweater and reached into a pocket on her blouse. "Ah! I got it." She held it out to me. "I gave him the paper."

"Whaddaya mean?"

She shrugged. "He wanted paper to write you a note, so I gave him paper. What's wrong with that?"

"Nothin. What does it say?"

"You think I read it?" She was genuinely horrified.

"Sorry, Dolores. Course not." I took the paper and unfolded it."

Dear Faye,

Sorry I missed you. Maybe next time.
Why am I saying maybe? Next time will
definitely come.

The signature, if that's what it was, was scribbled. I couldn't make it out.

"So?" Dolores said.

"I don't know who this is from."

"He didn't sign it?"

I showed it to her.

"Oy. Who could read that? So how many boyfriends you got, Faye, you don't know which one?"

"Dolores, I know ya don't believe me, but I don't have any."

"So why'd ya give this fella keys to your apartment?"

"I didn't. That's what I've been tryin to tell ya. Nobody but me has keys."

"Ya mean he was tryin to break in?"

"I think so. Tell me again what he looked like."

"Nice lookin."

"Is that the best ya can do?"

"I didn't pay attention to the pieces, I just thought, Faye's got a good-looker for a boyfriend."

"Okay. Thanks, Dolores."

"I'm sorry, Faye, if I done a dumb thing."

"No. No. Don't worry, it's okay."

"I shoulda called the cops, huh?"

I put a hand on her sleeve. "How could ya know?"

"Oy. I gave him paper."

"Forget about it. It's all okay."

"You think he'll come back?"

"Nah."

"He could murder us in our beds."

"Calm down, Dolores. He's not comin back."

"How can ya be so sure?"

"I'm a detective. I know these things." I didn't know anything. But I wanted to make her feel better.

"I think I'll go in now," she said.

"Good idea." I gave her arm a squeeze, and we each turned toward our doors. My hand was shaking a little when I put my key in the lock. Then Dolores cried out.

"Faye."

I turned.

"Maybe this'll help. He looked like Cary Grant."

"Oh, thanks, Dolores. Yeah, that'll help."

"Ya know who he is now?"

"No. But it gives me somethin to go on." At least she'd feel she'd done something for me. "G'night, Dolores."

Inside my apartment, for the first time, I didn't feel home free. This had always been my safe haven. No matter what else was going on in my life, being in my crib made me feel better. But now I felt scared. I wondered if my gate-crasher had wormed his way into my place somehow. Okay, so I had only two rooms and a bathroom. I could see the little kitchen and living room from right inside my door. He coulda been hiding behind a piece of furniture, but I didn't think so. That left the bathroom and bedroom. I placed my pocketbook on the floor. And then I couldn't move. It was like I was glued in place.

Hey, I had my gat! Yeah, but it was up in the bedroom closet. I leaned down and took off my pumps, then forced myself to tiptoe over to one of the drawers in the walk-through kitchen and slowly pulled it open. I reached in and took out the carving knife. It had a nice bone handle, and I got a good grip on it. I started to close the drawer before I realized how stupid that was.

The bathroom was the closest room but also the smallest and I might get caught in tight quarters, so I decided to give the bedroom a once-over first. My heart was thumping, but I didn't feel like doing the conga all by myself.

I made my way to the open door of the bedroom. Once again I felt paralyzed.

One of the big windows at the rear of the bedroom was open halfway. The thing was, I couldn't remember if that's the way I left it or somebody else had. But it didn't matter who opened it, it was a way in. On the one hand, if I could remember if it was me who did it, then I could be less scared. On the other hand, if I didn't, then I could be more scared and almost certain some crumb was in there waiting for me.

I couldn't just stand there with the knife in my hand. Well, I *could*, but that wouldn't get me very far.

I pictured myself frozen in place forever. Would anyone come looking for me? I almost laughed out loud.

All I had to do was take one step forward. If anyone was in my bedroom I'd see him right away. Unless he was in the closet.

I took the step.

Nobody.

Now I had to deal with the closet. I walked quietly around the bed and to the door. Had I left it closed that morning? I tried to picture myself getting ready for the day.

Nothing.

I knew what I'd worn cause I was still wearing it. But whether I left the door open or closed was a blank.

I reached out with my free hand, and it hovered over the glass doorknob. I raised my right arm and held the knife above me. If he had a gun I was a goner, but I had to make a move.

In one swift motion I turned the knob and pulled open the door.

Nothing.

Nobody.

I hadn't realized I'd been holding my breath until I let out what sounded like the sigh of a lion.

There was still the bathroom.

Again I crept around my bed and through the doorway into the kitchen. From there I could see the bathroom door. Closed, the way I always left it. I could hear my mother's voice telling me it wasn't proper to leave a bathroom door open. Funny, her telling me what was decent when she spent most of her life zonked on morphine.

I crept up on the door like it was a living being. Then I took the same position I'd taken at the closet in the bedroom and turned the knob with my left hand.

Nothing.

But there it was, the closed shower curtain. I didn't like the echoes I was getting from the last shower curtain I'd stumbled on. And when I was in the bedroom I'd forgotten to get my piece. Should I go back for it, get up on a chair, get the gun? Or should I keep going the way I was? I was in the home stretch, but it wasn't mopped up yet. I decided going back to get the gat was gonna put more strain on me.

Okay, knife high. Pull back the curtain.

I couldn't move.

I heard Woody's voice: *Ah, Faye, put it to bed.*

So I did. I flung back the curtain.

Nobody.

Woody said, *That's all there is, there ain't no more.*

I dropped my knife hand to my side. I was bushed and slumped against the cool tiles on the wall. So Dracula wasn't in my crib. At least I felt safe again.

I put the knife on the kitchen table and started to fill the coffeepot with water. It was then that Dolores's words hit me: *He looked like Cary Grant.*

I stood there, the pot in my hand, the water running from the tap.

"What a knucklehead," I said out loud.

I set the percolator on the stove, turned off the water, grabbed the phone, and prayed he'd be home.

"Hello, Bridgett, how ya doin?"

"Just fine, Faye. You?"

"Fine. Is Marty home by any chance?"

"No, he's workin late. Ya want I should have him call ya when he comes in?"

I started to say no, that I'd find him, but that wouldn't a been too smart.

"Sure, Bridgett. That'll be good."

We said goodbye and hung up. I dialed Smitty's bar. Coburn answered. I asked for Marty, and we went through the routine so Marty wouldn't be snagged by Bridgett. I wondered when he had time for his turtledove between work and his time at Smitty's bar.

A few seconds went by, and then Marty was on the phone. I asked him if he'd do something for me.

He said he'd take care of my request, then asked where to meet.

I told him.

He said sure, he'd be there soon as he could. I knew he wouldn't let me down.

After I hung up, I marched straight into the bedroom and headed for my gun.

THIRTY-SIX

ow many times in the past week had I stood outside the Wests' building? Once again I hadn't made an appointment. I didn't want to give them advance notice.

The doorman rang their apartment and told whoever picked up I was there. He told me it was okay.

Myrna met me at the door. Maid's night off. Or maybe they struggled through the nights alone.

"You should have called, Miss Quick."

"I know. But I wasn't in my office, and I didn't have your number with me."

"I see. Well, come in. Be careful what you say; Porter's got his dander up."

Poor, poor Porter, I thought, as I walked behind his wife on the way to the living room.

When I said hello, there was no response. He stared at me for a few secs.

Then he said, "Not only haven't you phoned me every day as we agreed, once again you've arrived here unannounced."

"I thought the doorman announced me," I said.

"Don't be facetious, Miss Quick. You know exactly what I mean." He took a deep drink from what looked like a mean martini. Cocktail hour. How nice. How genteel.

"Would you like a cocktail, Miss Quick?" Myrna asked.

"No thanks. Not while I'm workin."

"Oh," Porter said, "you're actually working?"

"I didn't come here for a social chat, Mr. West."

Porter pointed to a chair for me to sit, then took a spot on the sofa while Myrna perched on the edge of a straight-backed chair.

"All right, what *did* you come here for? Surely, you haven't solved the case. I know that's too much to ask for."

I realized Porter sounded slightly soused.

He wasn't finished. "Actually, Miss Quick, I was thinking of firing you."

"Porter," Myrna said.

"Yes, Myrna, that's exactly what I've been thinking."

"I wouldn't do that if I were you, Mr. West."

"Fortunately, my dear, you're not."

"Porter, you haven't discussed this with me."

He waved a hand at her like she was a pesky mosquito.

"In fact, Miss Quick, you're fired."

I knew I had to stall until Marty got here. "Would ya mind tellin me why?"

"I'd like to know that, too," Myrna said.

"Because for one thing you don't follow rules. Rules are very important. They're the basis of our society. Without rules we'd be savages."

"Seems to me some people are savages even with rules."

"Those people break them, Miss Quick. That's exactly my point."

"What kinda rules are we talkin about?"

"Basic rules. Perhaps you don't know them, Miss Quick. I don't know anything about your background. It's possible you weren't brought up . . . the way . . . Claudette was."

I couldn't believe it, but he started crying in this weird gulping way. I didn't think I'd ever see that. Myrna went to him.

"Oh, Porter, you're going to make yourself sick."

He pushed her away, and she stumbled, falling over the cocktail table to the floor.

Porter and I jumped up, and we went to her.

"Get away from my wife," he said.

"I'm all right."

"It was an accident, Myrna. You know I'd never hurt you."

He gently lifted her up.

"Yes, dear. I know it was an accident."

Porter led his wife to the sofa. "Are you all right?"

"I'm fine."

He patted her on the shoulder like she was a pet. "Do you want anything?"

"No. I'm fine."

I went back to my chair, and Porter sat down and picked up his drink. He said, "It *was* an accident."

"I could see that, Mr. West." I wondered why he would care what I thought? I also wondered where Marty was.

"What were we talking about?" Porter asked.

"Ah, you mentioned Claudette and that she was brought up with rules." From what I'd learned of her she didn't pay much attention to her father's rules or anyone else's.

"My little girl," he said.

Porter was more than slightly soused. He was getting good and drunk. And it seemed to bring out his sentimental side. I thought it might be a good time to throw some info his way.

"Mr. West, did you know a man named Warner Garfield?"

"Oh, Miss Quick," Myrna said.

I hadn't really promised her I'd never bring his name up to Porter. "I have to, Mrs. West."

"What's going on? Have you two been up to something?"

"Nothing like that, Porter."

"Then what? It sounds like collusion to me."

"Let's get back to the question. Warner Garfield. Name ring any bells?"

"No."

"What if I told ya that Garfield was an abortionist."

"I'd say he was barbaric. I suppose you're going to tell me that he performed one on Claudette, aren't you? But you can't because she was pregnant when that bastard Cotten murdered her."

"That's true. He never performed an abortion on Claudette."

"Then why should I know his name or care about him?"

"Your daughter knew him. She told some people he was her boyfriend and others that he was hounding her. Do ya know why she'd do that, Mr. West?"

"She wouldn't even know a person like that. I refuse to believe it."

"She met him at the HeartsinArts actin company."

"Claudette didn't belong to any acting company."

Myrna gave me a warning look that I took to mean I shouldn't say she knew about the group or Garfield. I gave her a tiny nod.

"Mr. West, I don't think you knew your daughter as well as you think ya did."

"I fired you," he said. "Get out."

"Let's get somethin straight. You can fire me all ya want, but I'm not leavin just yet."

"I'll call my doorman."

"Nah. I don't think ya wanna do that. If ya do, I'll have to tell him what I know and then he'll have to tell your neighbors and it'll get real messy."

I believed that Porter didn't know of Garfield. But I was stalling for time. I heard the front door slam. Footsteps down the hall and then the appearance of Cornell Walker.

"Miss Quick," he said. "I didn't know you'd be here."

"Why would ya?"

"I wouldn't." He smiled and cocked his head to one side. "So why *are* you here?" He walked to the liquor cabinet and poured some whiskey over ice. Then he looked back at me. "You're not drinking, Miss Quick?"

"That's right."

He sat down in a wingback, crossed his legs, and looked at me. "You didn't answer my question."

"I think I'd like to ask you a question, Captain."

"All right."

I opened my pocketbook and took out the piece of paper Dolores had given me. Then I handed it to him. "This yours?"

He gave it a glance. "Yes. I'm glad you got it and sorry I missed you."

"Ya have a lousy signature."

"I do, don't I?"

Porter said, "What's going on?"

"I went to visit Miss Quick this afternoon, but she wasn't home, so I left a note with a very nice woman who was cleaning the hall."

"What kind of a note?" Porter asked.

"The kind that says I was there," Walker said. "What's all the—"

A buzzer sounded.

Myrna said, "That's from downstairs. The doorman. I wonder if we have another visitor." She scurried outta the room.

I hoped it was Marty cause I wasn't sure I liked how things were going.

Myrna poked her head in. "Are you expecting a Marty Mitchum, Miss Quick?"

"I am."

"All right then." She disappeared.

Walker said, "Who's Marty Mitchum?"

"A detective friend of mine."

"A boyfriend?" He smiled and winked at me.

I wanted to give him one across the chops. But I didn't think that would accomplish what I'd come here for.

"No. Not a boyfriend. A colleague."

"I see."

"Why is he coming here?" Porter asked.

"Remember when I first came in, ya asked me if I'd solved the case and then ya fired me before I could answer? Well, yeah, I've solved the case." I hoped like hell that was the truth.

Walker said, "How great, Miss Quick. Tell us."

"I will. But I have to speak to Detective Mitchum first."

Myrna came in with Marty, who was without his hat. I couldn't remember if I'd ever seen him bareheaded before. She introduced him to Porter and Walker.

"Take a seat," Porter said. "The more the merrier. Want a cocktail?"

"No thanks."

"Detective, ya got somethin for me?"

"Yeah, I do."

"If you'll excuse us for a minute."

"Do we have a choice?" Porter asked.

I ignored his remark, and Marty and I went into the hall.

"So?"

"You were right."

"You're sure?"

"Oh yeah."

"Gimme a name."

"Corporal Edward Dunne."

"How'd ya do this over the phone?"

"I got my ways." He gave me a grin. "Threat of a court-martial is a great convincer."

"Swell. Okay, we're goin back in there. Be ready for anything."

"I always am."

We went back, and I sat in my chair and Marty sat on the other end of the sofa.

"Sorry for the inconvenience," I said.

"What's this all about?" Porter asked.

I saw that he'd made himself another martini. "Captain Walker, ya wanna tell me why ya came to my apartment?"

"I wanted to see you. Is that so strange? You're a very attractive young lady."

"Ya always make it a habit of tryin to break into ladies' apartments?"

"I beg your pardon?"

"Dolores, the one who gave ya the paper, said she saw you tryin to get into my place with a key." I wanted to throw him off balance before I got to the big stuff.

"Well, she was mistaken."

"She's not usually mistaken."

"She was this time."

"I don't think so."

"Then she's lying." He took a slug of his drink.

"Nah. Not Dolores."

Myrna said, "What's going on here?"

"I'm tryin to establish why the captain was attemptin to break into my place."

"But he says he wasn't."

"Yeah. I know what he says. Okay, let's let that one go for now. How about this? Are ya accustomed to callin on young ladies without makin a date? Ah, never mind. Dolores said ya looked like Cary Grant."

"That's very flattering but not accurate."

"I think it's the cleft in your chin that made her think that. It's what made me know it was you, crummy signature or not."

Myrna said, "Why are you harassing my brother, Faye?"

"Oh, so now it's Faye," Porter said. "I knew you two were plotting something."

We both ignored him. I turned back to Walker.

"Does the name Edward Dunne mean anything to you?"

"Of course. He's assigned to me."

"A loyal guy, huh?"

"Yes, why?"

Sweat popped out along his brow and across his nose. "So loyal that when the cops checked out your alibi for the night of Claudette's murder, Corporal Dunne said you'd been there all night, didn't he?"

"I had been."

"No, Captain Walker, you hadn't."

Marty said, "He admitted to me half an hour ago that you weren't there that night."

"Well, then he's lying."

"Everybody's lyin. Ya notice that, Detective?"

"Can't miss it."

"Everybody is lyin except the captain."

"Why would Cornell lie about where he was?" Myrna asked.

"Because he killed your daughter, Mrs. West."

THIRTY-SEVEN

All three of them rose to their feet. Porter was a little wobbly, but the other two stood at attention.

"This is outrageous," Walker said.

"Why would Cornell kill my daughter? His niece?" Myrna said.

Porter said, "I think we've had enough of this. You'd both better leave now."

"Not yet. I think you three should sit down." Surprisingly, they did.

"Cornell," Myrna said, "tell them you didn't have anything to do with this. He was in South Carolina when it happened."

"No, Mrs. West. He wasn't. He was in New York with Claudette tryin to convince her to go through with the abortion she had planned for the next day."

Walker laughed.

"What's so funny?" Marty asked.

"You wouldn't understand."

"Try me."

"I think Porter's right. You should both leave."

"C'mon, Cornell. We're just gettin started here."

"Myrna, buzz the doorman," Walker said.

She didn't answer, and she didn't move.

"Then we'll have to call the police."

"I *am* the police," Marty said.

Walker was starting to look desperate around the edges. I flashed on him in his uniform and realized that that's what had been nagging at me the night Birdie and I went to the USO. The uniforms were telling me something then, but I wasn't hearing.

Myrna said, "We called him in South Carolina the next day."

"What time was that?"

"I don't know. Everything was still so confusing and awful."

"It was late in the afternoon," Porter said. He seemed to be sobering up.

"Plenty of time for the captain to get back to Parris Island. What did ya tell Corporal Dunne when he learned your niece had been killed the night before?"

Marty said, "I can answer that one. Walker told Corporal Dunne he'd had a rendezvous with another captain's wife that night, so Dunne never put the two things together."

"This is getting more absurd every minute," Walker said.

"Is it? See, I know ya went to see Warner Garfield to arrange the abortion. When I heard the initials CW had been crossed out in Garfield's book two weeks before, I thought they stood for Claudette West and that she'd decided against it, then changed her mind, rescheduled for January twenty-first when the CW appeared again. But now I know the first set of initials stood for Cornell Walker, and Garfield had crossed them out because you'd been there, made the arrangement, and paid him."

"You don't know what you're talking about," Walker said.

"I think I do."

"Even if that's all true," Myrna said, "why does that make my brother a murderer?"

"I'm sorry to tell ya this, Myrna, Porter, cause this whole case is rotten enough, but Claudette's unborn baby was Cornell's. Claudette was in love with him, and they'd been havin an affair. But then she got pregnant."

Myrna was crying softly. Porter looked shell-shocked. Walker was trying to hold my gaze.

I went on. "Claudette had agreed to the abortion at first and then changed her mind. So Cornell had to get himself up here to try to convince her to have it. When she wouldn't agree, he killed her."

Walker laughed again.

"Why do you keep laughing, Cornell?"

"Sorry, Myrna. I'm laughing because she has it so wrong."

"Wrong?" I asked.

"Yes, wrong. It's true I made the arrangement and gave the money to Garfield, but—"

Myrna's gasp cut him off.

"I'll kill you," Porter said, trying to rise, but Marty held him back.

"Go on," I said.

"*I'm* the one who didn't want her to go through with the abortion. That's why I came up here. To convince her *not* to have it."

"Why?" I asked.

"Because I loved her and I wanted her to have our child. I'd agreed to the abortion in a weak moment. But her death was an accident, I swear it. We were walking along in the snow, arguing, and she kept on insisting she was going to have the abortion. I grabbed for her, and she slipped and went down, hitting her head on a cement step. She was dead. I didn't know what to do."

"Hittin her head on a step couldna caused all that blood," I said.

"It didn't. That's right, but I had to make it look like she'd been murdered so I . . . I smashed her head against the step until there was enough blood to make it look like a real attack."

"Ya know what, Cornell? You're still lyin. People don't bleed after they're dead."

His stare at me was cold. Those eyes glinting like chips off an ice block.

"Ya might as well admit what really happened cause we know ya killed Garfield, too."

"Really? How did I do that?"

I couldn't tell him about the undershirt and what Anne experienced when she'd held it in her hands and how the battle scenes were cause Cornell was in the Marines even if he never saw action.

"I'll leave that to the DA. I'll just say this. We know Garfield was blackmailin ya cause he'd put two and two together."

"He was scum."

"I agree with that," I said. "So what really happened with you and Claudette?"

"She was willful and disobedient. She insisted on going through with the abortion, so I smashed her against a building. No one was around."

Myrna was crying. "It's unbearable."

"You're the scum, Cornell, that's who's scum," Porter said.

"I wasn't going to have my child ripped from her."

So he killed them both himself. It wasn't logical, but then murderers often aren't. Especially when there's passion involved. I read that in a book.

I nodded at Marty and he stood up and crossed the room.

"Stand up, Walker."

He did. Marty turned him around and clapped the cuffs on him. "Let's go."

I wanted to comfort the Wests, but I didn't know how. There wasn't any comfort for something like this. They'd have to find their own way out of it.

If they ever could.

It took me a little while to feel clean again. But I wasn't sure how long it would take to get rid of the sick feeling I always got when I thought of the West/Walker case.

The day after Walker was arrested I got a call from Detective Johnny Lake.

"I hear you broke the case," he said.

"I guess so." I felt like a rat treading on his toes like that. But what was done was done. He could hate me for the rest of my life. I was sorry it hadn't worked out with him, but I knew I'd get over it.

"Why didn't you call me when you went up to the West apartment?"

"It's not a very nice reason."

"That's okay."

"I didn't think of it."

He laughed.

"At least you're honest, Faye."

When he said my name, I felt tingles.

"I'm always honest," I said.

"Were you honest about why you broke our date?"

"Yeah, I was."

"Then maybe we can try it again sometime."

The "sometime" line, I thought.

"Sure," I said. I knew I'd never hear from him again.

"How about Wednesday?"

That hit me like a bombshell. "Ya mean the day after tomorrow?"

"This is Monday. So the day after tomorrow. Right."

I wanted to shout my yes, but I said it just as casual as I could.

"I'll pick you up at your apartment at seven, if that's all right?"

I didn't have any pressing engagements or cases, so I said, "That's fine."

By five to seven on Wednesday he hadn't called to break the date. I was looking swell and feeling like a million bucks even though my insides were doing a tap dance. I took a last look in the mirror, and then the bell rang.

Hubba-hubba!

ABOUT THE AUTHOR

SANDRA SCOPPETTONE has written numerous other novels, including three under the pseudonym Jack Early. Most recently she created the five-book series of mystery novels featuring New York private eye Lauren Laurano. Scoppettone lives on Long Island in New York.

ABOUT THE TYPE

Designed for the Monotype Corporation in the early 1900s by F.H. Pierpont, Plantin is named for the sixteenth-century Antwerp printer Christophe Plantin. Although not based directly on his work, the model for Plantin was taken from the huge collection of type Plantin had procured. Like Times Roman, this typeface was designed to conserve paper: it has a large x-height and appears slightly condensed. Plantin is a fine text face for books, journals, and textbooks.